OUTSIDE LOLA'S

PAUL DIGGORY

Published in 2020 by FeedARead Publishing

British Library C.I.P.

A CIP catalogue record for this title is available from the British Library.

Cover design: Roy McCarthy at kulastudio.com

For Kate, Lauren and Joel

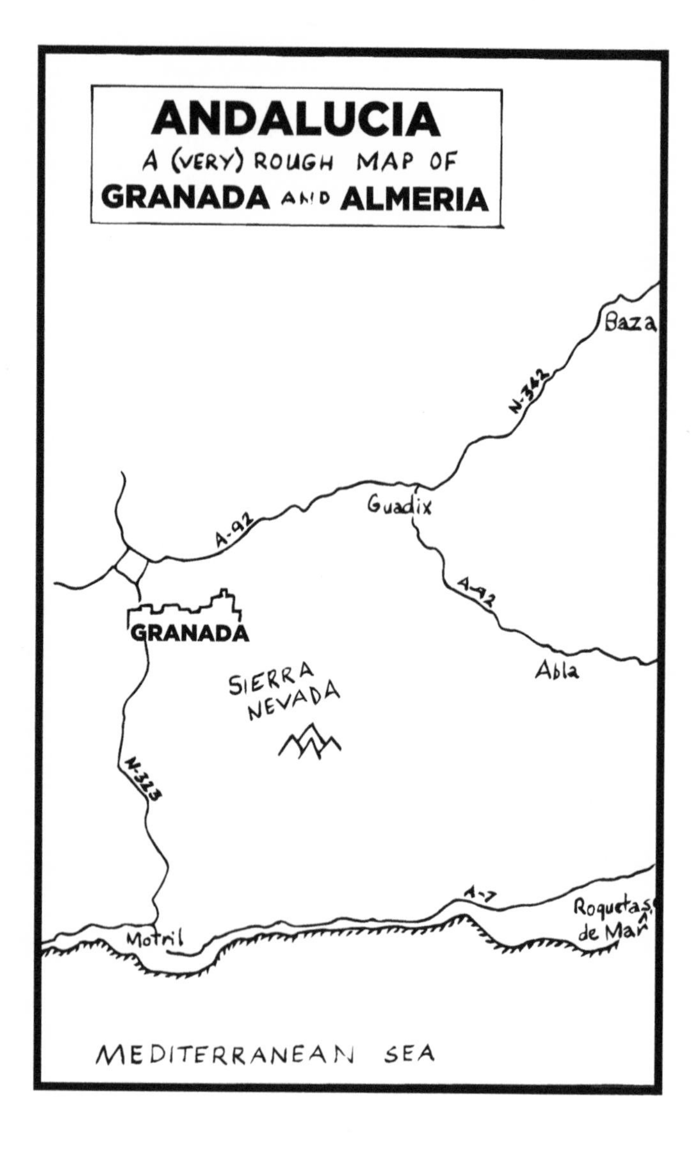
ANDALUCIA
A (VERY) ROUGH MAP OF
GRANADA AND ALMERIA
Baza
N-342
A-92
Guadix
A-92
GRANADA
Abla
SIERRA
NEVADA
N-323
A-7
Roquetas
de Mar
Motril
MEDITERRANEAN SEA

Vélez Blanco
Vélez-Rubio
Lorca
Cúllar
E-15
Huercal-Overa
SIERRA DE LOS FILABRES
Albox
A-7
Vera
Villaricos
Garrucha
Mojácar
Turre
N-340a
LOLA'S
Tabernas
OASYS
A-7
Carboneras
A-92
Níjar
ALMERIA
Rodalquilar
El Cabo de Gata
San José
Gulf of Almeria
NORTH AFRICA

Chapter One

Friday 15 June 2018

After two hours on the beach and absorbed in his novel Jack was in serious danger of relaxing. Exactly what he'd come out to Andalucia for, to put some space between him and his old life. He took little interest in new arrivals at the beach. Until, surprise, surprise... the cause of yesterday's distraction returned accompanied by the surly guy with the moustache. She was modelling a black bikini, matching her shining ebony hair, which she'd combed up and back at the front for a classically Spanish look. The cloak of peaceful inner calm that had wrapped itself around him quickly vanished. He put down his book and pondered why he was putting himself through so much frustration.

The woman's partner was not only younger than Jack, he was younger too than her, by several years he'd guess. As irrational as he knew his thoughts to be, it was nevertheless irritating to him. Having decided that beer, wine and the hot Spanish sun were a heady mix, today Jack had chosen to stick to soft drinks. So it was especially noticeable to him that her partner had put away several beers by mid-afternoon. Such that when he left her side and strolled into the sea Jack was perplexed to see him begin to swim out. From his own brief wallow in the waves yesterday he'd readily discovered that you're out of your depth on this beach quite quickly and you didn't need to swim far before the sea became choppy. 'What the hell's he doing?' Jack thought to himself.

Continuing to swim out, he's now well beyond other swimmers. Looking around him nobody else seems particularly alarmed. But as the swimmer approaches the yellow buoys, his strokes are increasingly ragged and he's visibly slowing. The buoys indicate the distance beyond which it's not advisable to go — he'd seen it on the signs. Now his companion sits up to look for him, removing her headphones. He's definitely struggling and she's definitely flustered. On her feet now, she walks briskly to the water's edge, hands on hips. Jack can't understand what she's saying but she looks like she's asking for someone to help. Her agitation is lost amongst the din of the beach, a din that seems to have grown in proportion to the need for attention. The chill-out dance mix from Lola's sounds suddenly out of place. There don't appear to be many takers as shoulders are shrugged and people look away or pretend they're unaware. At least Jack has learned surly bloke's name judging by the number of times he's heard her call 'Alfredo'.

'Oh, what the hell…' thinks Jack, lifting his six feet frame from his sun bed. If he sits there and does nothing and the guy drowns he's got to live with it. Better to do something. He heads across and gestures to the woman that he understands and runs off towards the coastguard, about 100m down the beach. On reaching the platform, he realises it's empty. He thinks the sign says 'gone for lunch'. This never happened in Baywatch.

He turns and runs back, trying to avoid sandcastles

and tiny children. One is buried up to his neck in the sand, just a laughing, gurning head and Jack spots him at the last moment and manages to hurdle over him. The kid laughs like it's the funniest thing he's ever seen. Everyone's giving him strange looks and his urgency seems out of place. He's too old for this, he thinks. She's beside herself now and in tears. Alfredo meanwhile has become difficult to see. He's somewhere near the yellow buoys but the movement of the waves in front is such that he's partially hidden from sight, just the occasional bobbing of his head locates him.

'There's only one thing for it' he thinks, his heart starting to beat faster.

Jack feels he's got to do something and a sudden rush of nerves and adrenaline overcomes him. Striding through the water, he plunges into the waves and tries to find his breast stroke rhythm. It's the only stroke he can sustain for more than 20m so he figures he's probably looking for a lifetime best. He's not exactly Michael Phelps but he's steady and makes progress out towards the yellow buoys. The waves are stronger than they look from the beach. Every now and then he goes under and the sound from beneath the waves is intense. He's struggling to keep Alfredo in his sight and he's gasping for breath himself and starting to tire. He wishes he'd put his goggles on. There's a briny taste of salt water in his mouth and it occurs to him more than once that he's not really up to this sort of challenge. There's no turning back now though.

Persisting until he recovers some sort of rhythm, Jack finds himself not that far away from Alfredo, who by now is flailing about and looking disoriented.

"Alfredo! Alfredo!" splutters Jack before his head goes under the water again.

The noise is deafening, a few seconds of rumbling

raw power pressurising his ears. Emerging through the waves Alfredo looks startled. He jabbers something back in Spanish. Jack's gone up a gear now and forces his way through the swell. Encouraged by coming this far he's determined to get him back. In his panic and with the roaring turbulence of the sea, Alfredo can't make out what Jack's saying. All things considered, language is the least of their problems. A very tricky twenty seconds passes while they try to lock hands and arms, shouting at each other but neither being able to comprehend a word. Finally Jack's able to grasp Alfredo under the arms and kicks for all he's worth in a sort of back stroke. Alfredo has enough left that he's able to put in some random kicks to contribute to their movement and, with a bit of one handed sculling, between them they move gradually towards the shore. It's desperately tough for the pair of them as their heads bob up and down and in and out of the sea, the swell building up, breakers riding over them with the incoming tide, each one pushing them further towards the beach. Jack can feel the undulating current beneath the surface as he kicks for all he's worth, gradually bringing the shore closer and the safety of the beach.

Now they can hear voices. They become louder as the water loses its depth. It's a euphoric feeling as Jack's right foot finds the sand and awkwardly he pulls and twists Alfredo into a standing position. To cheers and applause from those nearest, the two men collapse through the shallow waters and crawling, drag themselves onto the beach. Unable to stand easily, a few folks have come in to help them. They're met by Alfredo's woman, who's in tears, sobbing with relief as she smiles. She hugs Alfredo. Turning towards Jack who's kneeling close by, she's full of gratitude and he can see the joy in her eyes.

"Gracias, gracias, señor! Estoy muy agradecido.

Gracias de nuevo!"

Jack smiles and nods his head in appreciation. He looks up at the sky and thinks to himself 'I did it! My God!' Lowering his head, he lets his hands rest above his knees, still breathing heavily as ripples of sea water swirl around his feet. A man in fluorescent green budgie smugglers appears, a vision that once seen cannot be unseen, and thrusts a bottle of water into his hands.

It's only a short walk back to Lola's but Jack's lost count of the handshakes and backslaps he receives on his way. Alfredo approaches Jack and looks him in the eye. Shaking his head slowly, there are tears in his eyes. He holds out his arms and the two men embrace. Cue more applause from the Spanish audience.

"Qué puedo decir? Gracias. Eras tan valiente!" said Alfredo.

"Bueno" is all Jack can manage.

Then he thinks of a phrase he'd tried to learn on the flight over:

"Yo...no hablo Español. Inglés."

"Ah!" the lady intervenes. "He says he does not know what to say, he is so grateful and he wants you to know you were very brave. Thank you so much, señor."

Jack said "I had to do something. I could see you were distressed and that he was in trouble." Still gasping for breath, he added "The main thing is...everything's OK now. We're safe! And by the way...your English is very good."

"Thank you. Would you like a beer?" she asked.

"Oh, yes please. I could murder a beer!"

"What?"

"Ha! No worries, just an English expression. By the way, I'm Jack," he says, wearily extending a hand.

"Beatriz. I am so pleased you were here" she said.

As she spoke she beamed a smile that electrified Jack. He was transfixed.

As everyone returned to holiday mode and Jack enjoyed the most satisfying beer for a long, long time, Beatriz turned to Alfredo and fixed him with an entirely different look. It was a steely glare that spelt trouble. Whatever she was saying was delivered through gritted teeth and Alfredo was getting it in the neck. Both barrels. He looked down like a naughty spaniel as she berated him for going out so far when he's not a great swimmer, especially having had a few beers.

"How do you think I felt? Do you think it was clever, swimming out like that? You had no thought for me! All I could think was that I was about to lose you! How could I have explained to your Mama? Just imagine!"

Jack could see why she was cross. Despite his lack of Spanish he made out the gist of it. After she'd finished and calmed down, she came over to him.

"Señor, I would like to thank you properly and wonder where I can contact you perhaps?"

"Well," said Jack, "it's really not necessary but I'll give you my number."

She fetched her mobile to put the number straight in and then said:

"I don't know how I could ever thank you enough."

'It would be easier than you think' thought Jack but he actually said "Look, don't worry, it's only what any decent man would do in the circumstances."

"But none of the other decent men on the beach did anything. Only you."

With that, Beatriz turned and walked back to her sun bed. After a short exchange of words with the crestfallen Alfredo, they began to pack up their things to go. Before they left, he walked over to Jack. Looking humbled and embarrassed, he revealed that his English was actually quite decent.

"Thank you so much. What I did was very dangerous and you risked your life for me. I'm sorry."

Jack got up and they shook hands.

"Lucky, lucky, lucky!" called the North African jewellery seller, right on cue, with his long colourful robe and a dozen hats piled on his head.

The short bus ride up to Mojacar Pueblo was uncomfortable and in the late afternoon heat the shops were just starting to re-open. After putting his towel and swimming shorts to dry, Jack dragged himself upstairs to his room. Lying back on his pillow he reflected on what had happened. And only his second day out here. He'd arrived Wednesday evening, collected from the airport by a friend of Robert's and had not seen his host until he woke up yesterday.

He'd had that feeling of mild disorientation that you have when you wake up somewhere new. The room was lit only by shards of sunlight piercing the blinds. As he rubbed the sleep from his eyes he surveyed his new surroundings. If Robert's on Twitter, he thought, he sure as hell wasn't following Kelly Hoppen. Perched on the edge of the bed he cast a glance at his phone. He pulled on a t-shirt and hoisted up the blinds. A stained wall with a bit of a yard below greeted him.

"Buenos dias, Señor Jack!"

The door swung open and there was Robert, large as life and, well, just large.

"Roberto! Good to see you, man."

"Hope I didn't wake you when I came in last night, it was later than I expected."

"No, must have been flat out. Not bad for a first night. Bit warm, you must be used to it. Just admiring the panoramic view. I thought you might have had a mural or something done to brighten up that wall?"

"What, like a banner draped from next door's roof with something like 'Señor Jack, welcome to Mojacar' on it? What did you expect to see out of a Mojacar townhouse window…Sydney Opera House perhaps? The Hanging Gardens of Babylon? Herds of wildebeest sweeping majestically…"

"Thanks, Basil. Point taken."

"Anyway, come on down, coffee's on. We got some catching up to do."

Adjusting his striped boxers and scratching his arse he turned and whistled down the stairs.

Until recently Jack's route through life had been relatively conventional: a reasonably successful career in marketing, married with three kids. Robert's path had been more bumpy with more twists and turns than the Amalfi coast. Never short of ideas but invariably short in delivery. As often as he envied Jack's stability and sure-footed approach to life, Jack admired Robert's indefatigable spirit and optimism. And now they had something in common. The difference was that Jack didn't know that freedom was what he really wanted and he certainly wasn't used to having flexibility in his life.

"Won't be a minute with this" said Robert. "Help yourself to coffee."

"Cheers, mate" said Jack. "I was trying to work out on the flight over how long it's been since we last saw each other? Was it Rich and Tina's silver wedding bash?"

"Search me. Suppose it must have been. What was that then…five years ago?

"Yeah, something like that."

"Long time since University though, eh? Wow, where's the time gone?"

The baggy boxers and t-shirt didn't do much to hide the fact that Robert had put on a lot of weight over the years.

"You're not getting to the gym very often then these days?"

"Funnily enough…no. Gives me a point of distinction though with the locals. They seem to think it goes with my personality."

Jack laughed.

"I suppose so. Roberto, a man who can brighten up a room just by…well, moving away from the window."

"Hey! Thing is, Jack, you may see me as fat. I, on the other hand, identify as thin. I'm trans-slender, you see. Now shut up and get some of this down you. El desayunos is served. Breakfast to you, pal."

They quickly got stuck into a simple but authentically Spanish breakfast of chunky toasted bread drizzled with olive oil and spread with tomato pulp as they settled to each other's company.

"So what the hell happened then, Jack?"

"Ah, you know…the company wasn't performing well in a depressed market. Law of the jungle, along comes a bigger beast and swallows us up. They don't need two marketing teams so it's volunteers and over-50s over the side."

"And no lifeboats."

"Well, I'd been there a while so the redundancy terms were OK, I'm not going to go hungry just yet."

"Actually, it's the family I meant. You and Amanda.

You always seemed so together."

"I dunno. We just sort of got into a rut. Naturally work didn't help. Maybe we'd just run our course? Some days I feel right with it, others I wonder what the hell I've done. Or we've done I should say. Neither of us has been particularly happy."

Jack didn't know if this was the start of a new life or an intermission. Were they taking a break for refreshments before the players assemble for Act Two? He just wasn't sure what he was for anymore.

"Thing is...I've been a husband and a Dad and I've still got the kids I know, but do they need me? Losing my job too, it'd be hard enough with one or the other but both, it's been a bit heavy to be honest."

It seemed ironic to Jack. All the time he'd put in over so many years. And for what? Through his long hours he'd started to neglect their relationship and incrementally it withered and died. He'd always held this belief that loyalty was something to be valued but, when it mattered, found his company wasn't bothered.

"When I needed the support at home, it wasn't really there, it was too late. Maybe there just wasn't the love and care for each other any more, maybe we'd become tired...I just don't know. There came a stage where it sort of made more sense for me to leave."

"So when you left, did Davina McCall pop up and run through a summary of your highlights?"

"Yeah, right."

Robert stood up, walked round the table and put his hand on Jack's shoulder.

"Not a bundle of laughs then, mate? We'd better wipe that weary, forlorn look off your face. It doesn't suit you. Let's see what we can do to cheer you up."

A resident of Mojacar for over seven years, Robert was quite well known and popular with many of the locals who knew him. They liked his sunny disposition. One of Andalucia's small historic towns, Mojacar's buildings grip the sides of a hill and can be seen for miles around. Jack was looking forward to exploring it at his leisure. After making sure his guest knew where everything was around the house, Robert advised him that he'd be leaving him to settle in as he'd got some business to attend to and he'd be back in the evening.

"You haven't actually told me what you're up to these days" said Jack.

"Ah, that'll wait 'til later. A bit of this and that, you know? Gotta shoot, mate. You'll love Mojacar Pueblo, but it's bloody steep, so take it easy. And it's only a five minute bus ride to the beach at Mojacar Playa...very different but loads of bars and restaurants. If you want to chill out and acclimatise, that's the place to be. Not too busy either."

"Sounds good. I'll unpack and may well do that. See you later, Rob."

"Oh, by the way" added Robert half way out the door, "if anyone asks where you're staying, the locals know me as Señor Bobby."

"No! Señor Bobby? In your shape you're only a translator's typing error away from Mr Blobby. Love it!"

"Thanks a lot, you tosser. Don't forget your key. Adios amigo."

And with the two guys' friendship rebooted, Jack decided to spend his first couple of days attempting to unwind on the beach.

In the bedroom Jack's mobile rang out. He'd been sleeping, a bit late for a siesta, but not to put too fine a point on it, he was completely knackered.

"Robert! How ya doing?"

"Alright, thanks. Listen, I'm on my way back. Fancy a beer or something?"

"Sure, why not? Where shall I meet you?"

"Tell you what, Jack, there's a nice little bar in Turre. It's a couple of kilometres inland, so just go to the bottom of the hill and pick up the bus. It's called La Para and it's on the left just after you've gone through the main part of the town. I'll be there in about an hour. Get stuck, give me a bell."

An hour, plenty of time, he thought as he flopped back onto his pillow. His mind began to wander back again, tracing how he'd managed to save someone's life. How odd, he thought, that it was his own life he'd come out here to change. When he'd stepped off the local bus just before midday yesterday and he'd walked along the Paseo del Mediterraneo, the beach bars had looked much the same, but Lola's was the one he walked into. A few tables to the right, bar to the left, stairs straight ahead leading down to the beach. It had a level of cool, laid back sophistication that the outside hadn't led him to expect. The white tables had yellow director's chairs and there were tall white stools at the bar, which looked inviting. Palms gave it a tropical holiday feel and he was quietly pleased with his choice. A smiling young guy told him they'd be serving food from one and there was a charge for the beds but it's waived if he has food. Sounded great, so he wandered down the stairs to choose his spot. He dumped his towel and bag and went back up the steps and ordered an Estrella. The chilled beer hit the spot.

The beautiful long sandy beach slopes steeply into the waves. It's one of many along a curving stretch of shoreline that sits beneath the imposing and majestic Sierra Cabrera mountains, overseen by Mojacar Pueblo's hilltop vantage point. Lola's was central and looking back from the sea it stood out in a range of more traditional beachfront establishments, all with some sort of special offer to draw in the punters. The cream loungers were matched with oblong shades above. There were cream metallic tables and covered bed-like igloos to curl up in, sheltered from the sun. And the chill-out zone - its cream sofas arranged round a coffee table, bordered by palms and shades - really appealed to Jack, although unless the place was short of customers he couldn't see himself sat there on his own like Billy No-Mates. So he dropped onto this weird, wavy scrunchy bed.

Jack always loved walking along the sand, letting the breaking waves lap over his feet. It was on yesterday's walk he'd noticed the two lifeguards on duty, which he was pleased to see, a male and female, both sporting yellow t-shirts with red shorts and baseball caps. They looked so young that he wouldn't have been surprised to see their school uniforms hanging up under their viewing platform. He'd have thought their life saving training and skills would be better than his. Then again, would they look as good as David Hasselhoff and Pamela Anderson in slow motion? Probably weren't even born when Baywatch came out, he thought. On reflection, he was now rather pleased they weren't there when they were needed, it would have robbed him of his moment of glory.

Thinking about the time, he picked up his phone. Another forty five minutes yet before meeting Robert. But he's got to find the bus stop too. He thought he'd better make a move.

Last night when they'd been out for a drink Robert asked Jack if he'd enjoyed himself. Jack laughed, telling him about what he saw as the onset of delusion in his advancing years. When he'd decided to order lunch he'd ascended the stairs and on reaching the top level was startled by a large full length mirror. Seeing his image against the blue ocean behind made him feel just a little bit epic, as if he was in a magazine shoot.

"Cool Balearic beats, 30° of sunshine and a little cold beer conspired to allow me to feel like I was 25 again. Then I took off my shades. Lo and behold, the mirrors, aided by the brilliant light, swiftly lost their magic and brought me right down to earth. Pale and pallid was an understatement."

Luckily, the mixed paella had been surprisingly good. In his best posh voice he proclaimed to Robert that the vino rosado had been fresh and chilled, with a bouquet of lilies and just a hint of raspberries and Turkish delight.

"My brain turns to mush too after a midday drink" said Robert.

Then Jack had told him about the highlight of his afternoon. He'd said he couldn't help but notice a woman in a strawberry pink dress. With her malted Latin glow and long black wavy hair she looked gloriously resplendent as she scanned the location. Removing her dress artfully she revealed a red bikini. Despite rolling over to his other side and turning up Caribou on his iPod, he soon found himself turning back again. He confessed to having a moment and he'd been unable to do much about it. She was not only attractive but a more mature woman. Still considerably younger than him, no doubt, but what the hell, he thought.

"You're not used to having no-one there to slap you, that's what it is, mate" Robert interjected. "No withering put down!"

Yet on realising that she had someone with her, Jack had been almost relieved. He was around the same height as her - about 5' 8" - but thick set with short black hair and a moustache. Imagining him wearing white trousers and a short yellow military jacket, he'd decided that no, despite being a little silhouetto of a man, he didn't really look anything like Freddie Mercury. Despite the stud in his ear and a tattoo of what appeared a slightly deformed bull on his left bicep, he still contrived to look somewhat dull. 'How on earth could she be with him?' he'd thought, betraying that conceit commonly displayed by males the world over. Showing remarkably little interest, her companion spent most of his time asleep on the beach or listening to music.

After an hour or so she stood up to slip on her dress and tied it at the waste. If anything, she looked even more alluring. She proceeded to glide into the sea. Splashing water onto her calves, she washed the sand from her feet and slipped on a pair of sandals. Walking slowly back and up the stairs in front of the cocktail bar she disappeared into the ladies room.

"It was when she came back that I decided to throw the towel in. I'd taken enough punishment. First day in the sun and all that."

"Just feeling a teeny bit naughty, eh" teased Robert. "You don't need me to remind you of my lack of success with the female of the species" he said. "I mean, you can see I'm not exactly trying too hard to attract them. I thought if I relaxed a bit more around women then I might improve my chances."

"You've not given up though, have you?" said Jack.

"Oh yes. I've learned from my mentor, Homer Simpson… 'Trying is the first step towards failure'."

Jack admitted it was a bit of a novelty for him at the moment, although he claimed that the prospect of going out with someone else frightened the life out of him.

"Just tip me off before you bring anyone back" Robert warned.

"I should be so lucky!" said Jack.

Jack lifted himself onto the edge of the bed and ran his fingers through his dark, greying hair. A rapid shower, quick change of clothes and a scan for messages and he was out. He felt like he should have a spring in his step but he wondered what the hell had happened to his legs - his calves were as tight as gooseberries and his thighs felt like he'd had lead implants. He trundled off to wait for the next bus.

"What sort of day have you had then, Robert?"

"Pretty good actually. I've been learning about the fruit and veg trade in Spain and I think there might be some opportunities on the distribution side."

"Never imagined you as a sort of Spanish barrow boy."

"Thank you very much. I'm aiming a bit higher than that. It's having the right contacts that's the key here."

"Much risk involved?"

"Yeah, of course. If there's no risk it's probably not worth doing. It's manageable though. Food distribution generally interests me, you know. I've also been looking at the fishing industry lately."

"Oh. Scaling up, are we?"

"What d'you mean?"

"Scaling…fish?!"

"Bloody hell…"

"Imagine it's pretty important along this coast?"

"Not half. Ever heard of Garrucha prawns?"

"No."

"Best you can get, I tell you. Garrucha's just east of Mojacar, a few kilometres along the coast. I'll take you over there one day. We can watch the boats come in late afternoon, have a drink and a mooch round, then sample the fish at a restaurant later on. The place is full of fish restaurants but I know a few good 'uns."

"I bet you do" said Jack, before breaking into song and crooning… "There's a plaice for us…"

Robert threw back his head laughing then joined in immediately.

"Somewhere, a plaice for us…yeah, yeah, where were we when we did that? Outside that chippie somewhere."

"York, wasn't it? On Fergie's stag weekend?"

"That's it! What a great weekend that was. Ha!"

"Anyway," Robert went on, "you seem very chipper, how's your day been? No blurred vision and sordid thoughts today?"

"No, far from it. It's been fantastic actually. I can't quite believe what's happened, it doesn't seem real."

And with that Jack went on to tell the story of his day. From initially grinning and chuckling to himself Robert became quite moved as the rescue was re-enacted. There'd been a flicker of recognition at the name of the rescued individual but Robert simply listened with rapt attention. Jack finished his story, held out his hands, palms up, before taking another swig of cold beer.

"Fuck me!" said Robert. "That's heroic that is. You saved his life!"

He slapped him across the shoulder then went on.

"This guy Alfredo. What did he look like?"

Jack gave a rough description. There was more than a flicker of recognition in Robert's face. And for a minute

Jack thought he detected some concern in his eyes.

"I know him, I'm sure it'll be him. He does a few things for me now and then, works for me sort of thing."

"Sort of thing?"

"Yeah, all unofficial, under the radar, cash in hand, you know? He's not the brightest tool in the box but he's worth keeping sweet for me because he's got some friends that are quite handy to know. Like these guys in the fishing business I've been talking to. And he's a nice guy, you know, we get on alright."

A smile emerged and there was mischief in Robert's eyes as he looked intently at Jack.

"Hey! This gorgeous creature you've been telling me about with a glint in your eye, this woman with Alfredo, the one who couldn't thank you enough? That's not his girlfriend or his partner you chump! She's his sister!"

For a second or two, Jack was stunned. Yet as their behaviour together these past two days flashed through his mind it all made perfect sense.

Later that evening over a few tapas, Robert tried to tell Jack a bit more about Alfredo. It was difficult to hold a quiet conversation given that Spain were playing their neighbours and big rivals Portugal in the opening game of their World Cup group and it proved to be an evening of passion and excitement as they fought out a 3-3 draw. He only knew Beatriz by sight to say hello to and didn't know much about the family and the background, but Alfredo was someone you wouldn't want to trust with too much responsibility.

"Let's just say that as some people drink from the fountain of knowledge, Alfredo only gargles" said Robert. "For example, a few years back when he was younger, he was involved with these guys handling stolen computer equipment. He had one job. Pick up a box that had been left in a pre-arranged location, take it in his car to another location and leave it there. They told him to make sure he couldn't be recognised easily. So he turns up in a car, puts on his old motorcycle helmet to walk across to the box. Cracking idea, except that across the top of the helmet was his name in capital letters."

"Oh, no! Priceless."

"It's a shame. He's a nice lad really and he's not so bad these days, a bit older and wiser. So I look out for him a bit, I suppose. If I'm doing anything with him I try to think of everything just in case, you never know. So a briefing used to be anything but…you had to go through anything that might go wrong and try to head it off at the pass. But I'd like to think I've shown him a thing or two and he's learned a bit to be fair."

Just then Jack's telephone pinged.

"Oh, that's a coincidence" he said, slightly taken aback. "It's a message from Beatriz - I gave her my number - she did ask for it, honestly. Insisted, in fact. She'd like to buy me dinner to show their appreciation. Tomorrow night. Place called Cabo Norte?"

"Good restaurant, you'll like it. Oooh! Now who's a happy bunny? Bunny caught in the headlights by the looks of your face. Cheer up, mate. After the way you were raving about her last night? Bingo, my son!"

Chapter Two

Saturday 16 June 2018

The table had been booked for 9:30 p.m. Jack was still trying to get used to the Spanish custom of eating late, although 9:30 was positively early. He'd already learned that if you go out to eat somewhere any earlier you were likely to be dining alone or with older British tourists whose motto seemed to be 'when in Spain...do as you do at home'. Restaurants catering predominantly for the home market were very lively after ten. Robert dropped him off a bit earlier so he could go for a little aperitif first. He needed something to settle his nerves. He'd not felt like this since before he was married. Crazy, he thought, but he was quite excited too. He popped into Lola's as he'd wanted to feel comfortable. Growing darker outside with louder music and a variety of lighting effects, it felt edgy and different and he felt anything but comfortable. Nevertheless, he sat quietly in a corner with a San Miguel and a British newspaper that someone had left. 'Chaos in the Commons'...was that really news, he wondered? 'Wetherspoons to ditch continental beers' ran another headline. Jingoistic opportunism for the duration of the World Cup or a myopic reaction to a Brexiteer customer base? 'Welfare shambles' intrigued him but not for long. Learning that universal credit was increasing debt and hardship while failing to increase employment was, he was sure, what those who understood had predicted for it.

Enough, he thought, folding and discarding the paper. Almost immediately he started thinking about his wife. Sometimes he really missed her. Was it simply the younger version of her that he missed? He still loved her in a way, so had they just started taking each other for granted? Why must he think about her now? 'It's just nerves' he reassured himself. It felt like a date, although he knew it wasn't. 'It'll be fine.'

Strolling along the seafront and dodging between all sorts of families and groups out to enjoy 'el paseo', he found Cabo Norte down a side street across the road from the beach. It was a white traditional building with French windows at the side. Walking in, Jack looked round as a smiling lady walked towards him but just in time he saw Beatriz waving from a table for two outside in the garden. Standing to greet him she looked sensational. Deep red dress, black stilettos, simple jewellery. Jack's heart skipped a beat. He wasn't sure if he could cope with looking into those eyes all evening. Trying to avert her gaze he noticed her hair was pulled into a knot at the back of her head, accentuating her neck and lending her a look of elegant poise.

"I'm so happy that you could come here this evening. It is very important for me to be able to say thank you for what you did yesterday", said Beatriz.

"Oh, well, it's very nice of you. Thanks for inviting me."

Beatriz explained that after inviting him she had started to worry that she didn't actually know anything about him at all and perhaps had acted on impulse. Then she thought about what he'd done, and figured that he must be a good person. Jack nodded and smiled before explaining a bit about his background. Despite thinking beforehand about what he should tell her about himself, it just felt natural to tell her he was married, that he had children and after his redundancy how he had come to be staying in Mojacar. Just talking helped each of them to throw off some of the awkwardness they felt on meeting again.

"Isn't it strange", she said, "that but for your problems in life leading you here, my brother may have drowned yesterday?"

"I suppose it is" said Jack. "Who knows? Maybe it was luck, maybe it was fate, or destiny?"

Moving from the philosophical to the practical, Beatriz asked where Jack was staying just as the waitress arrived. 'When in Mojacar' Jack thought and asked about the manzanilla sherry that Beatriz had ordered. Would she recommend that he try one?

"Oh yes, of course. It's jerez! It's made in Andalucia and manzanilla is especially dry but it doesn't have the saltiness that some other types of sherry have. Try it."

He continued to tell her about staying with his old friend for a while and, although there were lots of details about Robert's recent life out in Spain that he still didn't know, they'd fallen easily into their old friendship and felt very comfortable. It was just what he needed.

"And what about you, Beatriz?" he said. "Where are you from, what do you do? And Alfredo too…I feel I should know more about him!"

Holding her hands up and rolling her eyes she replied.

"Alfredo? What can I say? He is a constant worry to me and my mother. He was always a bit lazy at school and so now he works, usually for some friends as he calls them, but I don't know. He is a little vague about what he does with them, which makes me suspicious. Sometimes it sounds a little, how do you say in English…?

"Dodgy?"

"Yes, I think. I would prefer that he find a regular proper job but no, things haven't worked out for him in regular jobs. I think this way of life suits him for now. Mama would just like to see him settle down, you know…a steady job and a nice young woman to take care of him. The old fashioned ideal."

Even outside it was still warm with the occasional delicate breeze coming off the sea. Jack asked about her father. Doesn't he worry about him? Beatriz grimaced slightly before trying to explain that they had a complicated relationship.

"Papa had always wanted Alfredo to follow him into the butcher's trade or something similar, a job that he would be able to have for life."

"Well, at least you'd know what kind of work he's out of" Jack commented, somewhat facetiously.

Ignoring his remark she went on to say that Alfredo was never interested. Mama supported him to follow a different path but he didn't really work hard at school so he didn't have the qualifications that he should. So he feels he let her down and his father too and sometimes there's a little unease at home. Consequently, Beatriz looks out for him as his older sister.

"Incidentally, I think my friend Robert knows Alfredo. He said he's done a bit of work with him now and again. But Robert's worked like that for years and I'm well used to it…in the UK we call it 'wheeling and dealing'."

"I must ask Alfredo about him then. Perhaps I've

seen him around."

"I hope what he does with my friend is not too dodgy, although I wouldn't be entirely surprised."

They both laughed.

"But he does like him, which is important. I'm sure he'd look after him."

"Oh, I do hope so. He needs someone to look out for him now and again, he has been in a few problems in the past, so…let's hope."

"Indeed. By the way, the locals apparently know him as Señor Bobby."

As they tucked into their calamar a la marinada Jack exclaimed that he'd never tasted squid this good and Beatriz told him more about her family.

"Me and my family are from a little town in northern Almeria called Velez Rubio. It's a very quiet place about an hour from here. It has a nice church, very attractive, but most visitors go to Velez Blanco nearby. Alfredo and me, we are very close. There is quite an age gap between us, so maybe that has made me feel a little protective of him. As I mentioned, Papa is a butcher, so he is known to lots of people in the region."

She went on to tell Jack that she lives in Granada, where she has a small apartment and works for a PR and communications company. Most weekends she likes to spend at the coast and generally stays with Alfredo. A good way to switch off and separate her career from the rest of her life, it also helped her to ensure he has some sensible influence now and again. Beatriz' enthusiasm for her work was evident as she talked about social marketing for clients, writing marketing strategies, developing content and managing events. Her passion was infectious and if there'd been a vacancy there, he'd have been tempted to apply.

"I presume you're single then?" said Jack.

Her vitality was quickly replaced by a wistfulness, a pensive frown overshadowing her features.

"Yes...yes, I am. I was married once, but it didn't go very well, shall we say?"

At least that was something they had in common, he thought. But before he could probe any further she changed the subject and asked him what it was like in the UK and in particular why people wanted to leave the European Union. Jack slumped back in his chair and sighed. He tried to explain it as simply as he could but wasn't sure if she was any the wiser, thus putting her in exactly the same position as most of the UK electorate. She tried to lighten the conversation.

"So it's Sunday tomorrow, what do you do with yourself?"

"I think Robert's planning to take me to Villaricos in the morning...to a local market?"

"That's right. It's a big street market close to the sea front. It's very popular and you can buy all sorts of things. The quality? I'm not so sure. For the food, yes. Locally made products, maybe some leather goods...it's good. But if you see designer socks for two euros, don't expect them to fit after you've washed them...there's a reason!"

Jack smiled in appreciation and they tucked into ravioli de rabo, washed down with some red wine from Valencia that their waitress had suggested. During the evening, the chef came out to talk to diners in between courses. Jack tried to explain how the ravioli had been 'melt-in-the-mouth' wonderful. Whilst it wasn't clear that she'd understood what he'd said, she recognised his pleasure and seemed to have found him entertaining. He and Beatriz had got on together so well that Jack was already quite besotted, but drinking the lion's share of the wine had no doubt contributed to his feeling of well-being. And it wasn't lust he told himself, oh no. OK, he thought, maybe a bit. But she was just so lovely and he'd not expected to feel so liberated, so joyful, so happy and at ease. And she made him have a dessert. A quite wonderful pear cake with toffee sauce and vanilla ice cream. But that was that. She paid the bill, Jack insisted on leaving the tip.

"How are you getting back to Mojacar Pueblo?" she said as they walked down the steps.

"Oh, I was going to look for a taxi."

"No, don't worry, I have my car. I'll drop you off at the bottom of the town."

Jack started to protest but to his inner delight she insisted, just as he hoped she would. As they strolled around the corner to the car, the evening was still warm, waves rolled gently onto the shore and the moon danced in and out of clouds and cast its reflection across the water.The trip in her Seat Leon took only a few minutes. Jack expressed how much he'd enjoyed himself and especially the opportunity to meet her and get to know her better. Beatriz could see his authenticity and it pleased her too that they'd got on so well.

"I hope you feel your impulse was not misplaced?" said Jack. "Intuition is invariably right. I've overridden it so many times in my life mostly to my regret."

"Oh yes, of course, it was right! And please don't forget why I asked you to have dinner tonight" she said. "I will never forget what you did for me and my family. Your impulse was definitely not misplaced."

Leaning over, she kissed him on the cheek.

"Multo gracias!" she added.

"Oh, the gracias was all mine" said Jack and immediately wondered what the hell he'd said that for. "I'm so glad I was able to help" he added, recovering his poise.

As he got out of the car he turned and held up his hand to say goodbye. But as he did, not really wanting the evening to end and realising there was something he'd forgotten to say, he turned back, lowered his head into the car and said:

"By the way, I'm sorry but I meant to tell you earlier, Beatriz, how beautiful you looked this evening. That's a gorgeous dress too."

He'd surprised himself and hadn't anticipated saying anything like that, however true it was. A nervous smile played on his lips.

"Perhaps we can meet again while you are here" she said, "maybe coffee some time?"

"Oh yes. I'd really like that. Adios" said Jack, quitting while he was ahead, shutting the door and turning to set off up the hill into town. He had to stop himself from skipping in case she was still able to see him. 'Oh yes, yes, yes!' he thought. 'I would so like that.'

Chapter Three

Sunday 17 June 2018

Sunday morning and it's around eleven when Robert and Jack reach the small town of Villaricos. The closer to the centre of town they drive, the tighter cars are shoehorned into small spaces, bumpers poking out at peculiar angles. Car parks? Jack had seen more order in scrap yards. Eventually they abandon the car on a grass verge and walk through the main thoroughfare. The sun is already strong, the pace is slow. Old Spanish boys sit outside cafés at pavement tables weighing up each visitor from under their flat caps, some of them chasing their espressos with something a little stronger. A hubbub builds from round the corner and as they turn into the street masses of people pore over both sides of the stalls, tourists rubbing shoulders with locals.

"Let's get a coffee, eh?" said Robert.

There's a place on the corner with tables outside. Robert gestures to one of the waiters who points to a single empty table near the door as they squeeze through the chairs.

"Dos cafés con leche, por favor, señor. Hey Jack, the

sticky buns are good here, fancy one?"

He did. A fabulous aroma of strong, fresh coffee beans and baking pervaded the air. The intoxicating, good-to-be-alive atmosphere, especially after his evening out with Beatriz, merely added to his sense of positivity. He'd already told his landlord all about it at the risk of opening himself to constant ribbing at the slightest opportunity. That said, he had found himself wondering about what had happened in her marriage; she'd changed the subject rather quickly, albeit very deftly. This was something he hadn't shared with Robert.

The waiter arrives, gracefully high-twirling his tray and delivering a plate of freshly baked magdalenas and torrijas. The magdalenas are small, delicious lemon flavoured cakes while Robert tells him the torrijas are made like French toast - typically using up the stale bread and finished off by sprinkling with cinnamon or drizzled with honey. Everywhere around the centre of the market there's fresh food. Robert promises that they'll try a few things and pick up some goodies on their way back. It transpired that Robert was keen to come to Villaricos this morning as he's meeting a few associates about some potential business. First he wants to catch up some more with his friend and find out first hand about the state of the nation.

"Not you as well! Even Beatriz wanted to know about Brexit last night. She's probably more confused now than before she asked."

"Hey, Boris is the man, isn't he? He's going to save the country, surely?"

"Boris Johnson!" laughed Jack. "If that man walked into a think tank he'd drown. 'So, Mr Johnson, is there any beginning to your talents?'"

"Glad I'm away from it out here in Spain. To tell

you the truth, mate, I couldn't give a toss what happens. You know, I can't see myself returning to the UK, so as long as there's no disadvantage to me, I don't care."

"Isn't that a bit selfish?"

"Probably. Don't get me wrong, I like the old idea of a common market but, well…I don't think the average person understands enough to make an informed decision on something like the EU, and I'm no different. And as I don't have to think about it too much out here, I'm not going let it upset me."

Jack suggested that maybe the Rt Hon Mr Corbyn might be the one to lead them out of the mire.

"What?" said Robert. "Couldn't pour piss out of a shoe if the instructions were written on the heel. Right. That'll keep us going for a bit" he added as he arose from the table.

"Where're we going now?" Jack asked, as they leave the din of the cafe behind.

"I'll show you the sea front just down this way. It's a lovely walk along the promenade, usually very quiet."

"Beautiful" said Jack, hands on hips and looking out to sea.

"Actually", Robert said, "you don't really need to come with me to meet these guys. Thinking about it now, you'll probably be a bit bored. It's not that you won't understand anything, 'cause we talk what I like to call 'Espanglése'. A bit of a mash-up."

"Are you sure?" asked Jack.

"Yeah, you can be having a look round the market, mate, pick up a few things. Stroll along the front, go for a beer. Chill out a bit. If you need me I'll be at Playa Azul, that small hotel restaurant we passed on the way in. Opposite Dreambeach if you get stuck."

"Alright, great. I'll have a mooch round."

Leaving Jack to his own devices Robert makes a call as he walks through the bustling streets. Within a few minutes, he's entering Hostal Restaurante Playa Azul. He's directed by the receptionist into a traditional dining room, white tablecloths, wooden chairs under a low, beamed ceiling. He greets the only two men present, sitting in the corner having a beer. Xavi and Luis give him a respectful welcome and order him a beer. Xavi is the senior partner here, a tall wiry individual, bald with grey hair at the back and sides with moustache to match. Luis is smaller, darker complexion, black hair and his cartoon t-shirt is amply filled. Sitting round the small table there's some general chat about this and that for a minute or two before Robert cuts to the chase.

"Anyway, guys, what's this opportunity you've got coming up? It sounded very intriguing on the phone. What's it all about then?"

Xavi, the older one, glanced quickly at Luis, then leaned forward towards Robert. Speaking quietly and furtively, he said:

"We have been notified of a special consignment of fruit coming into the country. This fruit is, shall we say, more valuable than usual. Do you understand?"

"I think so" said Robert. "What's in it then?"

"We don't know yet" Luis interjected with a slight tone of excitement that caused his colleague to shoot him a withering look.

"We don't know yet, this is true" Xavi confirmed. "We know it will be in small bags that have been hidden inside the fruit and…"

"What sort of fruit are we talking about?" said Robert.

"We don't know yet!" said Luis, his eyes again widening like a child on Christmas morning.

This time not a flicker from Xavi, just a tightening of his lips and a silent pause.

"We don't know yet what the fruit will be, but we know it will be delivered through the usual distribution system for fruit and vegetables and will arrive at a principal city in mainland Spain."

"Which city?"

"We don't know yet!" said Luis who almost immediately closed his eyes and tensed his shoulders, now resembling the child who's discovered the dog has dribbled on on his Terry's chocolate orange.

Xavi puffed out his cheeks, took a deep breath, then said:

"We will be told the relevant details a few days ahead of the arrival. What we want you to do is to be ready to go to the distribution centre on the appointed day to buy the consignment of fruit. The plan is to buy the fruit before it goes into the market for auction. We have a contact who will be expecting someone. If anything should go wrong, there is a back-up plan. The consignment of fruit will go in to be sold at auction. In that case you'd have to go in and bid. Because you know that the fruit is more valuable, you will be able to bid more than the competitors there, even if this is more than we have agreed with our contact."

"So I don't know what's inside the fruit. I don't even know what fruit it's going to be inside! And I don't know where the fruit's going to be sold," said Robert. "Should be a doddle, eh?"

"You will. After today we need to keep away, so we're not seen together, so we will liaise with you by leaving notes at your home. No mobile phone contact, OK?"

"OK. Just one thing, could what's inside the fruit be illegal then for it to be so valuable?"

"It could be. Are you in? We believe this is a low risk opportunity."

"Well you would, wouldn't you. You're not having to buy it, handle it and transport it back. Don't know about low risk but whether it's worth it depends what's in it for me. And I'll need to have someone working with me and they'll need paying."

"As long as they can be trusted."

"Of course. That's up to me, isn't it?"

The two men proceeded to thrash out what was in it for Robert, whilst Luis nodded and continued to look a little more excited than he should. That was it, the deal was done. Robert shook hands with each of them and left to find Jack.

"Time for something to eat, yet?" said Jack, as they met at the edge of the market.

"Yeah, let's find something like a Spanish Sunday lunch for you, shall we, although it's a bit early? Over here, lunch is traditionally the main meal of the day and it rarely happens before 2:00. Especially Sundays, you know, it's often a big family do where you get all the generations together. Nice really."

With that they trotted off, Jack with his shopping bags and Robert with a potentially tricky job secured.

Chapter Four

Monday 18 June 2108

Monday starts when Jack's phone bleeps. Text from Beatriz. He picks up the phone, plonks himself into a chair and moves his level of 'awake' up a notch. Would he like to meet her for coffee before she returns to Granada for the week? He replies immediately, his thumbs trying to keep up with his thoughts in vain. Only when he's hit 'send' does he notice that he's said 'Yes - great idea. Where Sharon we meet? Whatever Tim?' Bloody predictive text…he's half way through sending a correction when he receives Beatriz' response: 'Who are these people?'. After explaining and taking more care with his second attempt, he proceeds to smarten himself up without looking as if he's tried too hard.

"Effortless but artful, casual but chic…" he mutters to himself, as if he'd been following one of those smug guides on 'what to wear if you're over fifty' that provide some token men's interest in weekend style supplements.

Heladeria Blu sits on Paseo del Mediterraneo and has an open terrace in front. The young waitress greets Jack in Spanish that is too much and too rapid for him. He responds by trying out his newly learned vocabulary for eating out and when he gets to the end the waitress smiles sympathetically.

"It's alright, I'm English," she says in a home counties accent.

Just in time to save him from bathing in his own embarrassment, Beatriz walks in from the busy seafront road. Her wide smile brings the place alive as heads turn towards her and she extends her arms wide to give Jack a hug. Greetings are followed by a peck on each cheek as Jack thinks to himself it's already been worth it. Trying to stay cool, what he really wants to do is look around to see who's staring enviously at his pulling power…he's only prevented from doing so by self-awareness of his delusional thought patterns. Then she walks over to the outside counter and calls in to the couple beavering away in the kitchen.

"Hola Sofia… cómo te va?"

Sofia leans over and they manage a high-five as Beatriz sweeps back round to join Jack at the table.

"I guess you're a regular here then?" said Jack.

"Oh, how can you tell?" she laughed. "Yes, I love the coffee and I absolutely adore the ice cream."

Just then their waitress comes across. An americano and a flat white are ordered and Jack takes some advice before deciding:

"I'd like a nice piece of cake, I think."

"Cake? The cakes here are very good, for sure. But you should try the crepes with ice cream - you won't regret it, I promise you."

"If that's what you recommend, that's what I'll have. I think I'll go for the hazelnut and triple chocolate por favor."

This morning Beatriz was modelling a flowered sleeveless summer dress, tied at the waist. He was just thinking that he'd rather not be able to see his own reflection in her large round sunglasses when she removed them and placed them on the table. Oh, so much better, he thought, although the shades were really rather cool.

"These sunglasses are very stylish" he said, picking them up to have a closer look. "Probably not very cheap."

"Ha! Absolutely they are not cheap! But luckily I have a discount because they are made by one of our clients. They come from Malaga, just along the coast, and they are sustainable too."

As she leaned across the table to show Jack their tiny signature trademark on the inside of the arm, Jack tried to focus but his faculties were overwhelmed by her scent. It was heavenly.

As he tucked in, Jack asked Beatriz how her weekend had been and what was in prospect for her in Granada. He was genuinely interested but it also allowed him to get on with devouring an ice cream crepe that was as good as he'd been promised.

"Have you ever been to Granada?" asked Beatriz.

"No, I haven't" said Jack. "I believe it's a lovely city."

"Oh, yes. But you must see it. The Alhambra? It's fantástico!"

After a pause she added, "How long are you staying here for?"

Jack shrugged his shoulders.

"No idea really." He said in a matter of fact way. "Robert's said I can stay for as long as I like or as long as I need, so I don't know but I expect I'll be here for a few weeks yet."

"You must come to visit Granada. I have a friend running a great hotel and she'll give you a cheaper rate. I can show you the best places and we can tour the Alhambra, I haven't been round for a few years now."

"That sounds great, Beatriz. I'd love to do that. Are you sure?"

"Yes, of course."

"OK. Maybe you can suggest some dates for me?"

"I'll speak to my friend first and I can tell you when's best to come. It's done!"

They both smiled. Beatriz looked at her watch and said it was about time she was on her way. As they left, Jack noticed the chalk board advert at the entrance which said 'Skinny people are easier to kidnap, so eat lots of ice cream'. Well, that was his safety sorted.

That afternoon Robert picked up Jack to drive over to Garrucha. He gave him a bit of a taster of what to expect.

"It's principally a fishing town, that's historically what it's been about. But these days it does its best to attract tourists and, to be fair, the beach is decent enough. It's just that you've always got the fishing industry and the commercial side of things that dominate your views and that. Still, gives it a bit of character, you know, a real working place."

They parked a few streets in from the promenade. Given that it was June and that this is Europe's only officially designated desert region, it was unsurprising that the sun shone so consistently. Jack was starting to feel more at home with the heat and the pace as they walked towards the harbour, the town's central point. It felt like a quiet place with just small shops and bars, topped by apartments that for the most part looked like holiday lets judging by the towels drying on balconies. Then again, it was still siesta time. Emerging from the shade they crossed the promenade to be closer to the sea.

Looking down onto the beach there were quite a few families strewn across its sand. There was barely a ripple in the sea.

"Do you know," said Robert, "this is the only town beach in Europe with a blue flag? Considering the trawlers come in and out just over there that's not bad, eh?"

"That's impressive. Do they prioritise tourism then?"

"No, I wouldn't say that. Fishing is still the number one here, it's the main industry, biggest source of income to the town, important for jobs. But if they can maintain that and have a good tourist offer it's got to be be better for the local economy."

They strolled on along the sea front towards the harbour itself. As the boats weren't due back just yet, they popped into La Cantina de Floor to quench their thirst. Looking at a map on the wall Jack asked tour guide Robert about a place called Palomares, which looked quite close.

"Oh, Palomares is just a few kilometres up the coast near Villaricos, where we were yesterday. A bit of a blot on the landscape really. It's industrial and a bit smelly to be honest. It had a bit of a nuclear crisis in 1966 or somewhere around then. This Yank B-52 bomber had a mid-air collision with its refuelling plane! Can you imagine the media frenzy if that happened today?"

"Oh my God!" said Jack, looking simultaneously shocked and amused. "So did it go down in the sea then?"

"Nah, it just dumped its cargo - H bombs! Apparently three of them fell on land and another in the water. Incredibly none of them exploded, although one of them leaked quite a lot of radioactive material. They reckon they had a fleet of warships and subs looking for the one in the sea. Yet it was only found about eighty days after the incident when it became caught up in the nets of a local fisherman. They did some tests a few years back that showed there was still five times more radioactivity than anywhere else round here."

"Staggering," said Jack. "The pilot must have thought he was going down."

"Oh yeah, for sure. Selfish bastard must have thought…right, I'm not going down with these on board… I'll leave them as souvenirs for the fishermen and their families. Crazy. I mean, he wasn't exactly Pierre the famous French fighter pilot, was he?"

"What do you mean?"

"You must know that old joke?" said Robert. Then in an outrageous accent he tried to remind him… "I am Pierre, ze fameuse French fighteur pilot!"

"No, you'll have to tell me, mate, I can't remember that one."

"No, I can't tell that at this time of the day. It's a late night job after a few drinks. Remind me another time."

Trawlers can be seen just a couple of minutes from the harbour, returning with the day's catch. It's almost five o'clock and groups of people are making their way slowly in the late afternoon heat to see their arrival, small children straggling behind, some pulling in different directions but attached like bendy extensions to their parents' arms. The sea bed around Garrucha becomes very deep very quickly. Locals say it's possible to fish less than half a mile from the harbour wall and yet be over 1,000 feet in depth. Some of the coast line has a coral base, attracting tropical fish species. The rocky ledges and deep holes are home to conger and moray eels as well as octopus, to which the locals are quite partial. Of course, the stars on local menus are those large red prawns unique to Garrucha. Descending the steps to the quayside Jack and Robert head over to where the fish will be auctioned off as they're unloaded from the boats.

"Here we go, Jack, there's been fish unloaded here for thousands of years. It's inspiring to think of that, isn't it."

Jack murmurs his assent but really he finds it difficult to be inspired by seeing fish unloaded. What he wants to see are those red prawns, understand what all the fuss is about. Prized by chefs and considered by some to be the most delicious shellfish in the Mediterranean, their relatively small numbers mean they can be expensive even on the market. As boxes of prawns come in they're laid on flooded ground and ice blocks are packed around them. Buyers come in gradually and sit themselves down opposite the haul - as well as the prawns they can see John Dory, snappers, groupers and red scorpion fish. The men all look very studious and an air of expectation slowly builds. Jack takes some video footage on his phone to put on Twitter for his few hundred followers. The catch is so fresh that some of them look as if they're going to leap out of the box any moment. One man in the corner appears less interested in the fish than he is in Robert and Jack. Black jacket, black jeans, black t-shirt, his face is hidden behind sunglasses and a newspaper.

As the white plastic boxes of fish start to move along conveyor belts, the auction begins. The noise soon escalates as the buyers, seated in a tiered area along the side, start exchanging words. They've each got an electronic device and it seems that's how they bid. At the press of a button, out pops a label that drops into the tray they've bought. Then the boxes are iced and put onto pallets ready for despatching to whichever restaurant, hotel or shop has sealed the deal.

"What's going on, Robert?"

"No idea mate."

It all seems a bit chaotic but nobody's getting upset so it must be business as usual. A snapshot of working life in a modern Spanish fishing town.

"I'm surprised it doesn't smell more fishy in here, all these fish everywhere," said Jack.

"Fresh fish don't smell," Robert explained, with a simplicity that Eric Cantona could only dream of.

As Jack's eyebrows raised he wore a puzzled 'you learn something every day' expression.

Having seen enough, Robert said he'd take Jack for a short drive along the coast and inland, with the aim of returning for a table while the sun's going down. The man in black takes his leave at the same time and stays a good distance behind until they reach the car.

After their tour they did what the Spanish like to do in the evening, they took a paseo along the front. There was an unusually high number of English people in town, Robert thought. They soon discovered it was because it was England's opening group game against Tunisia, all looking for TVs in bars. It didn't make for the most relaxing of atmospheres in the streets as groups of mainly men in white shirts bearing the cross of St George warmed up for the game by singing songs and shouting a lot. By kick off, even the national anthem was out of tune. Eventually as the light began to fade the two guys went along to El Birra, a fish restaurant close to the marina.

"As a rule" said Robert, "never order fish on Mondays, 'cos the trawlers don't go out on Sundays and it won't be fresh. Unless, of course, it's Monday night in

Garrucha!"

They ordered a plate of the famous Gambas Rojas de Garrucha, along with a guiso marinaro to share - a local stew with monkfish, almonds, fried bread and wine sauce.

Toasting themselves with a glass of local cava, they proceeded to wax nostalgic about student days, what old friends are up to and the relative merits of weddings they'd both attended over the years. 'Ola Señor Bobby!' called out a Spaniard entering the restaurant. Robert waved in acknowledgement as a huge grin broke out on Jack's face and he slowly shook his head. After a couple of courses shared and well down the bottle of vino blanco, they became a little more serious. Talk changed to subjects closer to home, like families.

For Jack, it was too soon to say how he felt about this big change in his life. He thought he was just starting to enjoy being in Spain and was genuinely grateful to Robert for his help. In due course he needed to work, but what should he do and where? At times he thought his marriage was probably over for good, other times he thought more optimistically about it and saw some hope of getting back together with Amanda. For as long as that was a possibility his job-hunting would need to be mindful of location. Otherwise, the world was his oyster, what with the children grown up and spread around the country.

"How old are they now?" asked Robert.

"Josh is 29, Nicole's 26 and Seb's just turned 24."

"Wow, you could be a grandad anytime soon."

"That's enough of that."

They got on to talking about parents and especially their fathers. Jack's father had died three years ago following a heart attack.

"Do you think about him much?" said Robert.

"Yes I do, just at odd moments too. I'm never quite sure why he comes to me at particular moments. Although just lately I find myself asking what he'd have thought about my marriage hitting the rocks. Him and my Mum were so solid, passed their golden wedding anniversary. It was so important to them, they were so proud of themselves."

Jack felt a lump in his throat and his eyes moisten, then smiled and started laughing.

"What's up?" said Robert.

"Just something my Dad used to like doing. He used to have these classic quotes from films that he'd deliver in a dreadful attempt at impersonation. One he trotted out when things were not working out was from John Wayne, Lord knows which film it was from. He'd push his shoulders forward, his arms back at an angle and walk with his arse out and exaggerating his hips from side to side. I mean, how d'you make John Wayne look camp?"

"Can you remember the quote?"

"How could I ever forget it?"

He tried to conjure up an approximation of the great man's speaking voice.

"I think it went… 'Tomorrow is the most important thing in life. Comes into us at midnight very clean. It's perfect when it arrives and it puts itself in our hands. It hopes we've learned something from yesterday'. Optimistic or what?"

"Brilliant. And have you learned anything from yesterday?"

"Oh, I hope so. Every day I think about something I might have done differently. It's hard not to lately, especially around work and marriage. The sort of learning that I may never have the chance to apply again, which would be pretty useless really! But you never know…"

"Getting old's scary, isn't it?" said Robert.

"Yeah, it is, mate. I think we underestimate it, what older people go through as everything declines and fails, ugh! Doesn't bear thinking about."

"That's why we underestimate it, we put it away in a special compartment. And then, one day… 'Pass us my teeth, love, I wanna nibble your neck'."

"I've got to say, my Dad was always prepared to have a laugh at his own expense, always remained self-deprecating even in his old age."

"Self-deprecation's alright. Unfortunately my Dad was more into self-defecation, poor sod."

Robert's Dad had died around a year ago. He recalled how heartbroken he and his Dad had been when his Mum had died. Dad sort of gave up a bit, lost his spark. Eventually he'd had to go into a care home. He'd been lucky in that it was a good one, not cheap, but brilliant staff, couldn't do enough for him. Then he chuckled, putting his hand to his forehead…

"You wouldn't believe it," he said. "He seemed to become quite taken with this woman there, Dorothy her name was. I couldn't visit that often but when I did they were great at filling me in on what had been happening. You know, his memory had started to go a bit and we thought it was early onset of dementia. So I couldn't always rely on him to tell me himself. But there was this male carer who sat down with me one day and told me about Dad's relationship with Dorothy."

"It seems that every day her and my Dad would walk down to the bottom of the garden together. It was a very big garden, lovely trees and so on. This carer had gone down there to check they were OK one day when he saw them both sitting on this seat in a secluded part of the garden.

They were just sat there next to each other, but this Dorothy had got hold of his old man!"

"What! You're joking, aren't you?"

"No! Apparently, this happened every day. The two of them just sat quietly, Dorothy with her hand on my Dad's pecker! So this guy decided it was innocent enough and he didn't want to spoil their fun, so he left them alone apart from the odd covert check."

"One day, a new resident came into the home and about a week or so later, the carer said he'd noticed that my Dad had started going down to the same spot in the garden at around the same time each day, but with this new woman. He'd noticed that Dorothy was left on her own and was quite upset. She wasn't just feeling very sorry for herself, but appeared quite agitated. This one morning when Dad returned from his little trip down the garden with his lady friend, Dorothy went up to him once he was on his own… there was a bit of an exchange, the carer said. Then Dorothy said to him:

'What is it she's got that I haven't?'

And my Dad said…'Parkinson's!'"

"Noooo!" said Jack. "Are you winding me up?"

"No, that's what he said. The crafty old bastard, eh? They started trying to 'manage the relationship better' - I think they were the words. But it was only a couple of months later when he got pneumonia and that saw him off."

"At least he had some happy times before he went."

"Indeed he did," said Robert.

Chapter Five

Tuesday 19 June 2018

It's Tuesday morning and, just like the day before, it starts with a text from Beatriz. She's spoken with her friend, Christina, who manages a hotel in Granada and they're quiet over Wednesday and Thursday the following week, so she can do Jack a good deal. How would he be fixed for visiting Granada for those days? 'Let me see' he thinks, staring at a telephone calendar that shows the week ahead to be completely devoid of any activity or commitments whatsoever. 'Looking good' he replies. With that he proceeds to ask her to make the necessary arrangements and suggests they meet to discuss at the weekend. Soon after he reminds himself that he ought to ring his kids today, which should be a pleasant task. So why doesn't he look forward to it?

In Spain Jack has increasingly come to feel like two different men. One is relaxed, confident and colourful, he feels bright and optimistic; the other feels tension and his world appears in black and white, he's more dour, confused and pessimistic. The negative Jack comes in when he's dealing with things around the family, his job, his home. He knows he can't just disappear and cut himself off from his family, that's not an answer. It might be a struggle for him but he has to make a new future for himself and he has to look for some sort of balance in his life that enables him to play his part in the family positively.

Meanwhile Robert has left to meet Alfredo, having demanded of the young Spaniard that he keeps quiet about it…it's top secret! They meet at the Hub Internet Cafe in a small town called Huércal-Overa. It's not far from the AutoVia but which otherwise lies sprawling in the desert. Apart from its popular market, it's grown in recent years through an influx of European and Latin American immigrants.

They exchange greetings with a warm hug and Robert, not having eaten, can't resist the menu and orders sausage, bacon and egg.

"You British with your bacon and eggs…" said Alfredo.

"Nothing wrong with it, Alf. Now and again."

"Looks like now and again all the time maybe!"

Robert is not amused and shoots him a look.

"Hey amigo, at least built like this means I can float. Which is more than can be said for you!"

"What do you mean, Bobby?"

"Well…I heard you got into a little trouble in the sea last week. The word is, you had to be rescued by a British tourist."

Alfredo is somewhat taken aback that Robert knows about this incident.

"How did you find out about this?"

"It was on the front of the local newspaper this morning."

"What?"

"Nah, I'll tell you how. That guy who saved you is

called Jack, right? He just happens to be my best mate and he's staying out here with me for a little while. So, I'm glad you were OK and it's great that he was able to help you, but...what on earth were you thinking of? Don't go doing stuff like that and leaving me on my own. We've got great things to achieve, you and me. Be careful!"

He goes on to check that Alf knows that his sister is still in contact with Jack. He does and he concedes that it's a periodic reminder of his stupidity. He explains that's why it's paramount that he doesn't share any of their conversation this morning with his sister and he can't afford for his friend to know about it either. Alfredo goes from feeling slightly stupid to feeling ever so important as he awaits whatever precious knowledge Bobby is about to impart and he stealthily looks around the cafe. Robert tells him that he has some work for him but that it could be a bit risky and he asks if he can trust him. Alfredo is quite excited and says he can trust him, of course.

"This job involves travelling to a fruit market somewhere in Spain with a small truck. We're going to buy a consignment of fruit. Then we're going to bring it back to an agreed destination. OK?" said Robert.

"Is that it?" asked Alf, puzzled by the apparent simplicity of the task.

"Essentially, Alf, yes it is. But it might not be so straightforward. Plan A is that we do a deal when we get there with a contact at the market so that we can take the cargo, load up and get out as fast as we can. But we have to be prepared if anything goes wrong and we can't do the deal that way. To be clear, no deal is not an option for us. Understand?"

"Yes" said Alf, "but there must be a lot of fruit in the market, surely this is easy?"

"There may be lots of fruit in the market but if we just wanted lots of nice fruit we could get them from any market, anytime. This fruit is a bit different...let's just say it's worth a bit more than ordinary fruit."

"How will we know? Does it look different? What type of fruit is it?"

"We won't know what we're picking up until a couple of days before we go. The fruit will still look like fruit, whatever it is. It's the right boxes we've got to look out for."

"So the boxes will look different?"

"No, the boxes will be the same as all the other boxes. Each consignment of fruit has a different number or code or something and we'll be told what it is that identifies them from other fruit before we go. I'm expecting a message to tell me what it is we're looking for. And who we've got to meet when we get there".

"Now if it all goes pear shaped" Robert went on, "we need a Plan B."

"So we are collecting pears from the market?" said Alf.

"No, we're not, that was just a figure of...never mind. It's just fruit for now, right? Plan B is that I'll have to go into the auction and bid for the fruit. That just means we'll probably have to pay more for them. My associates will make sure I've got the cash to pay on the day and then we're off. The sooner we get them back here the better. Adios fruit market! Your job will be to drive the truck and help me load and unload the stuff. Can you manage that?"

"Sure I can."

"How about the truck? Can you get hold of a decent truck or large van at a good price?"

"Yes, no problem. When do we need it for?"

"Don't know yet, Alf. We might only get a few days

notice, so bear that in mind when you're looking at vehicles."

"OK. So what's in it for me?"

"You'll be well rewarded, Alfredo, well rewarded. I don't have the figures yet but I'll cut you a good slice, trust me."

"A-ha! So you are going to pay me in fruit, Señor Bobby?"

"Very funny. No, I'm not. And whatever you do, don't eat any of the fruit when you're on the job. Especially when you're driving."

"Not even one."

"Not even one. They may look like fruit, they may taste like fruit, let's just say this might be magic fruit. Comprendo?" Robert winked as he asked.

"Si, comprendo" said his voice. 'Non comprendo' said his face.

After reminding Alf that he can't breathe a word about this to his sister, they agreed to talk later in the week about the vehicle and any news on arrangements. As they leave the cafe together to go their separate ways, a man wearing a black t-shirt and shades lowers his newspaper and watches Robert cross the road.

Since the embarrassment of his ill-considered brush with becoming fish food, Alfredo has been subdued. It was a chastening experience. The meeting with Robert, however, has given him a little more belief, a feeling that he can be useful, that he's wanted, even though it's a task that sounds like it may not be entirely legitimate. At least he's only the driver. On the journey home he figured that if anything goes wrong he can always say he knew nothing, he was merely hired to drive the van. Would that wash with his sister, never mind the law? Then again, he enjoyed being with Señor Bobby. They seemed to click. Robert had time for him and genuinely appeared to be interested in him.

Arriving home, he took out his keys to open the door to his apartment and found to his surprise it was unlocked. Stepping inside cautiously, he immediately heard the sound of singing. Through the semi-strangulated vocals he recognised an old early sixties song called 'Cuando Calienta El Sol'. It could only be his mother. As he closed the door behind him, the singing stopped.

"Alfredoooo?" she yelled, as the sound of a brush hitting the floor went off like a shot echoing around the place.

Birds abandoned their rooftop perches and dogs in the vicinity skulked away to find a new sleeping spot.

"Mama!" said Alfredo, with a mock happiness that was betrayed by the slow delivery of each quivering syllable.

Mama marched from the kitchen into the hall where she stopped about four paces from her son. She put her hands on her ample hips, tilted her head down to look at him over her glasses and fixed him with a fearsome gaze. Alfredo shrugged his shoulders, his bottom lip quivering ever so slightly as he looked down. Then, letting go of her anger, Mama walked towards him…

"My son, my poor boy, what were you doing?" she said. "I'm so relieved, so happy to see you again. I love you, my son."

She hugged him. So tightly that he looked like he might need rescuing again as the colour drained from his face. His head was almost resting on the curls in her dyed auburn hair as first he patted her shoulder then, breathing more easily, he smiled and tried to reassure her.

"Mama, I love you too. It's alright, it's alright…" he said.

"Noooo! No, it's not alright you idiot!" she screamed as she pushed him away. "Don't you have any sense? Don't you care about me? Don't you care about Beatriz? Don't you care about your Papa and everybody in the family who loves you?"

"I'm sorry, really Mama."

"Sorry? You don't know the meaning of the word. And why do you not answer your telephone when I ring you? Every day I've been calling and calling and nothing. Stupid message."

"I've been so busy…"

"I've been so busy!" she mocked. "Doing what, hey? I never understood why you were in such a hurry to leave home in the first place."

"It's been four years now, Mama."

"You're still a young boy and if you want to come home your room is always ready for you, you know that. Nothing has been moved, it's…"

"I'm 26 now Mama."

"Oh Dios mio! You are 26. It's time you started to settle down, find a good job, find a good señorita, yes?"

Alfredo walked away shaking his head. All conversations with his mother sooner or later led to work and marriage. A 'good señorita' was somehow always the tipping point for Alfredo. She shuffled after him into the living room, where they sat down and had a more rational conversation. He tried to reassure her that his prospects were looking up and he could look after himself. She reassured him that she was only upset because she loved him so much. Mama had travelled over that morning on the bus. It had cost her €7 one way so Alfredo thought the least he could do was offer to take her home. She happily accepted but insisted on continuing with the cleaning she'd started. Almost worth the cost of the petrol and his time.

———

The man who'd saved him was having a quiet day and hoped to have a good look round Mojacar Pueblo. He'd managed to make contact with his eldest son, Josh, and by text they'd agreed to FaceTime at 8:30 before the start of his working day. Not ideal, his dad thought initially, but found it a bit hard to object as he had diddly squat to do for the rest of the day. It was now just over three months since he and Amanda had agreed to separate. When he and Josh managed to connect, it was good to see his son and it showed. He thought his Dad was looking very well, better than he'd seen him for a while. Spain must be agreeing with him.

Jack couldn't deny that he was feeling better but was also anxious to know how everyone was, and especially his wife. It was important to him to be able to communicate that whatever had gone down before, whatever the future held, he missed her in his life. Nicole and Seb were also fine according to Josh, but Jack knew there was perhaps an element of Josh giving his father the assurance he was looking for. As the oldest he'd taken on that leadership role that comes with the position, the extra responsibility and maturity that being the first born brings. He was more concerned about his Mum than Jack was expecting though, and that worried him a little. She'd been complaining of some pain and had been to the doctor, who was referring her to a specialist for a scan. Jack asked him to let him know the dates and arrangements and to be kept informed. He also promised to speak to her. The conversation left Jack with his stomach knotted. Freedom from a seemingly tired relationship and the prospect of a new career and even a new life and yet...He was still tied emotionally to his family and that was only right. He understood that. He just wanted to reach a point of feeling comfortable about it all and that still seemed unattainable.

—

For Alfredo the journey home to Velez Rubio was an opportunity to be the good son and spend more quality time with his mother. It was also an opportunity to experience how a 45 minute journey could be made to feel like three hours. By the time they reached Supermercado Dia, Alfredo knew everything about her neighbour's lumbago. He became thoroughly updated about the family and listened to certain old tales for the umpteenth time in his life. He also heard about the tragedy of the Priest's cat on the day of the Corpus Christi festival.

"Corpus Christi is to celebrate the presence of Christ in the the holy water," said Mama.

"I know, Mama, I remember."

"Good - I should hope so too. So the cat is found drinking from the holy water. He is chased out by dumb Angelo who looks after the church. The cat escapes down the road and is run over by the van leading the procession carrying the six choirboys to perform the dance in church! It's horrific. The priest is distraught and shouting at dumb Angelo, who becomes so upset he tells Father Mario that as the body of Christ is in the cat it may be back in three days time. Father Mario is so offended he says Angelo must pay for the cat's burial. Dumb Angelo said that the cat was so flattened he would put him in a take-away pizza box and bury him! Now there is no-one to look after the church. Oh

Dios mio!"

Then there was the shopping. It must have taken twice as long to do as usual. It felt like she'd stopped to introduce everyone she met to her son. Why must she assume that he knew everyone and their families, like she did, regaling him after each one with all their latest woes, ailments and feuds?

But she was in her element and Mama appreciated the help from her son. He stayed for some food but insisted that he must return home that evening, even though his bed was ready, of course. He watched Spain's game against Iran with Papa and, although they won 1-0, it wasn't a great game and La Furia Roja made heavy weather of it, so he left before the end. Before he departed, Mama told him that she had left food boxes in his fridge for him, enough for several days. He protested, of course, that she shouldn't have gone to the trouble but when he learned that the boxes included his favourite homemade tortilla, his heart gladdened. There was nothing like Mama's tortilla. And he absolutely must apologise properly to Beatriz for what he'd put her through. They embraced and Alfredo set off on the drive home. He didn't miss her inimitable advice and instructions from the passenger seat yet wondered about the possibility of using Mama's voice for a sat-nav app. He entertained himself as he drove home by imagining her voice giving him directions. Perhaps not a business idea with potential but it amused him nonetheless.

It was well after eleven when Beatriz' phone rang. She'd just removed her make-up and was only still awake because she'd worked late on a client's project. Who on earth would be ringing at this time of night? With a damp sponge in one hand and her mobile in the other she answered and sat on the bed in a simultaneous movement.

"Alfredo! Is anything wrong?"

"No, no."

"Why are you ringing now?. It's lucky I wasn't in bed already, I'm so tired after working late."

"I'm sorry," he said, "that's what I rang to tell you, that I'm sorry."

"What? I don't understand."

"I want to say sorry properly for what I put you through last week at the beach. I know I should have said earlier but…it's been a bit embarrassing and I'm not very good at saying things like that."

"Things like 'sorry' - even you must admit you've had a lot of chances to practice saying sorry!"

"That's not fair. OK, I make some mistakes, I know, but I don't mean to mess up. And this time was serious and I gave you a very hard time through being foolish. So I want you to know that I understand, I am sorry and I will try hard to be more sensible in future."

There was a pause before Beatriz spoke.

"Thank you, Alf. If I was there I'd give you a hug."

He went on to tell her about his visit from Mama, the lecture he'd had and the rest of his time with her. Except the flat cat of Corpus Christi. She already knew about that. Finally, Beatriz said it was nice to hear from him but he could have phoned in the morning. Alfredo was adamant that he had to ring her as soon as he got home, otherwise Mama would be ringing in the morning and disappointed if he hadn't already rung. Now he could sleep more soundly.

"So this was Mama's idea, she made you ring to apologise?"

"No, we talked about things today and I said I would speak with you…well, yes. Yes it was. But she was right. And I meant what I said."

"Well, you looked so bad when you came out of the sea…I don't think you'll be doing that again. Just take care of yourself."

"At least it gave you an introduction to your new English gentleman and maybe he will be the one for you."

"Alfredo!" she snapped back. "He's a nice man and it's not like that! And showing him around a little is the least I can do. After all, he took his life in his hands to save you, didn't he?"

"Sure, OK," and once again Alf had managed to say the wrong thing. Timing and sensitivity were never his closest friends.

—

Over breakfast Jack and Robert had swapped plans for the day. After hearing about Amanda's possible health problem from his friend's early morning Face Time, Robert urges his friend to contact her. It's been evident to him that he's worried, which is only natural. He feels Jack can't go wrong by showing interest and offering support but emphasises that the best reason for contacting her is that it's the right thing to do. Better to do the right thing than do things right, is what he always told his team at one of his many former workplaces. And judging by the number of times he'd been let go, it was advice his former employers had taken on board.

Robert's expecting to hear about a job he's been discussing and says he might have to spend a night away shortly, depending on the location.

"What?" said Jack. "You don't know where the job is going to be? That's strange, isn't it?"

"Nah, not really. Involves some pick-ups and they don't know where the goods are coming in yet so…it's all normal, regular. No problem."

"Maybe I could come with you, Rob? It'd be interesting to see another part of Spain while I'm over. Give you a hand perhaps too."

Robert hadn't seen Jack's suggestion coming. He felt flummoxed, having murmured vaguely in the affirmative. As he loaded the dishwasher it was almost possible to hear the cogs of his brain whirring round until he looked up and said:

"Oh bugger! Sorry Jack, but I've just thought. There's already two of us and it's not the biggest vehicle, just a van with a two seater cab. I think your incorporation into Señor Bobby Ltd will have to be delayed. Shame. I'll have to bear that in mind for another one, eh?"

"Oh, alright. I'm not riding in the back, that's for sure. Who's the guy working with you then?"

"Mmmm. It's someone you know actually."

"Someone I know? I've only really met two people since I've been here and - hang on a minute. It's not Alfredo?"

Robert smiled as he turned towards Jack and raised his eyebrows. Jack was amazed.

"You said you'd worked with him before but after what you said, you know, about him not being the sharpest and so on…I'm just a bit surprised."

"Well, he's reliable enough, he's available and there's not much can go wrong - he's only got to drive the vehicle. And after all, he's a decent kid."

"Look Rob, I hope there's nothing risky or dodgy about this job, his sister's desperate for him to stay on the straight and narrow."

"Oooh, his sister's desperate for him…" he repeated

like a sarcastic parrot. "Jack, of course it's alright. Trust me. And please don't start going all protective of him, just because she's the little light in your life right now."

"Get off with you!"

"On a job like this where you spend quite a bit of time with someone it's also important that you get on alright. And we do. So I'm not going to sell him short."

Later Jack decides that Robert was right, rather than continuing to think about how his wife is and whether there's any more he should know about her health, he ought to speak to her directly. After failing to get through twice, it's third time lucky.

"Jack, how are you?" said Amanda, trying not to sound too surprised to hear from him.

"I'm alright, thanks, Amanda. You know, it's a nice change to get away and relax, a bit of time out and so on."

"And how's Robert, it must be so long since you've seen him?"

"Oh, he's good, thanks, yes. He's just the same as he ever was really. He's out a lot of the time but I have to say I'm still not entirely sure what's he's doing. A bit of this and a bit of that without ever being too clear or specific. He's certainly happy enough, which can't be bad. Oh, he asked to be remembered to you."

"That's nice of him. You haven't painted too depressing a picture of me then?"

"Oh, come on, of course not. It's actually your health and well-being I was ringing about anyway. I was talking to Josh yesterday and he was telling me that you've been for a scan or something. He said it was a gynaecological problem and didn't really expand on that. You know what he's like for remembering the details."

"Quite. Definitely your son, isn't he?"

"Alright, alright. Give him some credit! What's it all about then?"

Amanda explains to Jack that she'd been having heavy periods with a bit more pain than she's been used to. In fact, it had become rather uncomfortable. She's been generally below par as well as needing to go to the toilet more frequently. That's also affecting her sleep. She sounded very low key and lethargic in telling him, Jack thought. This had gone on for a good few weeks so she visited her doctor and she carried out a pelvic examination. The doctor had been concerned about what she thought felt like some sort of abnormality and wanted her to have a further check "to see whether anything evil was going on down there" as Amanda put it. So about a week later she was into hospital for a laparoscopy…

"A whatscopy?" said Jack.

"A lap-ar-oscopy!" Amanda spelt out. "They stuck a little telescope into me with a tiny camera on the end then watched the pictures on a monitor."

"Wow! Were you awake, could you see as well?"

"I bloody well was not awake! They gave me a general anaesthetic."

"And what did they find then? Is everything OK?"

"Well, I don't know yet. I mean, they found a couple of tumours but I'm sweating a bit on the results. Of course, I'm praying they're not malignant. But if they are then… well, we'll see what the options are."

There was an awkward silence between them for a few moments before Jack let out a sigh.

"Oh God, that must be worrying for you. You've told the kids?"

"Not exactly. I just said it all looked OK but they're doing tests to make sure. I sort of bottled it a bit really. So I'll hope for the best and maybe I won't have to go there with them."

"Do you want me to tell them?" asked Jack.

"No, no. That's very considerate of you, Jack, but no. I should tell them, shouldn't I? I will."

Jack wanted to know what came next. Amanda groaned as she told him about potential treatments, including the removal of her womb. There was a response of cynical incredulity when Jack asked about the recovery time for a hysterectomy. She clearly hadn't thought he was paying attention. He took it in his stride. But he admitted he was worried for her. As people do, she told him not to worry, as if such absolution from concern would have any impact whatsoever. Together they struggled for words. The conversation began to peter out, with Amanda trying not to betray any emotion or weakness and Jack wanting to ensure that his interest sounded authentic and not platitudinous. He was glad he'd phoned. Yet instead of easing his mind, now he knew there was something to worry about.

Whilst Jack had been on the phone an envelope had been delivered. He picked it up and put it on the chair by Robert's desk. As it happens, he arrived home at lunch time as his lodger was tucking into a baguette that he'd made up.

"Any sign of a note or an envelope this morning?" he said, anxiously looking round the hall.

"Yes!" replied Jack. "I left it on your chair for you in case it was important."

He walked straight over to open the envelope. He looked very serious and read the note a second time.

"Important or what?" said Jack.

"Yeah, yeah, sort of. Looks like I'm going to be away next Wednesday and Thursday. That job I was telling you about."

"Oh, that's quite handy actually. That's when I'm going to visit Beatriz for my guided tour of Granada. So I couldn't have come with you anyway."

"What? You'd have rather gone away with a glamorous young Spanish woman and toured the magnificent Alhambra Palace rather than spend a night away with me in a van? I'm disappointed in you."

Jack simply arched his eyebrows and gave him a knowing look.

Naturally Jack was interested in the job and asked where he'd got to go. Robert didn't want to tell him much more than he already had but conceded that he had a strong idea that it would mean travelling to Madrid, somewhere that Jack would have loved to visit. Apprehensive of being forced to share more than he wanted to, he switched the subject to Jack's wife and whether he'd spoken with her. It worked. Jack was only too ready to reveal the details of Amanda's health issue and to assert his view that maybe the stress of their break-up had contributed in some way. With Jack absorbed in Amanda's health and trying to interpret anything underlying their actual conversation, Robert looked at his watch and butted in.

"Look, mate, I'm sorry to be rude but I've got to whizz. I'm sure she'll be alright. And give her my best next time you're speaking to her please. Whatever it is, it sounds precautionary to me and she'll get fixed up. What are you up to now?"

"Don't worry, you get off. I'm going to have a proper look round the old town this afternoon. It's about time really."

"Ah, great! Don't forget to go into Santa Maria, the old church, and the Mirador on top, brilliant views. Enjoy it. See you later, cheers."

—

From the open side of Plaza Nueva, Jack gazed out at kilometre after kilometre of agricultural land. Turning clockwise there was the coastline and beyond it a long band of azure blue to the horizon; further round, the Sierra Cabrera Mountains dominated the picture. As his line of vision returned to the dry fields he noticed there were no animals and, as Robert had indicated on his first morning, the complete absence of herds of wildebeest.

'Too bloody hot' he thought, when, as if from nowhere, he was surrounded by about thirty mature ladies aggressively marching around and pointing. As he tried to move out of what was possibly their annual pattern of migration he found himself bumped and jostled. They sounded Eastern European and Jack speculated that they could be former KGB guards who'd been given new identities. Becoming increasingly intimidated, he heard the voice of David Attenborough in his head telling him that '… on their journey the formidable beasts like to make time for birthing, mating and courting on the way…' He was determined that it wouldn't be with him but just then one of the pack leaders stood on his toes and as he lifted his foot to rub them, another rutting tourist pushed into him with a heavy shoulder bag. On one leg he had no chance and tumbled as if in slow motion. No chance of an apology either, as he realised he'd been trampled underfoot and left for dead. Looking up ignominiously from his vantage point on the ground, he saw his assailant marching off, unaware and unrepentant.

He was both relieved and disgusted to see the herd

trundling off presumably northward in search of food and vodka. It left him feeling decidedly pissed off at their lack of manners. And what the hell was in that bag? Their group supply of testosterone? Or sets of dumbbells for their daily training? Hoisting himself up off the marble-like floor of the Plaza, he looked around the square whilst dusting off his navy shorts and re-shaping his battered seagrass fedora. Too many tourists for his liking. So he meandered on up to the top of the old town.

The temperature was in the mid-thirties again and slow was the only pace available. Jack's efforts to cut a dash as a more refined tourist had been dealt a blow and how could they not have seen him in a bright green polo shirt? He was still struggling each time he left the house to adjust to the strength of the light, intensified as it was by the white walls of the pueblo. It's the sort of place that you see from a distance, its buildings hugging the side of the hill like something Hans Christian Anderson would have dreamed up, and think how lovely it must be to visit. Up close and personal, it was indeed lovely, just full of steep and twisting cobbled streets and narrow alleys and soon Jack was thinking it was the sort of place best visited in the cool of the evening. No matter, he strolled on. Small shops sold all manner of jewellery and trinkets, artwork and lots of ladies' clothes and accessories of a certain style; flowered, flowing, floppy and full of colour, it was either a celebration of the Summer of Love or they were expecting Stevie Nicks to turn up at any moment.

Jack eventually came to another square, Plaza Parterre. There were seats outside and best of all, a shaded area. A few locals sat around. A scruffy dog lay beside a bench with two old timers in flat caps putting the world to rights. The one with the heavy moustache coughed before delightfully hawking up something unpleasant, which he then directed out to the side. As it slapped onto the back of the dog's head its eyes opened, looked right, looked left, then slowly closed.

Jack bought a little tub of mango and passion fruit ice cream from Café Irene, sat peacefully in the shade, then realised that the building opposite was the Iglesia de Santa Maria, the church that Robert had told him to visit. Very handy. After polishing off his treat, he climbed the steps which led to Plaza Iglesia and the main entrance to the church. Standing under an imposing old tree in the corner next to a shop selling American vintage items, he looked around at what must be one of the smallest squares he could recall seeing. The church was built from natural stone, with an arched door and a similarly arched stained glass window above it. Climbing the half dozen or so steps he smiled at an old man sitting on a chair outside the door. Inside it was cool, refreshingly simple and so white that Farrow and Ball might have called it Seared Retina. Emerging from the church, he took a closer look at an unusual statue. It was called the 'Mojaquera', a special monument to those women of the town who, for many centuries, fetched water from the Moorish fountain at the foot of the village, carrying it right to the top of the town. The white marble statue showed a clay pot on the woman's head. Jack briefly imagined Beatriz walking up the hill in her red dress with a clay pot of water on her head. It was the wrong image and he quickly snapped it shut. He moved on to find the Mirador del Castillo.

'Made it' said Jack to himself. 'What a view! Worth the walk.' He sat down, took out his phone to take a photo and saw a message from Beatriz.

'How are you? What are you up to? What are you doing Friday? x

It made him smile just to receive an enquiry. Friday? He replied immediately.

'Trampled by tourists. Now on top of Mojacar. All engagements Friday cancelled. What have you in mind?' A few seconds later he added his own 'x' uneasily .

A minute or so later she replied. She said that she'd be working in Almeria on Friday - would he like to meet her for lunch and she'd arrange for him to be taken around the city? Jack's bruised toes and aching calf muscles all but faded away in an instant. He agreed to call her later for the details of where to meet.

Walking into the hotel bar Jack browsed around before sitting at an outside table to enjoy a glass of chilled vino rosado and a small bowl of olives. Just then the young barman came over to him.

"Everything is OK, señor?"

"Yes, wonderful thank you. Just what I need to recover from the walk up here."

"Oh, you walked all the way up? You know there is a lift?"

"A lift? You're joking?"

"No, no, señor. The lift was opened not too long ago but always it was breaking down, so they cut down the number of people allowed to use it, but still it breaks down! When it is working it saves you a lot of energy but it doesn't bring you all the way to the top, it just helps a lot."

"Well, thank you. I shall be asking my friend why he didn't tell me about that."

When Robert returned home, he breezed into the room muttering about the world going mad. He often thought it was the distance provided by spending so long living outside the UK that made news items appear as if they'd been invented by sketch-writers. Today he'd been bemused by hearing that Trump had attacked Angela Merkel about her open-door immigration policy.

"Good luck trying to tell a former resident of East Germany that she should build a bloody wall. I'd love to hear her response! And great news for pensions," he went on, clearly wound up by listening to the local Spectrum FM news. "Apparently 23 million people in the UK are likely to have to work until they're ninety-five before they get their pension, or something like that. I'm staying out here, mate. Then they get a bit of a hot spell and there's going to be a carbon dioxide shortage. That's a new one, that is. It could affect beer production…while there's a World Cup on, for God's sake. But it's alright, 'cos William Hague's calling for the legalisation of cannabis. That should make up for the beer shortage, eh?"

Jack made him a drink and they sat down together. The first thing he raised with Robert was how tired he felt, the soreness in his muscles. He made a big deal out of how much energy he'd expended and accused him in a light-hearted way of deliberately withholding information.

"The bloody thing's never working!" howled Robert. "The local council or whatever they are have been given so much stick. It can't take as many people as it was supposed to and it's still slow and evidently defective. But there you go. Progress of sorts I suppose."

"I'd have taken my chances with it" said Jack.

"Oh, a good few people have been caught out in that lift, I tell you. One young woman decided to let as many people as possible know that she was trapped by updating her Facebook status. Thirty five people liked her status but nobody could be arsed to help or raise the alarm! Another young couple were trapped for six hours. They'd been taking salsa lessons and found it the ideal place to practice. They hummed the tune together apparently and by the time they were let out they were bloody brilliant."

"It's not so bad if you all know each other. Imagine being trapped with some obnoxious family…or drunks!"

"Drunks!" Robert's eyes lit up. "There's some great stories on the internet about drunks in lifts. It's one thing to get into a mess like that, then they go and upload it online for those people in the world with nothing better to do than read such stuff."

"Like you."

"Alright, alright."

"Well, you're off the hook, I'm glad I walked with hindsight."

Chapter Six

Friday 22 June 2018

Within forty five minutes of leaving Mojacar, Robert and Jack were whizzing past the aeropuerto exit from the Autovia close to Almeria. To make things easy for his pal, Robert had offered to take him into the city and to show him round the Alcazabar. At least that was the version offered to Jack. The reality was that Beatriz had been unable to find someone to show Jack around the city in the afternoon so had press-ganged her brother into service. When Robert got wind of this he thought he could fabricate an opportunity to have a quiet few minutes with Alfredo to discuss the following Wednesday's job. His cunning plan was more cunning than he thought as he'd ended up being invited to join them for lunch.

From the east the Autovia heads high above the city, giving Jack his first sight of the Alcazabar, keeping watch imperiously over the city just as the Arabs had intended. The descent into the city takes in some brilliant views before Robert turns off the palm lined Calle de Nicolás Salmerón and down into Parking Oliveros. Walking back up into into the brilliant light of Europe's driest city, the two amigos cross

La Rambla and saunter through the central shopping area.

"What's this place?" asked Jack.

"Oh, the Iglesias de San Pedro. It's got something about it, hasn't it?" said Robert.

"Oh definitely. Unusual colour on the towers."

They look up at the twin-pillared facade, its two bell towers, each topped by a cross, its masonry a distinct shade of mustard.

"I love the arabesque pattern at the top of the bell tower, it's really striking" Jack remarked of the demi-globe on which the crosses were perched.

"Yeah, they're like two halves of one of those old plastic world cup balls" said Robert, skewering any cultural pretensions whatsoever.

Moving on through a few more narrow streets they found themselves entering the Plaza de la Catedral. They sat down under shade outside the Hotel Catedral and ordered coffee. It's another beautiful morning and Jack gazed round the square, lined with tall palms, softening the otherwise formidable image of the imposing 16th century Cathedral itself. Across the square sitting outside another café was the man who'd first appeared in Garrucha. Today he wore a black jacket, black jeans, white t-shirt and sunglasses. Perhaps the black t-shirt was in the wash. Keeping a watchful eye on the two men he sipped an espresso from behind El Pais.

"Looks more like a castle rather than a cathedral," said Jack.

"Yeah, it does, but then I guess it was built at a time when this region was frequently attacked from the sea. And that's probably what made it suitable for the sixties film 'Patton: Lust for Glory'. It was actually used as a fortress. Do you remember it?"

"Now you mention it I think I saw it when I was

growing up. War film."

"Yeah. Very successful. Got a shedload of Oscars I think. Still, you can have a look in there anytime, we want to get you into the Alcazabar before it's too bloody hot. Let's not hang about."

Crossing the square they headed along more narrow streets before emerging into Calle Almanzor, walking with the walls of the Alcazabar to their right.

"Now then" said Robert, becoming animated and jumping in front of Jack. "Imagine that this street is ram packed with North African folks with market stalls all along the side, there's a real din from all the shouting and haggling. Then suddenly a couple of vehicles come hurtling around the corner and there's people flying all directions. Who's in the jeep being chased, then?"

"Ha! This isn't an Indiana Jones film, is it?"

"Dah da da dah, da da dah, dah da da dah, da dada da dah… Oh, well done, it is indeed."

"Yeah, brilliant scene! There's Indy, his Dad…"

"And their local ally, guiding them."

"That must be The Last Crusade. So this is the street where that was filmed? Harrison Ford and Sean Connery?"

"Yep. All along here up to the gates of the Alcazabar at the Puerta de la Justicia."

On learning this Jack is as elated as a kid who's just got off Space Mountain for the first time.

"I just want to watch the film now. Have you got it on DVD?"

"Might have. Can't remember to be honest. Anyway, let's go in. By the way, it's free to EU citizens, so make the best of it while you can."

Entering the old fortress, the largest built by the Arabs on the peninsula and a National Monument since

1931, they followed a zig-zagged ramp up to the Torre de la Justicia. The heat made it a slow amble round, making it easier to take in the stillness and the beauty of the views.

"This place has featured in films as well, you know" said Robert.

"Such as?"

"007 was set upon by Arab bandits within these very walls in 'Never Say Never Again'."

"That was Sean Connery again, wasn't it?"

"It was, yeah. Kim Basinger and Barbara Carrera… wow!"

"So which camp are you in for the best Bond? Connery or Craig?"

"Argh, no, don't make me choose. Can't I be in the Kim Basinger camp? It's hard to go against Sean Connery, the original, he was so good growing up and all that. But technically, you've got to give it to Daniel Craig, haven't you? I love Bond films though."

"Anything else filmed here that I might have seen?" said Jack.

"Well, you been watching Game of Thrones?"

"Some of it, yeah. Every time I tuned in it was raping, pillaging, decapitation and a bit more pillaging for good luck."

"There was a Dornish dastardly deed filmed here in series 6. Oh, and there was another big film in its day made here. I'll give you a clue. Who was the most boring person in the Hyborian Age?"

"Er, I don't know."

"Conan the Librarian!"

"Oh, for God's sake! That's quite clever for you, that is. So when exactly was the Hyborian Age, professor?"

Adopting the learned tone of an elderly scholar,

Robert stood on a step and said:

"Well, it was a mythical age, of course, set in the period following the sinking of Atlantis but regarding the actual dates involved, I haven't got a facking clue..."

"Thank you, sir" said Jack. "Now, how are we doing for time? We've got to meet Beatriz at 1:30 at... what's that place I told you we were meeting at?"

"Right, we'd better get a jog on. It's Casa Puga, it's not too far from here...all downhill."

Turning back on themselves, they retraced their steps to leave. Robert pushed open a heavy wooden door. The man in black, who'd followed them from the cathedral, had been about to pull open the door from the other side. The cast iron handle rapped his knuckles and in evading the door he lost his footing and fell back into a large shrub.The subjects of his interest walked on, oblivious to him.

Just as they arrived in Calle Jovellanos, Beatriz and Alfredo were about to enter the old front doors of the restaurant. Jack called down to them and they hung back outside to wait.

"Oh, Alfredo's with her," said Robert, feigning surprise.

"Yeah, so he is," said Jack.

Greetings all round and an introduction at last for Robert and Beatriz.

"I've heard a lot about you from Alf and Jack," said Beatriz with a smile.

"Oh, I'm not that bad, don't believe them."

But Beatriz politely insisted it was all positive and they went inside. The volume from the locals two and three deep at the bar suggested it was a popular establishment. All sorts of people were having all sorts of conversations as they filed through to a quieter area and a table in a corner - the only one available. The obligatory TV was on in the corner but you couldn't hear it and nobody was watching anyway. Bottles lined the walls, hams hung from the ceiling, there were typical Andalucian tiles and old barrels. A variety of awards on the walls shared space with some football memorabilia. It looked and felt like it had been here since 1870.

Beatriz explained that she'd not been able to find any colleagues or friends available to take Jack round so had given the job to Alfredo.

"Oh great," said Jack, desperately trying not to sound too underwhelmed. "I didn't recognise you with your clothes on, Alfredo" he added trying to be chummy. Tumbleweed. "Well, you know, we've only met on the beach."

Robert and Alf exchanged sheepish glances whilst Beatriz laughed nervously.

The boys decided to quench their thirst with Alhambra beers whilst Beatriz ordered a sparkling water as she was working later that afternoon. It was quickly agreed to leave the ordering to Beatriz and Alfredo. They were served by a short, balding waiter and soon the raciones were arriving on a series of plates that covered the table.

They did a sound job. Boquerónes, stuffed pimientos, juicy fried prawns, small hake, pork loin marinated in garlic, queso curado all followed together with a bottle of the house white. After chatting about food, swapping thoughts on other restaurants in the city and exchanging local tittle tattle, Beatriz turned the conversation round to the two men's partnership.

"So, I believe you two guys are going to be working together next week?"

"That's right," said Robert, anxious to handle it lest

his junior partner foul things up. "We'll be away for a couple of days, but hopefully there'll be other opportunities if this goes well."

"What exactly is the job you're doing?"

"Erm, distribution, I suppose you'd call it."

"What is it you're distributing?" she added, looking puzzled as Alf nonchalantly gazed around the restaurant.

"Foodstuffs. Fresh food. Fruit, vegetables, you know? I have some associates who buy produce from different parts of the country who need it moving, basically. And I can charge a premium on that, depending how easy or difficult it is." He shut up abruptly while he thought he was still ahead.

"Interesting," Beatriz said. "Let's hope you're well prepared in case there are any banana skins…"

Robert was a bit thrown by the reference to bananas - he hadn't even told Alf it was bananas they were collecting.

"Yes, oh, we are!" said Robert, taken aback.

Alf looked like he'd just sat on a drawing pin before he stood up, pointed to nowhere in particular and said…

"Toilet."

"Ooh, good idea, I've been dying to go myself," said Robert, sensing relief on two fronts.

Jack and Beatriz smiled at each other and she began to shake her head. She thought it was a little cloak and dagger for something as simple as distributing food. Clearly suspicious that it wasn't quite what it seemed, she nevertheless laughed it off. Jack was on the same page and joked about them going out together now to discuss their business.

"I hope they don't hold all their meetings in men's toilets" he said.

"Oh, please, Jack!" she replied with a grimace.

Meanwhile, nearby in the restaurant's facilities,

Señor Bobby was explaining to his accomplice that they couldn't stay talking too long there, they must find time outside and before he took Jack round Almeria. Not least because there was no room. The Casa Puga's toilets were very small…in fact, one at a time. After a man walked in, saw Robert talking through the door to a man using the toilet and then walked out swiftly, he realised it wasn't a good look. Just before re-emerging into the restaurant, he put his arm around Alf's shoulder and praised him for keeping his mouth shut, emphasising that they couldn't discuss any details yet. Approaching the table Robert decided to act assertively.

"Alf and I are going to take our drinks outside for a minute or two - we just need to sort out one or two arrangements for next week".

With that, they sashayed through the customers cramming the bar and out through the front door to find that quite a few others had spilled outside onto the pavement. They stayed out for a while despite the fact that Robert had no new information to give Alf and he assured him that as soon as he received instructions he'd be in touch. For his part, Alf was confident that there wouldn't be any problems with the transport. Back inside, coffees were ordered and Beatriz took herself off to the ladies' room. Jack watched her walk through the room by virtue of a large mirror on the wall next to their table. Still enraptured, still disbelieving that his courage on the beach had been rewarded with her company several times already.

Looking round the room he became more aware of the religious imagery that was scattered across the wall displays. Oddest of all was a water tank against the wall that was festooned with cuttings and cards displaying pictures of Jesus and the Virgin Mary. He couldn't imagine anything similar in a British pub. It was evident that Roman

Catholicism continued to permeate many aspects of Spanish life, despite falling attendances at church. A few feet away a table of eight older people talked, argued and laughed as they had since they first sat down. Bar Casa Puga was a snapshot of Spanish life continuing unchanged over generations, accessible and classless.

Finally all four were sat down together again. Everyone seemed to have got what they wanted from lunch. Beatriz had explained to Jack that she'd be finished by around 7:30 and would meet to take him back to their hotels with a view to going out around 9:00. She was staying at the Hotel AC Almeria, on Plaza de las Flores, but as it was fully booked she'd arranged a room for him at the Hotel Nuevo Torreluz opposite. He did the honourable thing by offering to meet in her hotel lobby, although it had also occurred to him that he'd enjoy the frisson of emerging from a hotel with Beatriz. As he pondered his thoughts and wondered if they were fantasy or delusion, he tried to avoid noticing Robert, who he could see in the corner of his eye variously winking and raising his eyebrows as suggestively as possible. Still the naughty schoolboy at heart. Just then Robert turned, having seen in the mirror a large Spanish man with a thin moustache watching him studiously. He raised his eyebrows and cocked his head to him, at which the Spaniard simply lowered his head, peering over his glasses at him, before turning and walking away.

Beatriz and Robert having gone their separate ways, Alf led Jack towards the Cathedral. Admitting that he wasn't exactly an expert on the finer points of the city's culture and architecture was probably a good start. Almeria is known as a place that likes to party, especially at fiesta time. So much that the Pogues wrote a song about it called 'Fiesta' from their album 'If I Should Fall From Grace With God', and the Pogues knew a thing or two about partying. Right now though it's siesta and the shops are closed. When they arrived at the Cathedral, Alf was a bit embarrassed to find that it's only open until 1:30 each day. He hadn't done his homework. He may have been disappointed to have stumbled at the first hurdle, but Jack wasn't too bothered. All he wanted was to have a relaxing look round the best bits. He decided not to tell him he'd already seen this bit with Robert.

"So this is the highest place of worship?" said Jack.

"No" said Alf, "this is the Cathedral."

"Ah, right" said Jack, adjusting his level of expectation from Lonely Planet to Ladybird.

Alfredo told him a little more about the building before walking on, meandering through the Barrio de la Chanca, known as the Cave Quarter, where some families still live in the cave-like dwellings built into the rock on which the Alcazabar stands. Continuing through the Old Quarter they also passed the Aire de Almeria, where the ancient Arabic baths were recovered.

"It's part of our our cultural and social heritage" said Alfredo. "It shows Almeria has been a sort of melting pot of different people over a long period."

Gradually warming to each other's company, they headed towards the shopping area. Calle Navarro Rodrigo was still very quiet with just a few indications of people returning to work in the shops around them. Alf had been instructed by his sister to take Jack to Capri, a stylish café with a humongous selection of cakes, pastries and chocolates.

"Oh, this air conditioning is wonderful" said Jack.

"This is a very well known confiteria in the city," said

Alfredo, "run by the same family for many years."

Abandoning the menu in exchange for peering through the glass cabinets, the impasse was broken only when Alf pointed out that the almond pastry was a particular local speciality.

"More teas than a tattooed tart tittering in a tatty tutu!" said Jack, as bewildered by the list of beverages as Alf was by Jack's alliteration.

"So you live in Mojacar too, Alf? said Jack.

"No, Mojacar Playa. Not on the front but close."

"Ah, I see. And you don't mind Beatriz coming back to stay every weekend? It must cramp your style a bit?"

"Not really. It's good to have company. And it helps me pay the rent! I'd like to have more regular work, but right now there's not much that's permanent and interesting."

"You must be looking forward to this job with Robert next week. Maybe that will lead to something more regular. He seems very optimistic."

"Of course." Then he laughed, "But Robert is always optimistic. That's why I like to work with him."

After some very fine tea and wonderful cakes that each admitted they didn't need, it was time to move on.

"Well," said Jack. "What's next, Alf? Nothing too strenuous I hope?"

" Next we can go to the Casa del Cine. We must take a taxi because it's across the city and outside the centre. Beatriz will meet you there later."

"No more walking! OK, let's go."

About twenty minutes later they're outside the cinema museum at Calle Camino Romero, a large building, lovingly restored - white walls, terra cotta tiles, shuttered windows and palm trees outside. Alf has telephoned ahead and one of the guides, Ramon, is waiting for them.

“Welcome to Casa del Cine” says Ramon. “I’ll give you a quick tour, but please ask me anything you want.”

Jack thanked Alf for looking after him and they said their goodbyes. Ramon talked Jack through the history of the building, including one particular resident from 1966.

“John Lennon stayed here when he was making the film ‘How I Won The War’. When he first arrived he stayed in a small apartment at El Delfin Verde, near El Zapillo, the city’s beach. Then when his wife, Cynthia, came out to join him they needed something bigger. This house, Santa Isabel, reminded him of a children’s home in Liverpool near where he lived called Strawberry Fields and, although he started to write the song in the apartment, this is where he actually completed it.”

“No way” said Jack.

“Yes, it is true.

Sitting down for a few minutes, Ramon went on to tell Jack about his grandfather, a taxi driver In the sixties. Lennon had his Rolls Royce brought over whilst he was filming but there was a period of time after it had broken down when he needed a taxi. The taxi firm sent Fernando, Ramon’s grandfather. Lennon took a shine to him and insisted he drive him each time he needed transport.

“On one occasion” said Ramon “John wanted to look round the city and surrounding area to see the sights and, after learning that his fellow Beatle Paul McCartney had walked round London disguised as an Arab, he decided to try the same thing. My grandfather used to laugh telling me the story, because having an Arab in his back seat with a Liverpool accent was very amusing to him.”

“Did anyone spot him?”

“No! But then it’s quite common to see people from North Africa in Almeria - we have the ferry.”

Another day when Fernando was sent to Santa Isabel, Lennon emerged from the house with another man - Ringo Starr! He was visiting for his 26th birthday. He kept looking in the mirror because he couldn't believe he had half of the Beatles in his taxi.

"Every now and again," Ramon added, "Ringo would call out, 'Where are we going now, Johnny?' And whenever he picked him up, my grandfather would bring a small bag of Chupa-Chups. You know, the Spanish lollipops? He loved them and I think there's even a scene in the film where he has one."

"What an amazing experience for him" said Jack.

"Yes, for sure. By the way, you will also find a statue of Lennon sitting on a bench in Plaza de las Flores."

"Really? That's where my hotel is. I'd better look out for it."

"It was also here in Almeria that he started to wear his small round spectacles. So you can see he is very important to us."

On the way round they entered a room that featured holograms of all of the characters who've been through the house - David Lean, Yul Brynner, Brigitte Bardot, Clint Eastwood, John Lennon and more.

"Over here," said Ramon, "is the bedroom and bathroom, represented how it would have been when John Lennon stayed here. And you can see also some of the things - objects and places - that would have had some meaning to him at that time."

Just then the door opened and it was Beatriz, just to let him know she'd be ready in a short while. The two guys strolled back to the lobby area, where Jack flopped into a comfy chair to wait.

—

Outside the AC Almeria the uniformed young man took the car keys from Beatriz while she and Jack went off to their separate hotels. Up in her room Beatriz collapsed onto the bed, stretching out her arms and legs, letting out a contented moan as she flexed her neck. It had been a long week…too many hours at work. The room was modern, a smart feel of luxury with plenty of space. All that mattered to her at that moment was that the bed was just so comfortable. She reached over for the remote and brought the flat screen TV to life. What should she do? Fix herself a drink and catch up with the news? Take a shower? No, she thought, that could wait. Taking her key she left the room, headed for the lift and went up to the roof terrace.

That hour before the sun goes down is beautiful, she thought. Still very warm, the soft light bathing the city in a special glow. To her right was the imposing sight of the Alcazabar, straight ahead was the Mediterranean and beyond that North Africa. Just a couple of people remained on the terrace, one reading, one listening. Beatriz sat back in the lounger and smiled. Soon she felt, if not energised, then rebalanced. The view was what she'd needed and when she returned to her room, she felt lighter than when she'd left it.

Across the road, Jack checked into his cheaper hotel, which he'd later describe to Beatriz as 'perfectly fine and functional'. Apart from showering and changing ready for going out, he'd had a little snooze and was feeling better for it. Walking nervously into the AC he walked past reception and into the lounge, where he dropped nicely into a swish black leather chair that squeaked and creaked as he made himself comfortable. Flicking through an interiors magazine, he was suddenly distracted by the sound of heels clicking along the spiral staircase.

'Oh, good Lord!' he silently exclaimed when he saw it was Beatriz. 'Am I really going out for an evening with a woman who looks like this?'

"Hola," she said, smiling warmly.

"Wow! You certainly scrub up well," said Jack.

"I what?" said Beatriz, slightly bemused.

"Oh, sorry, just something we say, 'scrubbing up well'...obscure everyday English. What I mean is that you look fantastic."

"Gracias, señor. You're, how you say, scrubbing up well yourself, very relaxed. Perhaps Andalucia is starting to take a hold over you?"

"Maybe it is."

With that they headed into the Plaza, Jack doing his level best not to exude smugness from every pore of his body.

"Where are you taking me to tonight then, Beatriz?" Jack asked.

"I thought we'd try La Consentida. It's only five minutes to walk and if we're lucky we may be able to have a table outside. I think you'll like it."

The restaurant could be heard before it could be seen. It looked like there was no space outside but then Jack spotted someone about to leave. Eye contact with a waiter and a few gesticulations later they were seated under a cream canopy. Trees were dotted around the space, their large leaves an intensely bright green thanks to the illumination from discreetly hung lanterns. The residual heat of the day hung over the courtyard. They ordered manzanillas and the waiter left their menus. Outside it was tapas and Beatriz reminded Jack that there's one free with every drink.

"Interesting" said Jack, scanning the tapas menu.

"Yes, it's just a bit of fun really but it makes people laugh and adds some interest to the menu." said Beatriz.

Each selection was named after a female celebrity. So a Marilyn Monroe was secret de credo a la brasa, or a 'grilled pork secret'; ask for a Lady Di and that's lagrimas de pollo fritas, or fried chicken tears; somewhat predictably a Miley Cyrus was a perrito caliente, or as the Americans say, a 'hot dog'.

"I bet there's a lot of men who can't resist ordering the Monica Lewinsky" said Jack unthinkingly and without even averting his gaze from the menu.

"Why is that?" asked Beatriz.

"Seriously?"

"I don't know who this woman is…Is she a Russian actress?"

"Erm…not Russian, but she was famous for something that happened between her and the American President, Bill Clinton. She worked for him at the White House. Surely you will have heard of her?" Jack reasoned, shifting uncomfortably in his seat.

"When did this take place?"

"Oh, I think it was around 1996."

"Mmm, I was sixteen. I have a vague memory of all the girls at school talking about something like this. Did they have an affair or something?"

"Yes, allegedly. Although he said they didn't. In fact, he said he did not have sexual relations with that woman. But he sort of did."

"Sort of?"

"Yes, sort of. He did and he didn't. You know, it wasn't the full…the complete act…of…"

Jack was now resorting to actions including baffling facial contortions and tics. He thought about pretending to faint but was saved by the arrival of the waiter.

"You are ready to order?"

"Si" said Beatriz. "I'll have a white wine please with an Amy Winehouse. Are you going to have Monica Lewinsky, Jack?"

"Ha!" went Jack. "No...no, I'm going to have Madonna please, with a white wine too. Gracias."

For the record, the Monica Lewinsky was costilla de cerdo con salsa americana - or, if you prefer, a pork rib with American sauce. Naturally. From then on Jack took more care with his comments about the menu. Scarlett Johansson and Kim Basinger (so he could tell Robert what it was like) were followed by Sofia Loren and Audrey Hepburn. There was no way he was mentioning Pamela Anderson or Sharon Stone. Once the pitfalls of celebrity tapas had been overcome, the conversation flowed easily.

——

Robert and Alf, in the meantime, had been doing some planning. On returning home Robert found a note had been delivered by his contacts. Their destination would be Madrid, as he had expected. They would be buying a consignment of bananas and he now had some further details about the money involved. 'Better ring Alf' he thought.

"Alf? It's me, Roberto. Get back alright?...Good. Listen, I've had a message so we need to speak. Can you come round tonight?...Great. I'll do some food for us...Yes it will be edible you cheeky sod. See you at nine. Adios."

Just before nine Robert had a look round and was quite pleased with himself. He'd decided to make an effort for Alfredo. If they were to work together in the future then he wanted him to be loyal and reliable, so a bit of effort at relationship building wouldn't go amiss. Then again he wondered if the candles may be a bit over the top? 'What the hell' he thought. Three raps on the door and Robert was out to greet his dining companion.

"Good evening partner!"

"Hola, Roberto."

Bless him. He'd brought a bottle of wine with him. Robert was surprised but quietly impressed by his gesture.

"Beer?" asked Robert.

"Yes, why not?" said Alf.

"Sit yourself down" demanded Robert. "Try this Ambar Extra…little bit strong but lovely stuff."

"Woah!" said Alf, taking a bigger gulp than he should. "That's good. You're right."

There was bread on the table with a little dish of olive oil each, some slices of jamon and chorizo and a bowl of almonds. Very cultured for Robert…

"Right, Alf" Robert started, "let's talk about this job next week, our little adventure, in case we get a little bit borracho later."

"Well, maybe you" said Alf. "I've got the car."

"Yeah, but come on, it's not far to your place - you could probably walk at a push, or get a taxi. Shame to spoil a good night, eh?"

"I suppose yes, I could…" said Alf.

"Look, if it's easier you can always stay here, there's plenty of space. Especially with Jack out of town for the night."

"Oh, thank you. Maybe. Let's see how it goes."

Robert began by telling him what was definite. They need to be at Mercamadrid when it opens on Thursday morning. The consignment they're aiming to buy contains bananas - a lot of boxes but he didn't know exactly how many. On Wednesday morning they'll head off for Madrid around 10:00 but may have to meet his contacts somewhere in the evening. That's when they'd be given the details of the person with whom they'd be negotiating at the market. A sum of cash will also be handed over for them to make the purchase.

"Any questions so far?" asked Robert.

"Sounds OK" said Alf. "What do we do with the bananas?"

"Good question. They won't tell us that until Wednesday. They don't want any mobile phone calls or messages initially, so they'll give us an address where we're to take them on Thursday. They'll meet us there and take them off our hands. We'll have some sort of receipt from the market that verifies it's the consignment they wanted."

Alfredo nodded his head slowly as he thought. Once the cogs stopped whirring, he leaned forward and said:

"What about our money? When will they pay you?"

"Very good question!" said Robert. "We'll have our cash when we hand over the boxes. It's possible we'll have some cash left over from the deal at the market if all goes according to plan."

"And then you pay me?"

"And then I pay you. Indeed, young man."

Robert smiled a big smile. Alfredo sat back and smiled a big smile too. As they added nodding to the smiles they began to resemble two emojis having a face-off until Robert said:

"Another drink, my man?"

"For sure" said Alf.

And with that`Robert cracked open a nice bottle of red wine.

"I tell you what, Alf. If this job goes well next week, we'll be opening some fizzy stuff to celebrate, eh?"

—

It was around 11:30 when Beatriz and Jack strolled back to their hotels. When Jack saw how lively it was outside the Torreluz where most tables were taken and animated discussion filled the night air, he asked Beatriz if she fancied a nightcap.

The only available tables were free because they had an obscure view of the TV screen. Highlights of the day's World Cup games were being shown and right now it looked like Brazil v Costa Rica.

"So that's why everyone's here" said Jack.

"Ah, yes! While Spain are in the tournament, there is big interest. If they go out, maybe not so much. The national team brings people together, all over Spain - including Catalunya." Beatriz replied, shrugging her shoulders as if to suggest that she didn't really get it.

"It's probably Brazil in the yellow and green and everybody likes to see them play."

They each had a cognac with their espresso. Just then there was a collective uprising from almost everybody there. The football had finished. Handshakes, hugs and farewells duly completed, a peaceful calm settled over the handful of customers left. A few minutes later they drank up and Jack walked Beatriz across the small plaza to her hotel. And as he walked back to his own hotel he whispered 'good night' to John Lennon, alone on a bench.

—

Just along the coast in Mojacar, the partners in Spain's newest fruit distribution business were building their relationship on a foundation of Robert's paella, which both agreed had been rather good. They had at the same time ensured their assets were liquidated with the help of a second bottle of red. Alf stayed over to avoid either losing his licence or the embarrassment of falling over on his way home. All in all, it had seemed a good step forward.

Chapter Seven

Saturday 23 June 2018

Beatriz and Jack passed a myriad of shops in the narrow pedestrianised streets, from the smart and chic to the more prosaic. Turning into the tree-lined Paseo de Almeria, Jack's hunger encouraged him to take her arm and guide her away from the clothes and towards La Dolce Allianza.

"One of my favourite places for desayunos when I'm in Almeria" announced Beatriz.

They found a table inside and immediately began scrutinising the menu.

"It's never quiet in a Spanish cafe, is it?" said Jack.

"Of course not, this is Spain - we are never short of something to say, especially at breakfast" said Beatriz with a touch of pride.

The long, ornate room featured a glass counter that ran almost its length, a veritable palace of temptation. The wide variety of people sitting inside and outside demonstrated its ongoing appeal. They ordered tostadas topped with tomato, olive oil and serrano ham, a couple of cappuccinos arriving promptly via the traditional and formally attired service.

Afterwards, instead of heading straight back to the hotel to pick up the car, Beatriz insisted on a detour to the Mercado Central for some fresh food for the weekend. An impressive building dating back to 1892, its entrance alone with its wrought iron gates at the top of marble steps is enough to draw in the curious visitor, but it was the wonderful aromas that hooked Jack.

"Perhaps, Jack, you can take back some food for Robert - a nice surprise for him?"

"Good idea" he replied, wondering why he hadn't thought of it himself.

"If you come here very early the squid are so fresh that they're still changing colour." said Beatriz. "All the fruit and vegetables are grown in those large greenhouses you see all over the countryside close to the Autovia."

Encouraged by the vibrant atmosphere in the market, Jack got a little carried away. He even bought Robert a bunch of flowers. Having lugged the bags back to the hotel, there was one last thing. He insisted on having his photograph taken with John Lennon, still strumming his guitar on a bench in Plaza Flores, right outside his hotel. They collected the car and were soon on their way home in time for lunch and a barely earned siesta.

Robert and Alfredo had awoken not nearly so brightly. Breakfast for Robert was tea and toast around eleven. As for Alf, he must have disappeared early. Robert had a vague recollection that he had to see his mother today and had presumably departed quietly. Then again, a lorry could have run into the house and he'd have remained unconscious. He got up from the table to put his plate in the dishwasher, loaded in a very haphazard manner from the previous night. He popped in a tablet, shut the door and pressed the button. There was a gentle hum before the water started to whoosh quietly into the machine. Sighing, he leaned forward and kissed the top of the dishwasher gently…

"I bloody love you" he said, with feeling.

Despite feeling groggy in a typical 'morning after the night before' sort of way, Robert was upbeat. He was a little surprised how well the evening with Alfredo had gone but his food had been pretty good, the beer and wine had flowed and as for Alf…actually, they really had got on well. They discussed a lot of things, laughed together and shared their feelings in a way that had been unexpected. There was a good rapport between them and he thought he could trust him. He hoped that was how Alf felt about him too.

Sometimes Robert could feel quite low. He knew he was heavy and overweight, but it only affected him when he was tired and depressed. Uncaring about anyone including himself, he'd be unsmiling and almost weary of life. It was in those periods he'd realise he didn't have anyone that really cared about him. What did it matter to anyone else if he wasn't there? Would anyone notice if he simply was't around anymore? But today wasn't one of those days. He had a purpose and right now life felt worthwhile.

It was around 12:30 when the door opened and Jack's voice called out…

"Señor Roberto?"

"Señor Jacko!" replied Robert.

Jack walked into the kitchen and dropped his carrier bags onto the table.

"There we go. A few things to start the weekend off."

"Oh, cheers mate. You've been to the Mercado then? Presumably this was included within the Tour Guide Beatriz package, was it?"

"Ha, ha! Of course it was."

"I thought so. And that glint in your eye…is that telling me you took advantage of any of the optional extras on offer from your guide?"

"No!" Jack snapped back quickly. "It is not. We had a very nice time, thank you, and if there's a glint in my eye it's probably because I'm feeling very happy today and very positive about life, so less of your innuendo, sunshine."

Over a coffee they went on to tell each other about their respective Friday evenings. Robert was evidently proud of his culinary achievements in entertaining Alfredo, whilst Jack provided him with a touch of mirth in describing his problems in explaining what it was that had once made Monica Lewinsky a household name. Robert was left open-mouthed. As Jack noted, a position not unfamiliar to Monica herself during her time in the White House. After lunch they agreed a siesta might be helpful before popping down to the beach to catch a few rays.

"I hope Alfredo's tidied up my bed after him" Jack called as he ascended the stairs.

"What?" said Robert.

"Alfredo…I presume he had my room last night when he stayed over?" Jack said.

"Oh, yeah. Yeah, I think he did. The end of the evening's a bit hazy to be honest".

Jack pushed open the door and his room looked pretty much as he'd left it. It couldn't have been re-made like this, he thought, as there were things left strewn across the duvet exactly as he'd left them. He popped his head out of the door and called down again.

"Hey, Robert. No-one's been in here - I can tell from how everything's still exactly as I'd left them."

Robert stuck his head round the corner and looked up the stairs at Jack.

"Oh, really? Erm…well…oh, fair enough. We were a bit the worse for wear when we called it a night. He must have slept on the sofa. Come to think of it, the cushions looked a bit lived in when I came down this morning. I'm sure I told him he could have your room."

Jack shrugged his shoulders and retired to his room to lie down.

Chapter Eight

Sunday 24 June 2018

Siesta over, the boys had been revived and had spent the last few hours of the afternoon at the beach. Jack had promised himself he'd ring the kids when he got back. They were invariably on his mind and he wanted to know what was going on in their worlds. He'd left a message for Seb, who'd not answered. Probably out enjoying himself, Jack hoped. Rugby season had finished but he was a very active lad with lots of friends and plenty of interests too. Nicole had sounded pleased to hear from him and work was going well, even if her love life was up and down. She said she thought her Mum had a doctor's appointment on Monday. This was confirmed by Josh when they spoke - the appointment was mid-afternoon. He was taking time off work to go with her, despite her protestations. Jack found this both reassuring and a little sad - his son had developed a fine sense of responsibility, but ordinarily this would have been his role and not something his son should have to do.

"Please give my love to your Mum on Monday and tell her I'm thinking about her. I mean that."

Calls over, Jack sat back in his chair and stared into

space, alone with his thoughts. They'd grown from vulnerable children to confident adults in what seemed like such a short space of time. Where did the years go? Most of it was a blur, although reminiscing about his laboured attempt at telling Seb about the birds and the bees brought a smile. A complete waste of his time, it was like trying to give a fish a bath.

Later that evening Robert drove them the few miles to Turre, where he'd booked a table at Casa Adelina. After the previous night he was looking for something quieter and was happy to drive. This old traditional restaurant has evidently been around for years and fronts onto the main street through the town. Over a beer Jack told his friend about his conversations with Nicole and Josh and confessed that he'd been left a little flat. This sense of responsibility about Amanda keeps gnawing at him. And what if this tumour turns out to be cancerous? Maybe if she'd run off with someone else it would have been easier, a line drawn under things.

Before Robert could summon his inner amateur therapist, Jack was moving on, telling him how difficult he found it at times, the break-up of their marriage. He'd concluded that theirs was a relationship that often seemed to have more potential than it delivered. There was such promise in the early years when the children were growing up. Then again, was he guilty of underrating what it had delivered? Love, fun, happiness, the satisfaction of shaping little children into responsible adults…that can gloss over the difficult times, the times when you're absolutely sick of life and work.

"Nothing worth doing is easy" Robert interjected quietly, displaying the solemnity of a counsellor and the depth of a teaspoon.

Jack had wondered, not for the first time, if splitting up was taking the easy way out. It had reminded him of a bloke he used to work for who was fond of quoting an old African proverb. 'If you want to go quickly, go alone; if you want to go far, go together.' It was about teamwork and collaboration, but it might equally apply to marriage and family.

"A very wise man" said Robert.

"Not really" said Jack. "He was a complete twat most of the time."

He'd thought that 'going far' should be about more than just material things, it should be about personal growth contributing to the collective wealth. Of course, he thought there was nothing wrong with having material benefits too as part of a fruitful relationship.

"Don't forget, Jack, your kids sound like they've turned out really well. You and Amanda have clearly done a good job, mate."

"I suppose so, yes. And I am proud of that. Trying to look ahead though, it's just a bit depressing" said Jack. "The costs don't help. When you think about separation or divorce, only the lawyers ever win. What nobody sees are the hidden costs."

"Nobody apart from the poor bastards paying" said Robert.

"Right. But it's the emotional costs that I worry about most. What impact might this have on everyone?"

As their food arrived they started on the wine.

"Only time will tell, Jack, if this is your time to enter the free market and you get to play the field...or whether you stay inside the union of marriage. You sound like you've left but still feel trapped. You've sort of made a deal, but the deal isn't that good. You got to snap out of this and be optimistic that whatever happens, it'll be for the best, mate. And while we're at it, you've got to stop blaming yourself for all this, especially for Amanda's health - you said yourself, you both contributed to the relationship going tits up."

Jack checked the strength of the wine on the label, looked back at Robert and asked him if he'd been on anything else before he came out.

"Well, it's probably true what they say… 'Marriage is temporary, alimony is forever'."

"Oh, thanks a bundle, Robert.

On that doleful note they set about a shared seafood platter.

"Moving seamlessly from leaving the union of marriage to leaving the union of Europe" said Robert, "I read recently about a meeting of EU leaders that was held in Estonia. They were all invited to relax in the evening by attending a Sting concert. The reporter reckoned this was highly appropriate, given that Sting's a well known exponent of tantric sex. Like the Brexit talks, he also has the ability to go on and on for ages without showing any sign of a satisfying conclusion."

This seemed to draw a line under the seriousness of the evening's conversation so far and a lightness appeared in their faces.

"Right" said Jack, "forget my separation, my unemployment and everything else that I'm anxious about… let's enjoy ourselves and I promise to lighten up. Now how about the prospects for world peace under Donald Trump?"

"Oh God! The future is orange…I saw someone on the telly the other day asking if Trump's access to nuclear weapons should be restricted. Personally, I'd start at cutlery."

—

As it was Sunday, Beatriz and Alf travelled over to their parents in Velez Rubio for lunch, still the focal point of Spanish family life. More Spaniards in their twenties live with their parents than any other European country. So maybe Alfredo had been quite bold in moving out in his relatively early twenties and his mother's desire for him to remain may seem more understandable in the circumstances. And even when young people do finally flee the nest in Spain, they don't often fly that far away. Like Beatriz and Alf, it helps keep the family together. When the youngsters arrive, Mama's been hard at work in the kitchen. But you won't hear her complaining about it. She revels in her role as the principal player, the matriarch who takes centre stage in this weekly production. The menu might change, the guests will vary, but Mama's performance remains consistent and at the core.

It's a particularly hot day and they'll be eating outside, as is usual for this time of year. The terrace at the rear of the house has a pagoda with trailing flowers, providing shade in the afternoon sun for the diners sitting round the table. Papa has dug up the vegetables for today's meal freshly from the garden. The table's been set and he's also in charge of drinks. Beatriz and Alfredo arrive to a warm and loving welcome. Mama stands back, surveys them to make sure they've not lost weight and they're looking healthy. Papa will shortly drive over to pick up Beatriz and Alf's abuelo, Mama's father, who lives the other side of the town and who's now 87.

"Who's coming with me to fetch El Abuelito?" demands Papa.

"Can't you manage on your own?" asks Beatriz.

"On my own? What if he's in a bad mood and kicks off? You can keep him calm when I'm driving."

"Don't drive so fast," said Alf. "You scare him to death."

"I'll come with you" said Beatriz. "Mi Abuelito deserves to be looked after."

Mama just shakes her head and rolls her eyes. Most of the time she's happy to play a traditionally submissive role, allowing her husband to think he's the dominant partner. Then when the occasion demands she turns on the fire and that's when you see who really rules the roost. On such occasions Papa knows his place and pipes down.

When they return with his abuelo, Alf breathes a sigh of relief. Mama has been interrogating him about his forthcoming work. As they hear the door, she finishes with:

"When you have work like this every day and it becomes normal, then I will stop the worrying, my son."

The old man walks into the kitchen uneasily, wearing his flat cap and a slightly oversized jacket that looks like it could be the cause of his stoop, such that when he removes it you expect him to stand up straight. But he doesn't.

Taking their seats at the table Papa makes sure they've all got an aperitif, everybody drinking manzanilla except him - he's got a cold beer. As they help themselves to olives and almonds, they talk about the family and local events before gravitating to more weighty issues like jobs and unemployment. Naturally the question of migrants arises and the conversation, as it frequently does with Papa and the generation gap, becomes more animated. He complains about migrant labour on the fruit and veg farms.

"These people come in and take all the jobs across the region. What are local young people supposed to do?" he said.

"Papa, you know it's not like that" said Beatriz, first to take the bait. "These jobs are available because local people won't take them."

"They should be made to take them."

"No, no" said Alfredo. "This region has always relied heavily on migrant labour, especially from Africa, so it's nothing new. And when you talk about these jobs, you're talking about working long hours in baking hot plastic polytunnels. I wouldn't do it."

"It's very low pay too" Beatriz added. "That keeps the price down and makes more money for the owners."

"I think the most worrying thing now" added Alfredo, "is where the workers are living. Have you seen the shanty towns that have sprung up? They're a real eyesore and the conditions can't be good."

Papa went round topping up glasses, recognising that he wasn't going to find anyone to agree with his world view. He chunnered and moaned as he served, with the occasional shake of the head. Just when he thought it had blown over, up piped Mama…

"And don't forget how sensitive this can be. Remember what happened in El Ejido not long ago."

"It was at least 15 years ago Mama" said Alfredo. "I was at school."

"Maybe it was" she went on, "but it was a horrible event. The Moroccan man who was accused of stabbing a local woman was mentally disabled. But did the people wait for it to be dealt with by the police, by the courts? No. Instead they think it's OK to attack the homes of all North Africans, their cars and shops too. For days! Careless talk can be irresponsible and become very dangerous."

"You're right, Mama" said Beatriz. "We are a multicultural society and that's very healthy."

It was past two o'clock when the first course was brought out. Gazpacho blanco, a chilled vegetable soup with almonds, white grapes and garlic - perfect for a hot afternoon. Beatriz told them about their day in Almeria, when Alf had taken Jack round the city.

"Why did you not take him to the Museo Flamenco in the Arab Baths?" asked Papa.

"There wasn't enough time to do everything" said Beatriz.

"It should be the cultural starting point! No time indeed…"

They knew what was coming next.

"I'll put on some music."

The sounds of Papa's all-time favourite artist invaded the terrace, but nobody objected. Paco de Lucia was a legend, an artist capable of uniting a nation in acceptance of his brilliance as the ultimate Flamenco guitarist.

Next up, a large oval plate of jamon and chorizo with Andalucian piquito bread and an ensalada mixta. Papa opened a bottle of Ribera del Duero whilst Mama brought out her rabo de toro. The bull's tail had been simmering in the pot for over eight hours…with carrots, onions, garlic, paprika and plenty of red wine. It smelt divine and more bread was brought out to soak up the stew. Then finally, room was found for Mama's tocino de cielo, a creamy caramel dessert which she'd garnished with a few blueberries and mint leaves for presentation.

"Why do you think it is called tocino de cielo?" said Abuelito out of the blue.

They looked at each other as if they all knew but understood the rules of the game.

"Why is that, mi Abuelito?" said Beatriz, providing his cue.

Too late. He was asleep.

Afterwards over coffee, relaxing in the late afternoon

sun to a background of El Abuelito's snoring, the conversation inevitably came round to Alfredo and his work trip.

"So," said Papa, "you are away for a few days this week with some work?"

"That's right, Papa." Alfredo replied.

"What's the pay like? And the prospects…are they good?"

"As long as the job goes well, the pay is OK. If it goes well, hopefully there'll be more opportunities."

"And this man you work with…he's someone you can trust?"

"Oh yes, for sure. I've done a few small jobs with Robert before. He's a good guy."

"I've met him once, Papa" said Beatriz. "We all had lunch in Almeria and his friend, Jack, speaks very well of him."

"This Jack," said Mama, "he is the man from the beach, no?"

"Yes, that's right, Mama" said Beatriz.

"Well he's a very good man. We thank God for him, saving my bambino."

Alfredo winced at still being thought of as her bambino. Papa just shook his head and looked to the heavens.

"Aaargh…" he said. "If you drink like a fish, you cannot swim like a fish. It's crazy, no?"

"Alright, alright" said Alfredo, taking it on the chin.

"I don't want to go swimming" said Abuelito, waking with a start.

And so a lazy, hazy sense of quiet descended on a family overcome with sunshine, food and mild intoxication.

Chapter Nine

Monday 25 June 2018

Irritated a little by his anxiety throughout Monday, Jack is torn between ringing Josh late afternoon following his wife's appointment and mid-evening when he can be sure he'll have left. He doesn't want to risk a conversation with him in front of his mother and so concedes he'll just have to fret a while longer. Naturally he wants Amanda to be well. But there's also an element of not wanting his own life to become complicated. Jack doesn't like complicated. Isn't it because he doesn't want to be made to look bad, having just split up with her? Isn't it somewhat selfish on his part, he asks himself? Just another aspect of it, maybe. Deep down isn't he also afraid of a serious illness to her proving more emotional than he can perhaps cope with? The main thing is that she's alright for her self, so she can be happy, he reasons.

Robert's gone out to meet his associates and to see Alfredo. It's 7:30 and Jack feels that's probably a reasonable time to call.

"Hello son, alright to talk?"

"Yeah, sure, Dad. Just driving home from Mum's but I'm on hands-free."

"OK. How did it go at the hospital?"

"Not so great, Dad, I'm afraid. Hang on...just pulling into a lay-by...OK, so she's got a uterine tumour, I think it's called, which means it's inside the womb. The bad news is that they think it's malignant."

"Oh no."

"Yeah, it's been a bit of a shit afternoon. Mum's been very strong about it. The good news is that the consultant says they've caught it early and they can deal with it. Mum's got to have a hysterectomy as soon as they can get her in."

"Any idea of the timescale?"

"They expect it to be some time in the next week to ten days. They've given her leaflets and whatever but...I don't know, I'm going to have to Google this when I get home and find out a bit more myself."

"Yes, I will too. Bloody hell, poor Amanda."

Further thoughts, questions, considerations and sympathies are expressed and shared over the next few minutes. Despite the sombre mood they agree that it's lucky it's been spotted and at least the medics say she should be fine. Jack wants to know any details or arrangements as soon as possible.

Robert's purpose in driving to Villaricos was to meet his clients and to discuss what he hopes will be the finer points of the task in Madrid. Rather than be seen together for the second time in the same hotel they're to meet on a quiet stretch of the promenade, a bench looking out to sea. As he walks towards the meeting spot he sees Xavi and Luis up ahead, approaching from the opposite direction. Xavi still has that calm, detached persona, although his eyes dart around from time to time, lizard-like, as if he's worried that someone might be watching him. Luis has his perma-grin in place, his eyes rolling up to their corners every now and then to keep sight of Xavi, the young pup looking up to his master for guidance. A young pup wearing an undersized navy blue Rolling Stones t-shirt, that one with the big tongue logo, which on Luis means the end of the tongue is stretched right across his ample gut.

"Rolling Stones fan are we, Luis?"

"Who?"

"Your t-shirt" said Robert, pointing at his belly.

"No, no…it was in a box that I found."

"Oh, you just happened to 'find' a box of t-shirts, did you? I'd love to see you 'Move Like Jagger' mind."

"Like Jagger…? What do you mean?"

"Oh, never mind. How's Xavi?"

"Very well, thank you. Are you all set for Madrid?"

"We are indeed, just need some final details so we can fine tune the operation and we'll be set up nicely."

Xavi gestures towards a seat further along the path and the other two men follow him over. He sits just off centre with Luis to his left, leaning forward, elbows on his knees. Robert sits on the other end, his left ankle resting on his right knee, trying to look calm and relaxed. He can't help but notice Luis' resemblance to a cheap chubby Buddha, one you'd expect to find in a factory outlet shop selling seconds. Xavi opens by asking Robert about his timings.

"We'll be staying nearby overnight. Small place, cheap. False names. Paying cash. I've checked out the layout of Mercamadrid online to try to ensure we find the place as easily as we can. I know where the fruit warehouses are, I just need the details."

"So you understand the size and complexity of the

market?" asked Xavi.

"I do."

"It's bigger than big…it's bigger than very big…it's very very big!" said Luis, eyes bulging such that Robert was reminded of the fried eggs he'd had for breakfast.

"Gracias, Luis" said Xavi.

"It covers 222 hectares, it has 800 firms, it serves 20,000 people a day, it's visited by 15,000 vehicles a day, it employs 8,000 workers from 30 different countries and it provides food for 12 million people living within 500 kilometres. That's how big it is" said Robert triumphantly and looking smugger than a brace of Paxmans on University Challenge.

Xavi nodded and smiled. Luis was open-mouthed. He looked up at his master, then back at Robert and pronounced:

"That is very very really big!"

"Good way of putting it" said Robert.

"So," Xavi went on, "you need to make a note of a few things."

"Fire away" said Robert, taking out his mobile and bringing up the Notes app.

"You're not recording this are you?"

"No! Just making notes here where they'll be password protected. Don't want to leave little notes lying around, do we?"

"Good."

The key information was imparted. Robert now knew exactly who to contact and when. He also knew what to expect afterwards in terms of onward delivery of their cargo, although nothing would be revealed until he received a phone call afterwards. Xavi had also discreetly handed him an envelope and asked him to open it carefully and count the notes inside, which he did. The men all shook hands.

"Good luck" said Xavi.

"Yeah, good luck" added Luis.

Robert nodded, turned and walked away, leaving tweedle dee and tweedle dumb to head off in the opposite direction. There was a beautiful breeze rippling off the Mediterranean as gulls flew across the shallow waters looking for food, the waves unfolding along the sand. The image of Luis as some sort of Tibetan deity was tough to shake off and, recalling the advertising for the original vegetable oil spread, he muttered to himself as he walked along the promenade… 'I can't believe it's not Buddha'. Then, heading towards his car at the edge of town, he had a feeling that he was being followed. Turning sharply he saw no-one behind him. A man in black jacket, black jeans and black t-shirt had managed to slip into a shop doorway just in time.

Around this time Beatriz is telephoning Jack from her Granada apartment. Her friend Christina is the manager at the Euro Washington Irving Hotel and will meet him when he arrives. What time is this likely to be? Jack explains that he'd hoped to travel to Almeria by bus but the timetable just doesn't work out well, so Robert had offered him his car to travel to Almeria, he'd leave it at the station and Robert would pick it up on his way back from Madrid. His train will arrive in Granada at 17:31. This means he'll need to take a taxi - the station is two kilometres away on the other side of the city. She'll tell Christina to expect him around six. The prospect of seeing each other again and spending some time together elicits some excitement for both of them, although they each keep it just below the surface.

"How about we start at the Alhambra for 9:00?" suggests Beatriz. "It's important to see as much as we can before midday, when it becomes too hot."

"Sure. Fine with me, sounds sensible. Can't wait to see it" said Jack.

He lays on his enthusiasm for the Alhambra but it's her he's really looking forward to seeing. Call over, he slumps into the chair and lets out a sigh and returns to thinking about his wife.

Over in Calle la Fuente in Mojacar Pueblo, Robert is strolling up the hill to La Habanero, where he can see Alfredo sitting on a seat against the wall outside. They embrace and order a couple of beers.

"So, did you have a good weekend, Alf?"

"Si. We go over to my parents for lunch yesterday, El Abuelito also…it was very nice. Great food, lots to eat. And of course we talk about the usual things, the same things, you know how it is with family?"

"Oh yeah. I don't really miss that. Although I do miss my family sometimes. And how's Beatriz? She's got Jack coming to visit this week."

"Yes, but she doesn't say much."

"Do you reckon there might be a bit of an attraction there then?"

"Oh, I don't know, maybe? I only mentioned it once to tease her and she took my head off! So maybe there is."

"Ah…interesting. Anyway, down to business."

Robert proceeds to tell Alfredo about his recent discussion with his clients. When he tells him that they need to be at the market for 4:30 Alf thinks he means the afternoon. The shock is palpable as he realises that Robert really is talking about the morning. It's a long time since he's been out at that time of day. They'll be heading for Frutas Nave C, unit 40. That's where they'll find Pedro, or Señor

Nunez if he's a formal looking guy. Once they've successfully acquired the right containers they'll make their way out and go find breakfast somewhere quiet.

"It still sounds quite simple" said Alfredo.

"I'm sure it won't be. We've got to be prepared for things not to run quite as we've planned. One of the things I've learned through things going wrong is that plans are useless...but the act of planning is invaluable, my friend."

"How come?"

"Well, in coming up with a plan I've spent a lot of time learning about the market, the routes in and out, I've visualised it all. So if something goes wrong all that information I've built up can help us to sort out any problems."

Alfredo thought about this for a few seconds, then added: "I suppose it's what you would call common sense to plan properly?"

"It is, my friend, but common sense is not a flower that grows in everyone's garden."

"What?"

"Exactly."

With that they go on to discuss their time of departure for Madrid. Should they go across to Murcia and take the A-31 via Albacete? This has the advantage of being quicker but involves tolls. They decide it's best to get there quicker so they can get some sleep with such an early start. Robert would like to return by a different route, besides which he'll need to pick up his car from Almeria. It might be wise to keep a low profile on the return leg. So they agree on the fastest route there, the A-31 and A-43, returning on the A4.

"Now, tomorrow I'll book us a place to stay. Looking here at Google Maps it would be ideal to stay somewhere around San Agustin del Guadalix - it's right off the A-1 and we can be at the Mercamadrid in no time next morning. What do you reckon?"

"Looks good…away from the city, close to where we need to go, so yes."

"Great!" said Robert, leaning over and putting a fatherly arm around him. "I've got a good feeling about this, Alf. It's going to be very positive for us and we're going to enjoy ourselves too." He smiled as he finished speaking and squeezed tight on Alf's shoulder in a way that might just be perceived as a little more than fatherly.

—

Later that evening Jack and Robert caught up with each other, sharing the day's news, such as it was. They had a chuckle over some of the tabloid headlines following Harry Kane's hat-trick in England's 6-1 demolition of mighty Panama the night before - two penalties and a deflection off his trailing leg as he strolled across the penalty area checking for messages on his mobile were apparently sufficient for a knighthood. At least it had made for a memorable night's viewing in the bar.

Once Robert had told of his plans for Wednesday, their route and where they'd be staying, ever thoughtful he remembered to ask about Amanda. Jack leaned back in his chair, let out a long sigh as he stretched his arms out then settled for a moment, the back of his head resting in his hands. He told him what he knew and what he'd found out through the internet. Clearly serious in its potential implications, he was at least reassured that it had been diagnosed at the right time and she should make a good recovery. Nonetheless, Robert could see it was bothering him.

When he knows the date for the operation, should he return? Even if she didn't want him around, should he be there for his kids? Even if he wasn't needed, they agreed he couldn't go wrong by returning, by being there for the family. And really it was inevitable that he'd still feel responsibility, it hadn't been that long. Although he was relaxing and enjoying life in Spain, family would continue to draw him back. Deep down he knew it was time to give some serious thought to his future.

Chapter Ten

Wednesday 27 June 2018

Wednesday morning at eight o'clock as the day begins, quietly turning his back door key, stepping outside Alfredo is on his way to collect the van. He has his overnight bag with him and he's feeling a tingle of excitement about the day. He's got to walk along to Heladeria Blu where he's arranged to meet a friend who works at the van hire company. At around 8:30 he sits down to wait. After five slightly nervous minutes spent worrying about his friend, he finally shows up. Emerging from just along the road where he'd parked the big white van, he waves as he crosses the Paseo del Mediterraneo.

"Buenos dias, amigo. Sit down. Breakfast is on me. Great to see you!" said Alfredo.

After exchanging a few pleasantries they order desayunos. Afterwards Alfredo pays the deposit and his friend explains some of the basics about the van and so on. He texts Robert and heads round to pick him up.

"Right, Jack, here's my spare key for the motor. I've got mine with me. You've got my number if you should need to call me, I'm sure everything will be just splendid."

"Thanks, pal. This is so helpful. Hope everything goes smoothly for you and Alfredo. Look forward to hearing all about it when you get back."

"I hope it's not as exciting as what you'll have to tell me about, if you catch my drift!"

"Hey" said Alf, with Jack looking to the sky, "that's my sister you're talking about."

"Oh, sorry, Alf - forgot you were there."

"Take no notice, Alfredo, you know what he's like. Good luck spending two whole days with him," said Jack, "I know what it's like. Safe journey, guys."

"Cheers! Right then, Alf…fire up the Transit!"

Jack went upstairs to do some packing, while Butch and Sundance rode their van over the horizon and into the desert. The Ford Transit was only a few years old but it had seen some action and covered some ground.

"I bet this van could tell a few tales, eh Alf?"

"Oh for sure. But it drives OK, that's the main thing."

The plan was to stop near Murcia for a coffee then head on past Albacete for lunch. Traffic was relatively light and the motorway cruising was comfortable. Over in Granada, Beatriz was busy trying to get on top of her workload and at the same time squeeze in a little organising to ensure Jack's visit was a success. Christina had suggested they meet for a quick bite at lunchtime. Meanwhile Jack was skipping round the apartment in Mojacar having closed his case and overcome the pressure of trying to look his best for two and a half days. He wanted to make a good impression on Beatriz, and he had his own vanity to appease. He didn't want people looking at her and going 'what on earth's she doing with him?'. Then again, what if it did go really well, you never know? 'My God' he thought, 'how amazing would that be? Dream on…'

Then again, lately he'd been a bag of neuroses, prone to overthinking everything, and it wasn't long before Amanda began to prey on his mind again. Soon she'd be dependent on those around her. He'd spoken with her since Josh gave him the news and although she'd been typically stoical she also betrayed her vulnerability. It's a big operation anytime but because it's linked to cancer it felt more sinister. At least she had the satisfaction of the consultant's advice that it hadn't spread beyond her uterus and it had been caught early. Still, there was nothing he could do immediately and, if he was to return, he'd need to decide when would be best and how he might help her when she returned home. Best to put it to the back of his mind for now. He wanted to enjoy Granada.

By the time the lads had stopped for coffee and resumed their journey, Jack was speeding along the autopista on the first leg of his trip to Granada and Beatriz was meeting up with hotel manager Christina on the hotel's outdoor terrace.

"Hola Christina! How are you?"

"Ah…hola Bea! I'm very good, you're looking great. Are you all set for your visitor? I can't wait to meet him."

The two friends enjoyed some friendly banter and Beatriz had to withstand a little teasing about the nature of her relationship with Jack. Even though there was clearly nothing going on between them, Christina's intuition detected just a small frisson of possibility in Beatriz around her feelings. She promised to advise her by Friday morning on her views.

"I have a chart ready" she said, "giving marks for

looks, style, manners and sense of humour - very important - I like a man who makes me laugh!"

"You're assuming then that he can afford me?" asked Beatriz.

"Of course" said Christina laughing, "that's a minimum qualification before you can consider him. There's two more columns for assessment but I don't expect you to be able to report on performance and stamina for a few dates yet."

"Aaaargh!" she squealed. "That's outrageous!"

They went on to discuss the trials and tribulations of work: Beatriz's tales of clients and projects were juxtaposed with Christina's efforts to increase business interspersed with some of the odd and bizarre events involving their guests. Eventually they talk about arrangements for Jack's stay - it's a great deal she's sorted for him, given that it's a 5* hotel.

"Where are you eating tonight, Beatriz?"

"I thought I'd take him to Tajine Elvira - show him the city's connection to North Africa. Besides, it's my favourite Moroccan restaurant. What do you think?"

"Oh yeah, good idea, I always like it there.

"Great. So he's due in around 5:30. I'll still be working so I've suggested he takes a taxi here and I guess it'll be around six when he arrives."

"Fine. I'll watch out for him and make sure I'm told by Reception. I can't wait to meet him!"

Jack managed to negotiate the roads around Almeria and successfully found his way to Plaza de la Estación. The traditional old railway station, close to the sea front, provides him with a pleasant introduction to Spanish rail travel and soon he's on his way. He was simply looking forward to a relaxing journey and taking a scenic tour of the region. Running alongside the River Andarax to the eastern end of the Sierra de Gador, stopping at Fiñana at the edge of the Sierra de Baza, an ecological Natural Park, and Guadix, a town famous for its cave dwellings, the train should give him terrific views of the Sierra Nevada.

That Jack came to know all these locations and panoramic vistas along the route owed nothing to his research nor his travel guide. No, it was thanks to a man who had appeared in the carriage around two minutes out of Granada. Removing his rucksack and straw trilby, he sat straight opposite Jack and next to the window. He kept on his three quarter length mack, a strange choice for June, and smiled at his new friend. As he did so his eyes narrowed behind specs that were too small for the size of his head and served to exaggerate his ruddy complexion. Probably walking the length of the train he'd seen Jack sitting alone and recognised him as a suitable victim. Familiar with the well-known British concept, based on Sod's Law, of having the misfortune of sitting opposite the 'nutter on the train' - see also 'nutter on the bus' - he was disappointed yet curious to find himself sitting at a table seat opposite an example that demonstrated the international nature of the phenomenon.

"Hey there, do you speak Ingalazey?" asked the stranger in a most unusual accent.

"Yes. I do. I am…English"

"Well isn't that just great" he responded, "we can talk and understand each other." He smiled. Jack tried to. But struggled. Instead, Jack was focused on where he might be from. He didn't like to ask, although he thought it likely that it was an accent learned from American cinema and TV. After every comment or statement he moved his head forward ever so slightly and raised his eyebrows. Jack tried to read his book, he also tried ignoring him, but nothing would shake off his attention.

As the voyage continued the man at least proved helpful on places of interest that they passed. But he insisted on proving an absolute authority on the many places they passed of no interest whatsoever. By the time he thought of moving it was too late. Jack was resigned to having him throughout the journey. He asked questions between places of interest. If Jack couldn't answer or tried to avoid doing so, he simply asked something else. He had to acknowledge his intrigue at an exchange that took place somewhere around Benalua.

"Have you ever been to Malta?"

"Yes I have."

"I would like to go to Malta."

"It's a lovely island, very friendly."

"I saw it in a film, Black Eagle, with Jean Claude Van Damme. It was amazing!"

"Really?"

"Oh yes. He is Russian KGB…lots of kick boxing and kung fu…and they go to Madeena, I think it was called."

"Ah, it was probably an old town called Mdina, there's a big temple there, very old."

"Yes! Yes! That's the place. Is it real then? I only know it from Black Eagle. My father said he would take me to Malta one day. But that was before they took him back."

"Who took him back where?" said Jack, interested for the first time.

"My mother said they probably took him to Leningrad."

Then he leaned over the table after a furtive look around the carriage.

"He was KGB many years ago…like Van Demme!"

"I see" said Jack.

Before too long the train pulled into Granada. After briskly exiting the carriage he was hiding from his new bestie behind a kiosk when he received a text from Josh, which read simply:

Mum in for op Fri 6 July. Call later?

His stomach knotted and he felt sick for a few moments. He knew a date would be imminent but now this made it very real. He would have to make a decision quite quickly about what to do. He'd call Josh later from the hotel.

The refuelling pitstop on the autopista was functional and efficient, although for a time Robert regretted his decision to add cheesecake to his self-service tray on account of it winking at him repeatedly as he walked along the queue. Between animated bursts of conversation the silences became longer as the journey progressed. But the two guys were comfortable enough with that. They were soon skirting round Madrid on the A-1 and heading off and into San Agustin del Guadalix, a small commuter town whose population had grown significantly in recent years to over 9,000 people. There it was! The Hostal Bar-Restaurante Alpaca. A modern building with a nod to the past in the form of wrought iron balconies and arched ground floor windows, rather defeated by the shutters and grills added for security. More Alcatraz than Alhambra. No matter. It was the price that was important and they'd be out before the crack of dawn.

"At least there's a bar" said Robert as they entered with their overnight bags.

The bar-restaurant was a mix of small modern tables, 'olde worlde' barrels, leather-look comfy chairs and stools. And a few gaming machines of course. At reception a young man introducing himself as Ramon checked them in.

"So, we have Señor Robert Smith and Señor Alfredo di Stefano?"

"Yes" indicated the two men in turn, although Alfredo's new incognito surname had been a bit of a surprise to him.

"Are you any relation to the great man himself" asked Ramon, the excitement in his eyes betraying a desperate hope that he was in the presence of the family of the legendary Real Madrid centre forward.

"Er…no. I'm afraid we're not related" said Alfredo apologetically.

They went up to their third floor room. Alfredo was still puzzled by the name he'd been given.

"Just a bit of a laugh, mate" said Robert.

"What about your name then?"

"Robert Smith? Never heard of The Cure? Fine British band from my past. He obviously didn't recognise me without the eye make-up."

Inside it was bit tight on space, two single beds a few feet apart, the bathroom was also a bit cramped.

"It'll be fine" said Alfredo.

"Course it will, mate. We're here to do a job, that's all. A few more jobs like this and we'll be staying in better places, trust me."

"Do you fancy a beer?" asked Alf.

"Do I fancy a beer?" Robert pondered for a few seconds. "Well, now. If God had not intended me to drink the amber nectar, why the hell would he have given me a stomach like this?" he added, patting his belly. "Let's go."

—

In Granada the taxi turned off along the Paseo de Generalife and arrived at the Eurostars Washington Irving. As he paid the fare Jack looked up and saw a substantial, high quality, modern building. Walking into reception there was a feeling of smart, understated luxury. He looked around and felt a real buzz. As a couple in front of him moved off, a young woman whose name badge identified her as 'Carmen' asked if she could help.

"Habla Ingles?" he asked?

"Yes, of course."

"Great. I'd like to check in please. Jack Rivers."

"Ah, Señor Rivers! My Manager is expecting you. Please complete this while I call her. Thank you." She smiled as she handed Jack his registration form.

'Hola!' called the hotel's manager as she strode elegantly into the reception lounge.

"Christina?"

"Yes, that's right, delighted to meet you, Jack. I've heard a lot about you" she said, with a knowing curt smile and a polite handshake.

"Oh, that's worrying! I've been so looking forward to visiting Granada and what a lovely place this is."

"Oh thank you! Please sit down, I'll tell you a few things about it that may help you. Would you like a drink?"

"An orange juice would be perfect" said the message from his brain as it fought its way past an image of a cold beer.

"Great! I'll fetch you a fresh orange juice…" and even as she turned round Carmen was holding up her hand and going off to the bar.

"Ah! Great service. Carmen's on it like a car bonnet…" said Jack as if he was ordering a pint in the Frog and Ferkin in Ramsbottom. For a couple of seconds time stood still as Christina looked at him curiously then simply smiled.

Christina went on to tell Jack about his room and the hotel's facilities, including the rooftop pool. She also told him a little of the history, a hotel having been on the site since around 1870.

"Through the twentieth century it's received so many distinguished guests" she went on, "film stars like Gregory Peck, Brigitte Bardot, Anthony Quinn and Spanish legends too like Andrés Segovia, our famous guitarist."

"I feel honoured to follow in their footsteps!"

"And as a souvenir of your visit" said Christina, "you'll find a copy of 'Tales of the Alhambra' by Washington Irving in your room with our compliments. It's full of stories and legends of the characters who've been involved with the Alhambra through its history."

"Oh wow, what a lovely idea. Thank you!"

Finishing his fresh orange, Jack was taken up to his room. Christina explained that they'd had a late cancellation so she'd been able to upgrade him to a deluxe room, information which she delivered with a sly little wink. So after she left him to settle into his new surroundings he was feeling quite the international traveller. He'd be meeting Beatriz in reception around 8:30 and, of course, he wanted to speak to Josh, so he thought to himself… 'a shower or a nice soak in the bathtub?'

—

Robert and Alf downed their second and final San Miguels and agreed they'd toss a coin for the privilege of first in the shower. Tails! It was Alf to go first. Having manoeuvred himself into the small cubicle and hopped about in discomfort trying to set the temperature of the water, he'd just about got it sorted.

"Aaaaargh!" he screamed, arching his back and colliding with the screen.

"Oh bollocks" said Robert, turning off the wash basin tap. "Sorry about that, mate. Just filling up the kettle for after."

Alf moaned and huffed and puffed but otherwise refrained from letting out the volley of abuse that wanted to escape from under his breath. When Robert's turn to shower came he looked at the space and called to Alfredo:

"I don't want to worry you, Alf, but I could easily become wedged in here. Might need you to pull me out."

After raising his eyebrows, he replied "And what do you suggest I hold to pull you out?"

"Hey, you saucy little bugger" said Robert, laughing.

"You'll need to pay me extra for that."

Downstairs in the bar-restaurant they browsed at the menu.

"Weren't we supposed to meet your contact tonight?" said Alfredo. "About the arrangements in the morning?"

"Oh sorry, mate, must have forgotten to tell you. I had a message from Xavi saying it wasn't necessary, so we're OK tonight."

Alfredo confessed that he'd never had a great meal at any place where they showed pictures of each dish. The boss agreed but felt they'd be best eating in the hotel - keep a low profile, save time, get to bed early. So it was some sort of pork steak with chips for Robert and a pizza for Alfredo. Robert reckoned his just about passed muster and made the best of it, whilst the pizza looked nothing like the picture and wasn't helped by appearing to have a base made from cardboard, according to Alf. Another San Miguel or two compensated for the distinctly dull cuisine.

"Do you know why they put pictures alongside the menu items in places like this?" said Robert.

"Is it because their customers are stupid? Maybe they don't know what a pizza looks like?"

"Nah, nothing like that. I remember reading about this study a university did, I think it might have been Durham in the UK. They reckoned that if the dishes were fairly simple, having a picture made people more likely to go in and order. Whereas, if the dish had a more complicated name, or needed a bit of description, like you might have in a good restaurant, photos put people off."

"I had a friend who went to England and on the list of sandwiches in this cafe," said Alf, "they had 'Ike and Tina Tuna'. I suppose that would be difficult in a photo."

"Oh yes" said Robert laughing. "It certainly would. But I love the name though. Reminds me of a place I went once in America. They had at the bottom of the menu a 'Seven Course Irish Dinner' - then underneath it said 'Six beers and a potato, and you can't sub the potato for another beer'. I mean, these days that's borderline discrimination, but at the time I was almost tempted to order it."

Further south, Jack just about left himself enough time for a conversation with Josh before going down to meet Beatriz. Amanda's due into hospital mid-afternoon on the sixth, with the op presumably the following day, Saturday. At least the weekend made it easy for people to visit initially, Josh thought, even though she might feel groggy and a little sore. Jack felt visiting was the easy bit in many ways, what was important was to have people able to help her when she returned home. He was relieved that things seemed to be in place when Josh reassured him that Seb would be able to spend some time at home and Nicole would be taking some time off work to stay with her too. Added to that, she'd got a promise of support from her friend Joanne - cooking, cleaning, shopping and stuff like that. So that was all fine, but Jack continued to ponder about what he should do, whether anything was expected of him, what people would think if he didn't go back to see her or do anything. For now, thought the master procrastinator, plans would have to wait.

Jack saw Beatriz walking across the pavement towards the hotel entrance. He stood up from his seat and went to meet her at the doors. She was wearing a tight dress in true blue with a small black cardigan with short sleeves. Her hair was tied up in a pony tail by a black scarf with matching blue polka dots. Jack was wearing light chinos with a powder blue shirt, long sleeved. His dark brown latticed belt broadly matched his loafers and in an attempt to pull off a continental look he was completely sockless. How daring!

"So good to see you, Beatriz" he said as they embraced and went through the dos besos routine of a pretend peck on each cheek. "You look stunning and I love your hair." Steady on Jack.

"Thank you" she said coyly. "Welcome to Granada! Isn't it beautiful?"

"Absolutely. So far so good."

"And your room? Is it OK?"

"Oh, it's more than OK, it's fantastic. Christina said

they'd had a late cancellation so she upgraded me to a deluxe room."

"Whoah! That sounds great. You must show me your room before we go out, I want to see what it's like."

"Sure, although we don't want people talking about us."

"I don't care" she said, shrugging her shoulders. "You're looking very smart yourself so let people talk if they want."

"Right…" he said, a tingling sensation coursing through his body.

Almost at that moment, Christina emerged. She offered them an aperitif to start their evening but Beatriz wanted to show Jack a little of the city and agreed that they'd join her for a drink tomorrow evening. It was a little difficult to then go up to see Jack's room and so they walked out together and, as Christina watched them walk across the road and towards the centre, she noticed what a striking couple they made.

It was a five minute walk to La Tana, a small taberna painted white and yellow with black wrought iron balconies and old style lanterns. Inside, Jack looked around at its lovely range of old photographs on one wall, with a large rack of wines and all sorts of foodstuffs hanging on another. Beatriz decided it was time Jack tried a vermut. He protested. I mean, sweet vermouth, dry vermouth, he'd tried them both at home and they were a bit naff.

"Clearly you've not tried a proper Spanish vermut rojo. This is a dark one, rojo means simply red but this is a nice deep colour, served with a slice of orange. We'll drink it with some salty black olives too - they're just perfect together."

"Well," said Jack, taking his first sip, "I've got to say

that's not what I expected. Mmm…that's rather good. Oooh, so are these olives!"

After a pause for drinking and chewing on an olive he added: "I wouldn't have tried nearly so many things without you. At least if you're ever stuck for work you could get a job as a tour guide."

"Maybe I could but, you know what? It's not a big ambition."

Next they headed off across the city to Tajine Elvira. It looked more like a simple tea house from the outside, but its Arab influence was unmistakeable.

"I recommend we order a jug of mint lemonade" said Beatriz. "It has no alcohol but I just find it a lovely accompaniment to this style of food."

"OK" said Jack, "When in Morocco…"

They started with pastela - flaky pastry stuffed with chicken, almonds and cinnamon. Then along came lamb tagine and cous cous with chicken and caramelised onions.

"My favourite used to be dulces Arabes - they're like super light pastries coated in sweet honey yet crisp and fresh. I haven't actually had them since before I was married."

"Is there anything significant in that?" he asked.

"No, not really."

"Well, we'd better try them then. Although I'm so full I don't know how I'll manage."

"Let's share then!" she said with a big smile.

The dulces Arabes were served on a cake stand and they each picked the ones they wanted. He bit into his first, then rolled his eyes and groaned.

"Oh they're so good. In fact, with this piping hot, spicy tea they're damn near magical."

Beatriz laughed. When pressed by Jack as to whether they were as good as she remembers them, she was in no doubt they were. As they began to slowly meander back he remarked that it was something they had in common, a marriage that hadn't worked out. That may be so to a point, she agreed, but when Jack had three children and was married for so long, it wasn't really the same. Perhaps she would tell him about hers some time. He put a friendly arm around her shoulder and gave a little squeeze.

"Hang on, Beatriz. How far is it to the hotel from here? And what about you? Would you like me to walk you home? I'm sure I could find-"

"It's alright, no problem. At this pace it's at least, oh... twenty minutes? Then I can get a taxi home."

"Whereabouts do you live then?"

"Just on the edge of the centre, so it's maybe a kilometre from here, perhaps two from the hotel?"

"But I don't want you having to go back alone, it's late."

"Oh Jack, the city is very safe and don't forget I live here alone all the time!"

"True. Sorry, I just..."

She took his arm and nuzzled her head into his shoulder.

"Besides... I'd like the walk after all that food and maybe we can have a drink at the hotel before I call the taxi."

"Good idea. A nightcap."

"A what?"

"In the UK we call the last drink before bedtime a 'nightcap'"

"A nightcap? I like that...Right, let's go have a nightcap."

The hotel was quiet but there were still a decent number of guests sitting around the bar. After finding some comfy seats in a corner and ordering, a waiter brought over two glasses of licor de hierbas. Jack told Beatriz how much he was looking forward to visiting the Alhambra with his personal guide. She claimed she'd spent each evening this week learning everything about its history so that he wouldn't be disappointed. The hotel was close to the Alhambra, so she said she'd join him for breakfast at eight.

"That's wonderful! A perfect start to the day!"

"Right now, I must go home, there's a taxi outside and a tour guide needs to sleep well to perform well."

They walked over to the doors. Beatriz turned to face him just outside the doorway, a cool breeze running through her hair. Jack placed his hands either side of her shoulders and looked into her eyes.

"It's been a lovely evening" he said gently and smiled.

They embraced.

"My pleasure" she said, then kissed him on the cheek before turning and walking to the taxi.

Chapter Eleven

Thursday 28 June 2018

As they made their departure, Robert noticed something odd.

"Hold on" he called to Alfredo. "You just sign the visitor's book?"

"Yes. I thought it would be helpful to leave an honest comment."

"What's this mean?"

"I have written 'There's no room to swing a cat', signed by a member of PACMA."

"What's that then?"

"It stands for the Animalist Party Against Mistreatment of Animals."

"Ah ha! And how many members have they had elected to government then?"

"Er...none."

"Interesting. Very amusing, Alfredo. I didn't know you had a dark side."

The big white van started second time and they

drove out of the parking area, off the estate and towards the A-1 Autovia del Norte.

"So, Alfredo. This is it. Big job today. Mercamadrid here we come!"

"Which way at the roundabout?" asked Alf, keeping his mind on the task in hand.

" We want to be heading north and then look out for the M-963. That'll take us straight to the 'capital of markets'. That's what they call this place, you know."

"It looked a big complex on the map. You're happy with where we have to go?"

"As much as I can be, Alf, at this stage. It's not your normal market, that's for sure. It covers 65,000 square metres, it's got six warehouses and 342 sales positions. And that's just the central bit that does fruit and vegetables. Then there's a separate warehouse of 8,880 square metres that's got 120 chambers with 1,800 square metres just for ripening bananas for God's sake!"

"So that's the one we want, yes?"

"No. I've got the directions here but we're aiming for Frutas Nave C. The unit we're looking for is called Felix Sanchez. So forget the bananas for now, keep your eyes peeled. Then we've got to ask for Señor Nunez...Pedro."

"My eyes peeled?"

"Never mind, stay sharp and just look for the signs."

Beyond the headlights on the motorway they can see the market. Alfredo thinks it's lit up like a space station.

"I can feel the force is with me!" Alfredo suddenly lets out.

"You what?"

"I am Biggs Darklighter piloting my craft towards the brilliantly illuminated entrance. Hold on! I'm going down."

"Going down? One of us is going mad. Unfortunately it's the one behind the bloody wheel."

"So you're not a Star Wars fan then, Roberto?" Alf says while chuckling.

"Yeah I am actually, but who the hell's Biggs Firelighter or whatever his name is?"

"Biggs Darklighter is one of the top X-Wing pilots in the Rebel Alliance. If you want to find out more about him you can check it out on Wookieepedia."

"Wookieepedia? Good God…you've got too much time on your hands my friend."

Just then they see a row of toll booths and the large sign announces that they've arrived at Mercamadrid. Pulling into the right hand lane and passing the Zone Commercial they head off to the left for the Mercado Central de Frutas y Hortalizas. The white van proceeds carefully along Calle 44 as they look for the turn off. Each lane is full of vans and trucks of all sizes, some of them absolute monsters, jostling for position to find their collection points. Winding down the window, Robert passes across his credentials and hopes that Xavi has done his job properly. He has. Soon they're parking up, ready to walk round and find the right unit. In the night sky the moon is still set to full power, as people swarm around loading bays. The frequency of forklift trucks weaving through workers and customers adds to the sense of organised chaos. The market itself is a wild palette of colours. Even at this very early time there are shopkeepers galore moving around the place. The air is warm and humid and a generic aroma of fruit is all pervading. Everywhere there's piles of boxes and containers with their contents waxed and gleaming. It's all super clean and there's nothing of the disorder you expect from local markets where much of this stuff will eventually be sold.

"It's like entering another galaxy, this place," said Robert. "Remember those weird bars and places in Star Wars? Reminds me of that. Folks wandering around with big boots and gloves, strange headwear, protective clothing…all the shouting too. And all at 5 o'clock in the morning!"

"Roll on breakfast" said Alfredo.

"If you looked at this lot from above I bet it'd look like a load of worker ants milling around shifting stuff."

They pass so many varieties of fruit as they walk through - apples, avocado, mango, cassava, lemons, pineapples, persimmon, kiwi, peppers. The bunches of grapes make them want to reach over and grab a few, glistening and dazzling like precious jewels. Eventually they find their way to Unit 40 in Nave C, the premises of Felix Sanchez.

"Buenos dias, señor" says Robert addressing a man in red overalls.

Pleasantries out of the way the boys ask for Señor Nunez…The reply comes back and Alfredo looks slightly perturbed as he translates for Robert.

"He says he's not here…he's not well today."

"He's not well! Oh bollocks!"

"What do we do now?"

"Right, let's think. I've got his mobile number…I'll ring him. Not well…Jesus! Great timing, Señor Nunez."

Robert looks around as he waits on a reply. He's agitated.

"Damn! It's gone to voicemail. Thank you so much. If Nunez isn't here there's not really much we can do. We've got the details of the boxes we need to buy…so I guess we just need to find out how to go about buying them. Ask him when the bananas are selling."

A conversation between Alfredo and the man ensues.

Eventually, Alf turns to Robert. It seems that the main consignment of bananas will be available for bidding from 5:30. Fifteen minutes to wait.

By the time the clock comes round there's quite a number of people gathered at Felix Sanchez: buyers from supermarkets, shops, food distributors and markets. Suddenly Robert feels a little worried. What seemed like an easy task is now looking a bit vague. He knows which boxes he has to buy. What could possibly go wrong? Well, for a start, he hadn't reckoned on having to rely on Alfredo to tell him what's going on.

The auction starts…they're waiting for consignments 125 - 145. This gives them a bit of time to figure out custom and practice. Robert's surprised how quickly and efficiently it all proceeds. It's nearly time. Next lot. Here we go…Robert drums his fingers along the top of his shoulder bag and watches the auctioneer.

"Los números ciento veinticinco a ciento cuarenta y cinco…"

"This one!" Alfredo says urgently. "May the force be with you!"

"Fuck off, Firelighter!"

Robert is trembling inside as the bidding starts for the twenty boxes of bananas. There are a few clear competitors who start it off at a pace. Robert puts in a bid. It's beaten by a man in a blue jacket and chinos. Another man goes higher, a bald man with glasses and a white t-shirt. Robert goes again. It occurs to him that it could be quite easy - he just has to have these bananas so he just has to keep bidding until they drop out. Genius! He's noticed these guys have already bought consignments so he figures they must be from a big store. Well they can do without these, he thinks. The pattern continues for a couple of minutes, every increase in the price matched by a similar increase in Robert's heart rate.

Then a pause occurs, the auctioneer looks round, the bald man shakes his head…he's not bidding any more. The man in the blue jacket looks up from his notes and mouths something. But what's this? An old guy in brown overalls and a straw hat has got his hand up. Robert's heart sinks…more competition. The auctioneer is checking with him and the new bidder nods affirmatively, then looks round at everyone, grinning a bit too manically for Robert's liking. The auctioneer tries to continue the bidding but he's distracted by a few people and appeals for "un momento, por favor". He listens to what's being said by the men in the crowd and Robert starts badgering Alfredo.

"What are they saying? What's happening?"

"I think they are saying they know him and he's… how can I say?" Alf struggles for the correct words. "He is a man with problems. Mental problems."

"What? You mean he's not the full Euro?"

Suddenly a security officer is summoned over and he moves into the crowd to sensitively remove the disruptor from the auction.

"Bananas! Bananas!" shouts the man in the straw hat.

The auctioneer restarts proceedings by advising those present of the highest bid to date before inviting further bids. The blue sleeve goes up again and once more Robert responds. A signal from the man in blue and it looks like he's out. Yes! The auctioneer looks over to Robert and indicates that he is the successful buyer. It's all over. The boys have the bananas. One of the officials walks over to Robert and hands him a ticket of some kind. Alf explains that he told him where to go to pay and that he'll be given the collection arrangements. So they head over together to sort out the transaction. Robert looks at Alfredo and blows out his cheeks. Relief. He thinks to himself about what might be in the bananas but feels happy that at least the chances of him being knee-capped have diminished considerably.

Round at the loading bay, Alfredo reversed into the space. Once the numbers on each container had been checked, with the help of a strong young man it was a relatively quick and easy job to pack them all in. As they pulled out Robert asked Alf if they should have a look round the rest of the market whilst they were there. Alf said he could use a coffee so they parked up and wandered off to find somewhere. A few minutes later they're knocking back some fine strong coffee and tucking into a selection of pastries. The mood has lightened. The hard task is out of the way and life's good when the going is easy.

"I tell you what" said Robert. "I'd love to see the fish market. It's supposed to be amazing. Let's go have a look round. We'll be quick, then we're off back to base my son."

They flash their credentials not even knowing whether they'll access all areas or they're solely for the fruit and veg market but in they go.

"Do you realise," Robert asks "that this is the second biggest fish market in the world despite being land locked?"

"Is it? What's the biggest?"

"Oh, the one in Japan. I think it's called Tsukiji Fish Market. But they let tourists in there. It's quite a surreal image, isn't it…a massive fish market full of tourists? Can you imagine them all taking selfies with huge blue fin tuna?"

Alfredo likes this image and laughs.

"But how do you know about this fish market in Japan?"

"Research, my friend. I Googled everything I could

about Mercamadrid and you know what the internet's like. It's not content with giving you what you've asked for, it has to suggest other places you might like to have a look at. I saw the link and wondered what it was like.

Alfredo is impressed.

"The thing is, Alf," Robert continues, "it's a dangerous place for tourists. I watched a bit of a film about it on YouTube and the workers don't give a stuff about the tourists. They've got their jobs to get on with, it's highly pressurised and they're all rushing round, driving little cabs and fork-lift trucks and all sorts. Easy to end up on a slab. One minute selfie stick, next minute sushi stick."

Alf just shakes his head and smiles. Job satisfaction.

Having lingered longer than planned the white van is back on the road, complete with its cargo of bananas. The motorway is quite busy, no surprise given that it's the tail end of the morning rush into the city. Alfredo's under instruction to drive calmly and not to attract attention. It prompts further questions from his driver as to the nature of the bananas but Robert's not giving anything away and claims not to know himself. To a certain extent that's true. Then again he knows it's got to be something illegal. He wonders himself about the true value of the load but even he will probably never know and he's happy not to. It's about 9:30 and Robert suggests popping into a small suburb south of Madrid called Pinto so they can pick up some water.

"Ah, Pinto" said Alfredo, " that's where the lead singer of Saratoga comes from, Tete Novoa."

"Who are they then?"

"They're a heavy metal band, I used to love them. Tete is from Pinto."

"So is he like the Spanish Ozzie Osborne then?"

"Not exactly..."

They pull up outside a row of shops and Robert buys a few bottles of water, ambles back out and jumps into the passenger seat.

"Might as well carry on down the A-4 and through Pinto. We can join up with the motorway again on the other side," he says.

As they attempt to pull out onto the highway a police car zooms past, sirens wailing, lights flashing. In no more than 250 metres two more police cars join the route and some way down the road they see about five or six police vehicles parked somewhat randomly outside a Lidl supermarket.

"What's going on there?" said Alfredo.

"Goodness only knows. But look, there's handlers and dogs getting out the back of that van."

They've no option but to drive slowly past the scene as everyone else is doing the same, all trying to get an idea of what's going on.

"No signs of anything especially wrong" Alfredo said.

"No. Interesting though. I'd love to know what's going on, very odd. Still, best crack on, Alf. We should make Valdepenas comfortably for lunch I reckon."

—

As planned, Beatriz arrives at eight to take breakfast with Jack. Christina sees her at the door and the friends embrace and exchange a few words about the evening before. Jack, sitting casually with a glass of fresh orange juice, is trying to make sense of *El Pais.*

"Your guest has arrived, señor" announces Christina with a smile as the they walk over to Jack's table. "Oh, you are reading *El Pais*! You know more Spanish than I thought?"

"No, really I don't" says Jack. "I'm just trying to make myself look more intelligent. My tour guide!" he says as he rises from his seat with his arms wide to embrace Beatriz.

"So," says Christina, "we have a buffet breakfast. Just help yourself to whatever you want. If there's anything special you'd like, we can whip up some eggs, however you like them, whatever. Just ask. Now, how about a glass of cava to give you the perfect start…?"

They can't resist. Bring on the cava…

Beatriz leans back into her chair, puts her rucksack on the floor alongside her and they begin to discuss how they've slept and reflect on their evening out in Granada. She looks very cool in a white t-shirt, beige chinos and a short cerise cardigan. The white leather trainers are for comfort, she maintains. Jack is looking at her like Robert looks at a freshly opened packet of Dorritos. They're spoilt for choice for breakfast - fresh breads, cold meats, fruit platters, raciones of Trevélez ham and Montefrío cheese have all been elegantly prepped and set out.

Beatriz drizzles a little Alpujarras honey over the goat's cheese. Two glasses of cava arrive and breakfast proceeds very gently. There's a tinge of excitement coursing through him but at the same time he feels calm and is content simply to enjoy the moment. He thinks of his father reciting John Wayne. He looks at the sky, already a brilliant blue and marvels at the remarkable quality and clarity of the light. Background chatter mingles with birdsong, pierced intermittently by the random percussion of glasses, cutlery and china.

Following tree-shaded paths they're soon at the imposing Puerta de las Granadas, standing strong and looking down at the steepness of Cuesta de Gomérez, the narrow road that leads all the way from Plaza Nueva in the centre.

"Glad we haven't had to walk from the middle of the city" said Jack.

"Yes, it's very steep. It's worth remembering that whenever you see a road called '*cuesta*' it will be steep - in English it is a quest."

"OK…very practical."

"This gate was built in 1536" said Beatriz, flexing her tour guide credentials for the first time. "It was a tribute to the wedding of King Carlos. The marriage actually took place in Seville, but he and Isabella spent their honeymoon here at the Alhambra."

"It would be an amazing place for a wedding though! I can almost hear the bells ringing out."

Beatriz did her best to explain the complicated political and religious position at that time. She explained that Carlos I was also Charles V…which came from his being Holy Roman Emperor, she thought. He became King Carlos in 1516, by which time two big things had happened: Christopher Columbus had been sent way out west and discovered America; and the Moors were no more, with the surrender of the Emirate of Granada being the final act that removed the al-Andalus family from the region once and for all. Follow that, Carlos!

Walking slowly along the path, Jack tried to understand and appreciate.

"Right, so Carlos has become King of the whole of Spain as we know it…what about places like this then?"

"OK, so the last sultan was Muhammad XII and he went to Morocco, where he lived in exile. But this palace, the greatest symbol of the power of his regime, remains."

"I suppose it's quite helpful today in the multi-cultural society that we have, to be able to see the significant contributions made to our countries in the past by people from other parts of the world. Do you know what I mean? It might encourage people to show more tolerance."

Beatriz agreed. They looked around in quiet reverence for this outstanding example of Islamic architecture, strength and beauty set against the backdrop of the snow capped Sierra Nevada. Returning to old Carlos, she pointed out that he wasn't entirely happy about the Alhambra being such a monument to his predecessors, so he set about trying to alter it and, well, she said she'd show him the changes he made as they go round.

Reaching the top of an incline they come to Puerta de la Justicia, built in 1348 by Sultan Yusuf I and originally the main entrance. Nearby, the 'Pillar of Charles V' or Carlos is evidently of a different style, a sudden interjection of Renaissance, illustrated through the self-aggrandising swagger of Hercules and Apollo.

"I guess here he was trying to make a statement that we're now European" said Beatriz.

"A bit desperate to impose himself perhaps?"

The Alhambra nevertheless rises above it, powerfully and regally and not looking the slightest bit bothered. Jack finds it incredible that it's still here to see and experience in such splendid shape…its courtyards are epic and the gardens idyllic.

"Imagine if the palace was just a thing of the past?" said Beatriz. "It managed to survive the change to Spanish rule, even though the new regime wanted to put its own style into it. But there was a period later in the 18th and 19th centuries when it was simply neglected by the authorities.

"Why?"

"I don't know, but it was just left to decay. Then it became home to groups of beggars, thieves and people like that. For a time it was even used by Napoleon to accommodate his troops. Worst of all, parts of it were destroyed when it was used as target practice by the military."

Jack was quite shocked to hear this, it was hard to imagine. Good sense finally prevailed towards the end of the 19th century when it was made a national monument. Of course, now it's a Unesco World Heritage Site, and the most popular monument in Spain.

"What?" said Jack. "More popular than the big attractions in Madrid and Barcelona?"

"Absolutely! Around 2.5 million people every year - that's more than the Sagrada Familia in Barcelona."

"Well I'm not surprised about that, it's still not finished! Must be the worst building contract of all time."

Walking on they reached an enormous pile of Renaissance, the Palacio de Carlos V. At least Carlos will have had the joy of his very own magnificent imperial residence, Jack thought. Apparently not. By the time most of the work had been finished he'd been dead for 79 years. Largely completed by 1637, the roof was finally finished in 1923.

"1923!" Jack shrieked. "Ridiculous! It couldn't have been because they were busy on the Sagrada Familia."

Smiling, Beatriz pushed him playfully. They strolled round the Palacio, with the Museo de Bellas Artes and the Museo de la Alhambra telling its story. They came to a very regal-looking wooden chair used for state occasions. What is it about chairs behind ropes that makes you just want to climb under and sit on them?

As the sun's strength increased, they sat down for five minutes after grabbing an espresso from the small café bar. Waiting for their timed entrance to the Nasrid Palaces, Beatriz was about to explain their importance when Jack's phone bleeped with a triumphant text from Robert, which said simply 'Mission accomplished amigo!'

"Oh, the boys have got their job done" he said.

"Thank goodness for that. Let's hope their return journey goes smoothly."

"Yeah, we can but hope. So, what's life hold in store for you next, Beatriz?"

"Oh, I don't know. Why do you ask me that now?"

"Just thinking. Sitting here, surrounded by this wonder from the past, makes me think about our place in life, the future. You know, my life's at a bit of a crossroads… and I wonder what you're wanting from life?"

Beatriz tilted her head away from Jack then, looking back at him for a moment, she shrugged, her palms turned up towards the luminous sky.

"It's something I think about a lot. Yet…it's not something I talk about. Maybe because I'm not really sure what it is I want from life right now."

She smiled meekly. Jack sensed a vulnerability about her that he hadn't seen before.

"You seem to love your job" said Jack, "so is it about your personal life that you have some doubts?"

"Yes. I'm happy in my work. But apart from a few girl friends that I'm close with, and my family of course, it can be lonely. And I don't get any younger!" She laughed. "Remember I told you my marriage didn't work out?"

Jack nodded.

"It wasn't just that it didn't work out well. The impact on me has, I think, left some scars. And ever since,

I've found relationships with men too hard. So…I tend to keep men at a distance. I'm sure I've missed out on some potentially nice relationships because of this."

"Can I ask what it was that hurt you so much?"

She sighed.

"He turned out to be a very controlling person. Lovely on the outside to me and everyone else. It was just small things with me to start with, then over time they grew." After a pause, Beatriz looked at Jack and said "Maybe we should carry on with the Alhambra now? I don't want to spoil your day out, but if you like I can tell you a little more later, perhaps over dinner. It might be good for me to talk about it. And I believe I can trust you, Jack."

"Of course, Beatriz" said Jack. "Of course you can. I'm sorry to have deviated a bit from our tour." He took her hand. "Let me just say I'm so pleased that you invited me to Granada. To be here, walking around this beautiful place with you, is amazing. You're a good tour guide too!"

Laughing, they stood up. Jack gave her another of those little squeezes around the shoulder and they walked on.

It was as if they'd exited a time capsule, wandering through corridors, rooms and halls that had seemingly changed little since the time of Al-Andalus. They took in the Royal Residence, once the height of civilisation. On through the Mexuar Hall, where ministers once discussed matters of state. Outside in the Patio de las Leones fountains splash playfully whilst the lions look on stone-faced and dribbling. They admire the sophistication of the Palacio de Comares. Gentle alcoves in the bath house, the dome's star-shaped openings allowing the brilliance of daylight, then it's out into the wonder of the Patio de los Arrayanes - the Courtyard of the Myrtles. Every visitors' favourite postcard except that none can do it justice. Its combination of beauty and tranquillity are hard to convey. It's simple and simply incomparable, intricate and ornate pillars and arches, yet minimal and ordered, its long pool reflecting it all with barely a shimmer.

"No wonder Washington Irving was so enamoured of this place…it's just so special" said Jack. "As you go round these palaces, they've got this stillness and quality…it's hard to explain."

"It's better just to take people here" Beatriz replied and smiled.

Jack put his arm around her and gave her another little squeeze as if to say 'thank you' again. He was clearly enjoying these little squeezy moments.

They strolled on, basking in their surroundings and the heat of a Spanish summer. And each other's company. Beatriz told Jack that if he read his copy of 'Tales of the Alhambra' he'd see that Washington Irving felt his writing to be unworthy of the place, pretty much acknowledging her view that you have to bring someone here to allow them to appreciate it fully. Exploring the ramparts of the Alcazaba, they gazed down on the glimmering, shimmering Rio Darro, Granada resplendent on its banks. Walking around they reached the Generalife.

"The Generalife?" said Jack. "Sounds like an insurance company."

"Maybe in English but here, it means 'the gardens of the master builder'. They're lovely but not Moorish as they were re-designed in the 19th and 20th centuries. A good place to have a little lunch perhaps?"

Walking on through jasmine and cypress groves they found a spot to sit awhile in the shade. Beatriz pulled out a cool box from her rucksack with a selection of lunchtime treats. They sat back and relaxed whilst beyond lay even more courtyards, water features, gardens, the Palace and the Romantic Mirador. Jack thought this sounded the perfect spot at which to end their wonderful sojourn to the Alhambra and proposed they climb its staircase.

"Oh I don't think so" said Beatriz, failing to recognise the slightest potential in Jack's suggestion. "It's a modern building of no interest."

'Good try, Jack,' he thought to himself.

The leaving of the Alhambra was compensated by a short walk to the Hotel Alhambra Palace, a decision which initially puzzled Jack as it was clearly a huge and hugely unattractive orange building with a dome on top that resembled a big buzzer. Inside it turned out to be rather palatial. Beatriz told him that it had been built by an aristocrat, opened by King Alfonso in 1910 and had since welcomed all manner of royalty and superstars. It stood at a similar elevation to the Alhambra itself but, as soon as you walked through the ground floor café/bar to the balcony, you understood the attraction. Jack's jaw dropped when he saw the views of southern Granada and the mountains beyond. He was almost speechless.

"I had to bring you here" said Beatriz, smiling, "just for this."

They sat down, ordered a glass of white wine and a beer - a bottle of Alhambra, of course - and spent the best part of an hour entertaining themselves with idle chatter.

Just over an hour into the journey towards Valdepenas, Alfredo spies a blue light in his rear view mirror. Its headlights are on too.

"Police" he says calmly.

"Police?" replies Robert, turning round to see and wearing the pained expression of a man who's grabbed hold of an electric fence.

As they come close the patrol car slows and an officer gesticulates to them to pull over. Swearing under his breath, Robert tilts his head back into his head rest. He knew Alf hadn't been speeding so feared the worst as the two officers got out and started to approach. They open their windows.

"Is this your vehicle?" The preliminaries begin.

"No" says Alfredo.

"Have you stolen it?"

"Yes…no! Of course not, officer."

"It's rented" says Robert from the other side.

"You are not Spanish, sir?"

"Er, no, but I live here."

This brings about identification procedures and so on until one of the officers asks them what they have in the back. Robert's explanation that they've been to Mercamadrid to acquire a consignment of fruit on behalf of a trader in Villaricos leads to knowing glances between the officers.

"What sort of fruit?"

"Bananas."

"Ah, bananas. Perhaps we can try one, I'm feeling a bit peckish" said the officer smugly, grinning at his colleague.

"They're not ripe yet" says Alfredo.

"Of course you can" Robert interjects as he elbows Alfredo.

Opening the back doors of the van, Robert invites the officers to help themselves…

"It's bananas or bananas today, I'm afraid. We've sold out of ice cream."

Alfredo is taken aback but the boys in uniform pretend they haven't heard him. They can scent a conviction…but for what? After rooting round to find something that will open the boxes they settle on something from the van's tool box to jemmy the tops off. Cars and trucks are whizzing past on the Autovia, old people on bus trips strain to see what's going on for fleeting seconds as they pass the van on the hard shoulder. The older of the two policemen takes out a banana, peels back the skin, smells it, looks it over carefully, then takes a bite.

"You're right" he said to Alfredo, "they're not ripe. You open a few more" he instructs his younger colleague, "and check if there are any packages in the boxes. I'll radio in for advice."

Robert looks at Alfredo and screws his face up into a grimace. Taking his mobile out of his pocket he sneakily photographs the officer rummaging through the boxes. Then to Alf's horror he turns his back on the scene and takes a selfie wearing a big false smile on his face with the policeman bent over in the back of the van behind him. He shows it to Alf who tenses his shoulders, doing his best not to laugh out loud.

Just a moment after, the other policeman returns.

"Right" he says, "we're going to escort you to a place just off the Autovia at Madridejos. It's only about two kilometres."

"What for?" says Robert.

"My colleagues in the drug squad would like to take a proper look at the contents of the van."

"The drug squad?"

"Yes. It's procedure. I'm sure there's nothing for you to worry about but because of a crime committed today we are being extra vigilant."

"I see. OK then."

They get into their vehicles, start up and off they go.

"There's nothing for them to find, is there?" asks Alf.

"Not that I'm aware of, mate" he says, trying to disguise his fear. "It's just that, well, I wouldn't be entirely surprised if there was. It's all been a bit cloak and dagger and I always thought there was a chance there was something naughty going on. Bloody hell, what's happening? I can't believe this, I really can't."

There are services just off the junction and Robert can see a van marked 'Policia'. Another two officers emerge from the van. The male officer goes round the back and when he reappears he's got a black dog on a lead. The lead officer explains to the two banana dealers that this is a precaution, that they have reason to believe that drugs are being smuggled in certain consignments of fruit acquired at Mercamadrid and they need to do this to eliminate them from their enquiries. She says it won't take long and in the meantime she'll be asking them some questions.

"OK, officer. The dog looks nice and calm anyway. I suppose he's been listening to a bit of Mozart has he?" says Robert.

"Carry on" says the policewoman to her colleague with the dog, ignoring the remark.

She walks to the van to fetch a notebook.

"What was that about the music?" says Alf, perplexed.

"Oh, I saw this article in the paper and it was about the sniffer dogs in Madrid - they all have heated beds and listen to classical music. Apparently it's been shown to reduce stress. I'm going to need more than Mozart for my bloody stress if this goes tits up. Why don't you put that band on the cd player in the van? What are they called…?"

"Saratoga!" says Alf, suddenly enthusiastic.

"Yeah, that's it. They don't like heavy metal, upsets them. Upsets me and all if I'm honest. They quite like pop and a bit of reggae…"

Sgt Dogandla introduces herself formally and starts her interrogation. It's mostly straightforward stuff about their whereabouts the night before, what they've been doing today and so on. She's especially interested in their hotel stay the night before.

"So you stayed last night in Hostal Bar-Restaurante Alpaca in San Agustin del Guadalix?"

"That's correct, we did."

"Did you meet anyone there or outside in the evening?"

"No, officer, we didn't and we went to bed early because we had to be up very early this morning."

"And what time did you leave this morning?"

"About 4:30."

"Now I have reason to believe that you are members of PACMA."

"Members of what?"

"PACMA."

"PACMA?"

"You remember" says Alfredo, "the Animalist Party Against Mistreatment of Animals?"

"Oh, yes. Thank you for reminding me" Robert said sarcastically. "No, we're not members, it was my friend's little joke but I'm sure he could explain better himself."

"Well" said Alf, "it was a very small room at the hotel with no room to swing a cat…so I thought…"

"Yes, I can see what you thought. Very amusing…to some people I'm sure. But not to me. And not to PACMA, whose time we have had to take up today also."

"Sorry" said Alfredo sheepishly.

Just then the other policeman went back to their van with the dog.

"I didn't hear it bark so I'm assuming that everything is OK," said Sgt Dogandla. "Wait here."

After a quick conferral she returned and confirmed the good news. They were all clear and free to continue their journey. She was sorry for the inconvenience. They tried not to show their relief as they climbed aboard the banana express and tootled out of the car park towards the Autovia and Valdepenas. It would be about another hour, a later lunch than they'd planned.

Once the van had slipstreamed onto the highway Alfredo accelerated through the gears then let out a big false sigh.

"Wow! What about that? It was really interesting, wasn't it?" he said, looking quite animated.

"Interesting? Interesting? That wasn't my idea of interesting, I'm telling you. For a while there I thought we'd been set up."

Robert reminded Alf what he'd told him when they first discussed the job, he knew there'd be something unusual about their cargo. He felt relieved but he looked very tired all of a sudden. It had already been a long day and the sooner they could hand over the bananas the better. After a minute or so of silence, Robert decided to level with his partner.

"Look, Alf. I know I sort of indicated that there might be something about our cargo today that wasn't straightforward, but maybe I should have been clearer with you. I had a good idea there'd be something illegal about what we were picking up, although I genuinely didn't know what it would be. Honestly. It seemed straightforward enough. But when we got stopped there, I was expecting the worst. Now, I don't know what to think. I'm glad we're OK, they didn't find anything. On the other hand, I'm sure there should have been something in there - otherwise they wouldn't be paying decent money to a mug like me. So I'm just a bit worried about what'll happen now."

Alfredo nodded

"Sorry, mate."

"No, it's alright. You told me enough for me to work out. But I was glad you didn't tell me anymore. We'll be alright."

"I hope so."

This episode had taken quite a chunk out of their morning and the boys began the next leg of the journey in a subdued mood. Robert's plan had been to eat in Valdepenas but now lunchtime was upon them and he wasn't sure he had the desire to go into a big place and hunt for somewhere decent to eat. Surely there must be somewhere close to the Autovia they could try?

"Yes, I'm sure" said Alfredo. "It's not very far to Puerto Lapice."

"Hold on, I'll have a look at the route…Oh yeah, not far at all. Anything in mind there?"

"I just remember there's a place called Venta del Quijote I've heard of and that's meant to be a nice place. Literally it means 'the sale of Don Quixote', I don't know why, but it's on the trail of Don Quixote and I think it's where he was knighted. Papa went there on a trip."

"Let's do it! Come on, Alf…some good food, a glass of wine and a bit of history."

Robert revived somewhat with the prospect of lunch

being closer. They drove on through the La Mancha countryside and clocked a few windmills that are so typical of the region. Alf whet his employer's appetite by telling him about the local wines and the the cencibel grape. Known as tempranillo in Rioja, the wines of La Mancha were comparable in quality, he believed, but half the price. Who'd have guessed, thought Robert, that Alfredo would turn out to be a regular source of cultural information.

Pulling off the Autovia they headed towards the town of Puerto Lápice and soon found the restaurant with its statue of the great literary character outside. The wooden tables and chairs were dressed in red and white gingham and, although outside, were under shelter of the tiled roof, bringing shade from the sun's intensity. With its white-washed walls, true blue woodwork, terra cotta pillars and cacti it felt very traditional, very La Mancha. Alfredo ordered some water, a coca-cola and, for Robert, a glass of beer. A sharing plate of the local manchego was followed by *estofado de conejo*, a rabbit casserole, and *cordero guisado*, lamb stew. Robert sampled a large glass of Vina Albali Reserva and for this recommendation Alf significantly increased his chances of a bonus.

Having paid the bill they were lingering at the table discussing the chances of their visit being recorded for posterity like Don Quixote and Sancho Panza, but as Señor Bobby and Alfredo the Great revelled in their delusions of grandeur, Robert's mobile rang. The caller's number was hidden. He asked for a moment to move away from earshot of other diners and to grab a pen from his bag. It wasn't Xavi, it was his client for the operation. If he was pleased to hear that they had the goods he didn't show it. It was a purely functional exchange in which confirmation of progress was rewarded with details of the delivery point.

"Was it them?" asked Alfredo.

"Yeah, it was them. Come on, let's get on the road."

It would be around three and a half hours before they reached Almeria to pick up Robert's car. Add in a refreshment break and they were looking at being there around six-thirty. Then they'd have to find the lock-up in Cabo da Gata, another 45 minute drive.

"Providing this offloading goes to plan," said Robert, "we'll sleep like babies tonight."

———

The bells rang out for eight o'clock as Jack and Beatriz left Plaza Santa Ana to walk through Albaicin to the restaurant. Pointing up in the general direction of where they needed to be, Beatriz struck a pose - showing off her fitted knee-length white dress with thin shoulder straps and two broad, navy diagonal stripes below the hip.

"It looks uphill" said Jack, vaguely, having been not entirely focused on where she was indicating.

"Er…yes, Jack, it's uphill all the way. It's actually only about ten minutes or so but we don't want to rush, do we?"

Jack simply raised his eyebrows. They began to stroll and took a turn up Cuesta Aceituneros and Beatriz told him about the Albaicin, how it was in some ways the origin of Granada as a city. She said its fortunes had fluctuated over the centuries, but gradually it returned itself to be an important part of Granada life again.

"For me, it's a magical place with its own unique atmosphere and character." Jack simply smiled and nodded in agreement.

The narrow, whitewashed streets with their windows bordered in coloured ceramic tiles had an overtly Islamic feel. They passed small tea shops and restaurants run by Algerians and Moroccans, interspersed with stores selling souvenirs, jewellery, scarves and the like. Cluttered and chaotic, every now and then an opening afforded a new and unexpected snapshot of the Alhambra, each new angle as impressive as the last. Beatriz was right, this whole area was wonderfully atmospheric and Jack loved its colour and noise. Music, singing, people calling out to each other across the street, the glorious smells of street food, bougainvillea tumbling down walls, flower laden balconies, all so intoxicating…the persistent hawkers were a small price to pay, trying to sell him anything from flowers for his loved one to those plastic mirror sunglasses and genuine silk scarves made from cheap shiny polyester. As they approached the top of Cuesta de Granados, Jack could feel his calf muscles starting to ache but didn't want to let on. 'Not another *cuesta*.' The randomly crazy cobbling of the streets were taking their toll, not to mention the gradient.

"Not far now" said Beatriz, almost as if she'd sensed the twinges in the back of his legs.

A couple of streets on, Beatriz stopped and gesticulated across the road.

"This is the Mirador of San Nicolas. It's very popular with tourists because of the view. Come on, we've got a few minutes before we go to the restaurant - it's very close."

Standing on the square next to the church of San Nicolas, which dates back to 1525, they looked out at the Alhambra. It wasn't as busy as Jack would have expected.

"Oh, but at sunset it will be more crowded. That's what everyone wants to see. I think it was in 1997 when President Clinton visited from the USA and he said it was the most beautiful sunset in the world."

"Ah, interesting. So you can remember his visit here but not the incident involving Monica Lewinsky?"

"Is that the pork rib tapas lady?"

"Yes" said Jack, laughing, "she's the pork rib tapas lady."

"So are you hungry now?"

"Hungry? After walking up that hill? I could eat a whole pig never mind a pork rib! Lead me to the restaurant, señorita."

Las Estrellas de San Nicolas was a typically traditional white house decorated with colourful plants. Jack stole a glance at the menu in a wooden box frame on the wall outside the main entrance. Inside they were met by a waiter who welcomed them and asked if they'd like a drink before their meal.

"Oh yes please" said Jack, looking at Beatriz for affirmation. But instead of the beer he'd been fantasising about on the mean cobbles of the Albaicin… "Do you have a Negroni?"

"Yes, of course" said the waiter.

"I've never had a Negroni" confessed Beatriz. "What is it?"

"It's gin, martini rosso and Campari. Not for the faint-hearted."

"Ooooh! Well…why not? Make it two please."

"That's the spirit!"

They collapsed into a couple of deep chairs. The waiter was soon back with two Negronis, the colour of polished ruby, served in martini glasses and decorated with a coil of orange peel. A clink of glasses and they simultaneously sipped as if they'd entered some sort of pact.

"Mmm…This is…bitter and sweet at the same time. A little smoky too."

"But do you like it?" Jack wanted to know.

"Yes. Yes I do. It's quite sophisticated and a little racy, I'd say"

"I like your thinking" said Jack, grinning. "And I like racy too" he added in a manner that was just a little too lascivious for the first drink of the evening.

Escorted upstairs by the waiter, they were shown to their table. Jack was stunned. They had a table in front of the window. It was like a giant MacBook with the Alhambra as its screen saver. The sun started to set and still Jack couldn't stop looking at the view.

"Did you book this table specifically?" he asked.

"Of course" she replied with a shrug.

"Wow! Thank you. It's breathtaking…it's gorgeous."

The whole Palace was illuminated, an effect that would intensify as the sun went down and darkness descended. Beatriz asked him what he thought of Granada.

"Oh…" he said, "I've fallen in love."

He said no more but looked away across the sky. Was it the city he'd fallen for? Or Beatriz? She kept her gaze on him until he turned to face her again, then said:

"Shall we choose?"

The menu was good. A little expensive inevitably, given the location. They started with gazpacho, accompanied by a glass of Albariño, a crisp Galician white. It was between courses, after their bottle of red had arrived and the first glasses poured, that Jack ventured to ask about the sensitive subject they'd started on earlier at the Alhambra.

"Don't feel you've got to talk about difficult things tonight" he started. "We don't want to spoil the evening, do we? But if it helps I'll happily talk about my problems too."

"So we can both be sad and depressed?"

"No, absolutely not like that. Maybe it would be good for both of us. It might help. Who knows? After a few more drinks we might find it all amusing!"

"OK. It's a deal. I'll go first" said Beatriz.

They laughed, clinked glasses and drank a toast.

"To openness and honesty" said Jack.

"And future happiness" added Beatriz.

She started by explaining how she first met Mikel when she was twenty one and in the final year of her Communications and Media Studies degree course, studying at the University of Granada. They'd met initially at a social event and got on well. He was kind and considerate, interested in her and what she was doing. Nothing happened between them for about a year or so. By then she'd completed her degree and, no longer a student, she was working for an agency in the city. After meeting him in a cafe one afternoon, he invited her out to dinner. She accepted and their relationship grew.

"What did he do? Was he a student too when you met?" asked Jack.

"No. He was a junior lecturer on the Psychology course. A little ironic perhaps. Bright, articulate and a confident man."

"Older than you…"

"Yes, he was 25 when we met. He'd moved from his home in Bilbao, in the Basque region."

Beatriz took a deep breath and began to describe how they became very close and the relationship developed into a serious one. Mikel had initially been very affectionate, especially when they were out with friends when he was particularly charming. He showered her with attention, which she'd been flattered by, and often bought her gifts. He made her feel special. Marriage somehow appeared a logical next step for them to take. It was a nice wedding, everything went well and they were happy. She was by now twenty six and felt ready for the commitment. But very soon afterwards she began to notice some differences about him.

"Over time he started to question me more…little by little it increased. Then he became more critical of me - my decisions, my clothes, even my choice of friends. When we went out with people he would also be very challenging, argumentative. And he was always right of course. Everything contrary to his view was a personal affront. People started to make excuses not to come out with us, I felt, because of his attitude."

"How did he get on with your parents, your family… Alfredo?"

"My parents…it was OK face to face, otherwise he was often rude about them. It came to a point where I didn't want him to visit with me. Alfredo was very young then but Mikel didn't like him. He would make fun of him and he'd be rude to him a lot of the time. I saw less and less of my brother as time went on, which I was unhappy about."

"So how long was it before you thought you needed to get out of the relationship?"

"Oh, about two years" she said, just as the waiter brought through their next course. "The emotional manipulation became clear, he was such a narcissist!"

"This looks wonderful and it smells divine" said Jack. "Let's enjoy it." Then, putting his right hand on her left, he said quietly "I don't know how anyone could treat you like that, I really don't."

"Thank you" she almost whispered, forcing a smile that was betrayed by the tear that she wiped away with her napkin.

Reaching a point where she didn't want to finish

what was left of her duck, Beatriz began to pick up the thread of her story. By the third year, the relationship had become toxic she realised. It had reached a stage where the emotional manipulation made her feel everything was her fault. She recognised that she was becoming isolated from friends and family. He'd accuse her of spending his money and tell her that she'd changed since they were married. Occasionally finding him looking through her mobile phone or laptop, it was like living with a detective. If he was challenged he'd shrug it off by saying that 'if you've not been up to anything to worry about then you shouldn't mind me looking'.

"Once when we were out at a social event some friends were there and one rang me the day after to ask to meet for a coffee, which I did. She said she was worried about me - she'd noticed that every time I spoke he corrected me, or contradicted me or belittled me in some way. She said not only that it wasn't nice to see but that I wasn't looking well. It was very upsetting but perhaps a turning point for me. I knew I couldn't go on like that."

"He was never physically abusive to you?" Jack asked.

"No. But he did make me very fearful. He just made me feel worthless and I knew it was going to be hard, but I had to get out. I tried to have a discussion with him. That didn't go very well. I said I intended to take a break and move back to my parents' home and that was when he started making threats to harm himself. He was angry, reminding me of all the things he'd done for me and saying that he'd make me regret it if I left. I was afraid to stay, I was afraid to leave. It made me so unwell."

She let it lie for a few days and was as quiet and compliant as she could be. Beatriz knew he would be away for a whole day at an event at the University of Seville in the coming week and planned to make a move then. Naturally she'd had to forewarn her parents. She asked them to trust her and she would tell them more once she was home. When she'd raised it with her employer, her manager had been very understanding and was accommodating about taking time off. And that was how she came to leave him.

"That must have taken a huge amount of courage. I bet he didn't accept it very easily."

"No" she replied, shaking her head. "No, he wasn't exactly happy."

"What did you do about work?"

"After two weeks I returned to work, but part-time at the office and some hours working from my parents' home. Visiting clients continued so it was business as usual. Eventually, I saw the friend who I told you about, the one who told me they were worried about me? She and her husband agreed I could stay with them when I needed to, just until things were sorted out."

"And did Mikel try to do anything, did he try to change your mind?"

"Oh yes. When he realised that I wasn't responding to his threats, he changed. He started making promises about how he could be different, that he was sorry. Yet all the time it was still my fault - I must have misunderstood him, he'd not been serious, all sorts of bullshit that he expected me to believe. But I was done with him. Finally, at the end of that education year he got another job. He moved to Barcelona. And that was really the first time when I felt it was over and I'd got my life back."

"Would señor y señora like a dessert?" asked the waiter, unknowingly lifting the mood.

They would indeed and so it was crepes with

chocolate for Jack and a coconut pannacotta for Beatriz.

"What about a dessert wine?" said Jack, wearing an impish grin.

"Yes" she replied eventually after a coy and mischievous smile, "I think so. Whatever you think goes best" she told the waiter.

He returned with a Moscatel for the pannacotta and a Pedro Ximenez for the chocolate. As they tucked into their puddings and rambled on about the wine, it appeared that the evening was evidently reaching that peak smiling and giggling period where everything appears wonderful and the volume has turned up. Largely because everyone else in the room has drunk a similar amount. Jack fumbled around with his mobile under the table such that he had to confess he was checking to see how England had got on in their final group game.

"They lost to Belgium 1-0, but they were already assured of qualifying, so no problem."

Spain had qualified a few days earlier with an unconvincing draw against Morocco, so everyone was happy.

"Maybe we both need therapy" said Jack, trying to make light of their previous discussion, "but it's not as much fun as wine."

"Agreed" said Beatriz, laughing more than Jack's remark deserved. "Here's to therapy!" she said loudly.

"Mmm…have you ever thought of therapy?"

"Now and again, yes. But not seriously I suppose." Then she added, giggling, "Wine is cheaper."

"If it continues to give you problems with relationships, if it's still a barrier, maybe it would be worthwhile?"

"Maybe. For now, for this evening, you're my therapist, Jack. Here's to you!" And she raised her glass again, looking very pleased with herself.

"Indeed" said Jack, taking another slurp. Then after a pause..."Do you know how many therapists it takes to change a lightbulb?"

"No, I don't."

"Just the one...but the lightbulb has to want to change."

Jack sat back, putting on his look of detached amusement, despite his little joke being older than she was.

"I don't understand?" she said.

"It's just...erm...oh, lost in translation I think."

And with that he downed what was left of his wine. Beatriz even found that amusing, such that she followed suit.

"And how did you like your Pedro Ximenez?" she asked.

"Beautifully sticky, sensual and cloying on the palate in a good way. A perfect complement to my chocolate. Well done the waiter. To the waiter!"

Realising that they'd already emptied their glasses induced more mirth. Beatriz toggled her glass around between her fingers in a manner which suggested she might fancy another little tipple. Trying to be sensible Jack pretended to look sternly at her, raised his finger and mouthed 'No'. She put on a little girl scolded act, to which Jack responded.

"Coffee first" and the smile returned to her face.

Returning with two espressos, the waiter also presented them with small complimentary glasses of a pale green local herb liqueur, the typical after-dinner gesture.

"Oh dear" said Beatriz. She'd got the hiccups.

"Hold your breath" said Jack "for as long as you can. Always works for me."

She held her breath...a bit longer...a bit longer

still…and finally opened her mouth and breathed in before letting out what sounded like a very poor frog impersonation. That worked well then. Deciding they'd better settle up, they argued over the bill and came to a compromise.

"I know where we can go for a nightcap" said Beatriz. "Would you like one last drink? Perhaps to help us enjoy the moonlight?"

"Well, if you know somewhere good it would be rude not to accept your invitation. Give me the moonlight, seńorita!"

"*Hora de las noticias…*" said the announcer on the radio.

"Ah what's been happening in the world then, Alf?" said Robert, shuffling to a more upright posture in the passenger seat.

Alf leaned forward and turned up the volume. Robert could pick up some of the key words but the announcer spoke too fast for him to make any real sense of it. He picked out familiar terms… '*drogas*'… '*supermercado*'… 'Lidls'… '*platanos*'.

"What's been go-"

"Silenciar!"

The announcer moved on to another story. Alfredo looked across anxiously.

"She said that Lidls have discovered cocaine in some of their supermarkets. Packets of cocaine… mixed in with boxes of fresh bananas! Hundreds of thousands of euros worth! That's why we were stopped, isn't it?"

"Yeah, I mean, they said they were on the lookout for fruit which may contain drugs…so it is actually bananas they were after. What else did she say on the radio?"

"She said there were a dozen stores, I think. In Madrid, Plasencia, Caceres and Pinto."

"That's obviously what was happening when we went past this morning. Shit!"

"They know they were bought from Mercamadrid. One of the workers started to open the boxes to put on the shelves and found the cocaine wrapped in packs. They're checking their other stores to see if there's more."

After a period of stony silence between them, Alfredo had a question.

"Does this mean anything for us?"

"It could do. That's what I was worried about. I wonder if that's what we were supposed to be carrying back? If it is, we were stopped by the police and they found nothing…so whilst that's good news, it won't be good news for our clients when they find they've only got bananas. Assuming they were up to no good after all. Bananas that they've paid over the odds for."

"You're sure we got the right boxes?"

"Well, they're the numbers they specified. Maybe there was a switch or something. It's a bit odd, isn't it? That guy we were supposed to meet fails to turn in for work and this lot kicks off."

A few kilometres from Almeria the two guys turned up the volume for an updated news bulletin. It seemed that police had now recovered twenty five 'bricks' of cocaine from Lidl stores in and around Madrid with a likely street value of €4.5m. This figure was met with gasps of shock and astonishment by the two men. The bananas had been shipped in from Ecuador and the Ivory Coast. It was suggested that drug smugglers had made an error in failing to acquire the consignments, leading to the bananas being bought and distributed to supermarkets. Lidl estimated that over a tonne of bananas would be destroyed. A police spokesperson said that the crooks had gone as far as stripping out some of the bananas, leaving a hollow skin, to ensure the weight of the boxes was unaffected by the cocaine stashed inside. During a studio discussion it was stated that in the last year Spanish police had seized more than 14 tonnes of cocaine, which had been smuggled into the country in stuffed animals, nappies, seafood and, much to Robert's amusement, a picture of the Sacred Heart of Jesus.

"I bet there's a few naughty young shelf-fillers at Lidl who cottoned on to this first. Imagine them running round the warehouse, off their faces on bananas. I don't know why I'm laughing" he said. "Actually I feel a bit sick. I've got this ominous feeling that something's not right, even though I'm confident we've done everything right."

"What can we do?" asked Alfredo.

"Nothing. Nothing at all, other than do what we've been asked to do. So we'll pick up my car from the station car park in Almeria, you follow me and we'll find this lock-up and off-load these blessed bananas."

Stepping out from the air-conditioning of the van at the car park, Robert felt as if he'd been plugged into a power source as the heat from the late afternoon sun coursed through his body. He opened the door to the solar-powered oven that was his car. Reaching down he lifted the driver's rubber mat to reveal the car park ticket, just as he'd asked Jack to hide it. It was a thumbs-up to Alfredo, then he set the sat-nav to its new destination. Next stop, Cabo de Gata, an area that Robert loved for its quiet, ruggedly unspoilt beauty. He'd promised Alfredo they'd stop for a drink there and some food before returning to Mojacar.

The twenty seven kilometre route took them out of the city and past the airport. Between the road and the sea were the canals and lagoons of Las Salinas, where salt has been mined for centuries. Birdwatchers were in evidence too as the road meandered, attracted by the hundreds of bird species known to populate the area. There was no doubting the cover stars though, as the pink flamingoes high-stepped their way through the marshes, heads darting intermittently as they moved along slowly. As the road climbed, leaving the flat marshlands behind them, they passed further credentials of the region's commitment to environmentally sustainable business and then, as if to remind them of the importance of nature, they had to stop for a herd of goats. Strolling and bleating their way casually across the road they were in no hurry. Robert held his hand out of the window and gestured to Alfredo. Once underway again they soon moved off to the right, down to the region's namesake, the village of Cabo de Gata. Finding the traffic island easily they drove slowly towards the sea front, looking for Calle del Cuartel.

'Here we go' Robert muttered to himself. He held his arm out and put up his thumb. Alfredo acknowledged him, then pointed to an entrance to take the van. Robert parked his car on the side of the road and got out. He walked over to where Alfredo had pulled up the van.

"OK. It's number 17 we want," he said. "Then we've got to find the key."

Robert had been given directions to locate a key safe and the four digit code that would open it. He disappeared round the back of one of the buildings and after a couple of minutes emerged from an entirely different row. He'd got the key. Alfredo reversed the van close up to the doors. The door unlocked, they began to cart the boxes of bananas into the far corner of the musty space. Keen to get it over with, it only took a few minutes.

"Right" said Robert "let's get gone, mate."

Alfredo jumped behind the wheel again whilst Robert returned the key. He was a little longer than expected. Almost skipping back to the vehicle he leaned on the door and slapped Alf on the shoulder.

"Job done, my friend. Time for some R and R methinks."

"Some what?"

"Rest and recuperation. Not only do we need it, we bloody deserve it. "

"Do you know the way to San José?" sang Robert, badly.

"Yes, of course. Do you know the tune?" Alfredo shot back.

"Oh, listen to you, eh? Yes I do. Can I sing it properly? Can I fuck!"

Following Robert's car out of Cabo de Gata, Alfredo smiled and reflected on their little exchange. He'd enjoyed being with Robert on this expedition. He may have been tired after all the driving, but it was a satisfying feeling to have finished the task. They'd got on well together. There hadn't been many times in his life where he he'd genuinely felt trusted, let alone respected. And now he could look forward to a nice evening out with him before returning home. The way to San José was by returning inland to pick up the main road then look for another right to drop down to the coast. A bigger place, it's very popular with tourists and there's no shortage of accommodation and places to eat. They headed for Calle del Puerto, the road that leads to the marina. Shortly before they reached it, Robert pulled over, jumped out and walked towards the van behind him. He was whistling 'Do You Know the Way to San José?'. Alfredo grinned and nodded along.

"So you do know the tune" he said, laughing.

Robert grinned and simply explained that he wanted to park down one of the side streets and they could walk round to the restaurant. Having parked the vehicles, they began walking to El Jardin, where Robert knew the owner.

"Sorry to mention it, Robert, I'm not wanting it right now, but when will we be paid for the job?"

"A-ha! Good question. Well, I can exclusively reveal to you that I have 60% of the cash in my hot sweaty hands now...or to be precise, my hot sweaty bag."

"How come?"

"There was a package inside the unit which I picked up before we loaded the bananas. I agreed this with them in advance, a 60/40 split - 60% on delivery, the other 40% on their satisfaction that we've brought back what they asked for. I'll sort it out later when we get home if that's alright with you, Alf."

"Sure, yeah. That's great. Let's hope they're happy."

"They'd better be..."

El Jardin is the smallest in a row of restaurants elevated above the road and, according to Robert, the best. They walked up and sat down at a front table, looking towards the beach with the marina to their left. It was relatively early by Spanish customs to be eating but they were thirsty, hungry and needed to be back in Mojacar later that evening. A waiter emerged to serve them but Robert asked if Pepe was in. He was and he turned to call him. A tallish man with black hair combed back and wearing white shirt with black trousers, Pepe cut a smart figure. He embraced Robert warmly and said it had been too long. Alfredo liked being introduced as his colleague, it made him feel valued. The boys decided they'd like beers.

"Have you tried Origen Siglo XXI?" asked Pepe.

Neither of them had tried it.

"Oh, it's very good, one of my favourites. It's brewed in Almeria to a very old recipe, very traditional. Malty, full bodied, but very refreshing. 5.5%, so quite strong too."

Robert and Alfredo looked at each other and nodded enthusiastically.

"Sounds like a winner, Pepe. Thank you my friend."

"Coming right up. Hey, by the way, you not watching your boys in the World Cup tonight? Big game against Belgium."

"If I wasn't so tired I probably would, Pepe, but we're already through so I'll catch it later on the highlights."

The beers arrived. Pepe was right - damn fine beer it was.

Later they ordered their food when Robert, having decided he didn't want to be on show out front, just in case, decided to move inside to a table behind the arches. By then, the white town buildings had been gradually brought into sharper relief as the hills behind faded to black and lights began to flicker and sparkle. The restaurant had a warm, traditional feel, with its white walls, old lanterns and vines growing across the ceiling.

The food came and went gloriously…*provolone, berenjenas*, *cazuela de bacalhao* and *spagueti nero*. They'd worked through most of a bottle of local chardonnay from Almeria. Robert had reasoned that they'd be taking the back roads to Mojacar. Alf had countered more sensibly that the back roads to Mojacar may not have any police around but were far more hazardous and he'd got to drive a van! Then just as they were trying to choose a dessert, Robert's phone rang.

"What do you mean?"

"Look…what was your name again?"

"Where's Xavi? I need to speak to Xavi, he's the one I've been dealing with and-"

"I was given the numbers of the boxes to buy and that's what I did. You can see on the boxes. I haven't seen inside them, they're bananas, aren't they?"

"No, what do you mean? You've got what you ordered, exactly what you asked for."

"Are you threatening me?"

"Yes the boxes have been opened but not by me… they were opened by the police who stopped us on the autovia on the way back."

"Look, mate, I suggest you get hold of Xavi and get him to call me. I'm not having this. No! I don't like your attitude. Adios."

Robert looked angry but was visibly shaken and was breathing quite heavily. He told Alf they'd opened the boxes and found bananas. Clearly they were expecting something extra in there…just as he suspected. This guy sounded a nasty piece of work…threatening all sorts. He wasn't happy with this. Now Alfredo looked just as worried. His phone rang again. It was a different voice.

"Yes, I'm Robert."

"As I tried to explain to your friend, we were given the reference numbers for certain consignments of bananas. By Xavi. They are the boxes that we purchased this morning."

Robert rose from the table and walked out of the restaurant.

"Well I'm sorry if you were expecting anything different. Nothing has been removed, I can assure you. I explained very clearly to your colleague that we were stopped by the police on the autovia."

"It was near Madridejos and no, they didn't take anything."

"Look, I can tell you're disappointed. So were the

sniffer dogs, they obviously didn't get what they were looking for either. But I bought exactly what you asked for."

"Yeah, well, if something's gone wrong don't look at me - my part of the exercise went exactly as it should."

By now outside the back of the premises, Robert was becoming exasperated with his interrogator.

"I don't know what you're talking about. I haven't passed anything on to anyone else. I have not double-crossed anybody. Now I need to speak to Xavi about this, he's the one I had my instructions from."

"No, I don't particularly want to meet you in San José or anywhere else until I've sorted this out with Xavi. Hey?"

"Just calm down! There's no need for threats."

"Hello? Hello? Fuck!"

He walked quickly back inside to the table and told Alfredo about the conversation. He was genuinely worried about what was going to happen. He'd told him they knew he was speaking from somewhere in San José. They must have tracked his mobile somehow. Robert wouldn't tell them where they were but it's not a big place and they could probably guess from the background noise that they were in a restaurant or bar and it wouldn't take long to find them.

"Let's go home now, straight away" said Alfredo.

"They know where I live and he promised they'd find me."

"They don't know where I live!"

"I don't want you implicated, Alf. Let's keep you out of it as far as possible. This is my responsibility. Where's Pepe?"

Spying him in the corner he walked over and quietly asked for an urgent word. He explained that he'd done some work for someone and there'd been a misunderstanding but that these men were intimidating. They'd threatened him and said they were coming to San José to find him. He said he was scared for his safety and that he'd explain more fully later, but could he suggest anywhere he might stay? Pepe beckoned over to Alfredo before shepherding them outside and giving them instructions.

"It's a small place towards the edge of town" said Pepe. "You have a car?"

"We've got a car and a van" Robert answered.

"OK. Take the car, there's a place to park round the back where it won't be seen. It will be safe. The apartment is for tourists but we have no-one in right now. Where's your van?"

They described the location nearby and Pepe assured them it would be fine.

"Once you're in, stay there and just keep your heads down, alright? We'll speak in the morning."

"Thank you so much, Pepe, I owe you."

"Go!" urged the restauranteur. "Wait! Here…"

He threw a loaf of bread to Robert.

"Desayunos…"

They soon found the street and after a struggle in the dark discovered where to leave the car at the rear. It was a first floor apartment with stairs at the side. The accommodation was pretty decent too. There were a few basics in the kitchen including coffee and olive oil. Alfredo boiled some water. There was a double bed only.

"Very cosy" said Robert. "You've driven all this way, Alf, you can have the bed. I'll take the sofa, it'll probably be a sofa bed anyway."

"It's a big bed…plenty of room!" said Alfredo.

"It's alright here, actually, isn't it? Thank God for Pepe, he's a real star."

They looked at each other. Relieved for now, but looking worn out. And it had been going so well.

Stepping out into the street, Beatriz looked wobbly and disguised her inability to walk straight by linking arms with Jack. They waxed lyrical about their evening out. And it wasn't over yet, as Beatriz proclaimed, then faltered as she thought about the best route to take to reach a bar she knew. About to turn down another street, she remembered the moonlight and dragged Jack back to her spot. Pointing up at the moon, she held her left arm around his shoulder and nuzzled her head into Jack's such that his interest in the moon almost drained away completely. Manoeuvring her vaguely into a waltz position, he began singing as he moved her around in a circular direction.

"I'm dancing in the moonlight, doo de doo de doo doo, it's got me in its spotlight…"

Colliding with another couple walking by brought Jack's impromptu performance to a halt and they both laughed. Then suddenly she was away again, jerking his hand as he followed and it was all happy smiles and tottering down the sloping uneven streets. They walked for nearly twenty minutes, Beatriz stopping from time to time to point out landmarks that she couldn't really remember or when she did, couldn't speak clearly enough for Jack to understand. Finally, they arrived at their destination.

The name on the wall outside was separated by a saxophone and unsurprisingly El Son turned out to be a cocktail and music bar. Jack was given the choice of staying downstairs, where there was a dance floor, or upstairs for some Latin. Wisely eliminating the choice that might have led through encouragement or provocation to him pulling out his moves, he said he felt like a bit of Latin. Of course he did. Beatriz responded with a fatuously vacant grin which suggested that it was either the right answer or that she'd had too much to drink. If only Jack hadn't had too much to drink he might have spotted that himself.

Jack was very clear that he wanted to try something Spanish and so he went for an Oloroso Martinez, some sort of sherry, vermouth and cherry liqueur concoction. In choosing a White Lady, it was as if Beatriz was experiencing a premonition of her appearance. Including gin, orange liqueur and half an egg white, its silky foam clung beautifully to the curve of the champagne saucer in which it was served.

"OK, Jack, now your turn…" said Beatriz, head tilted but looking up into his eyes inquisitively.

"My turn? Oh, yes. Well…I've told you before what happened with me and my wife. Nothing dramatic, no game-changing event, just a slow decline in our relationship. I suppose a bit of boredom set in. No. A lot. A lot of boredom really, by the end. No-one was to blame especially, yet in a way we were both to blame."

Jack explained how he sometimes looked back and, with the benefit of hindsight, could see how their relationship started to slide downhill. Little incidents stood out as junctions where signs were ignored or wrong decisions taken, things said unwisely. The slippery slope was littered with them. Why had neither of them had the courage or the determination or the passion to do something to stop it? He'd reluctantly accepted that neither of them had wanted to, the desire for a different outcome just wasn't there. Something had to give and eventually, once Jack had been made redundant, he realised that he had to make a change in his life.

"I just felt it would be easiest if I got out, got away… gave us both a break. See what happens? See how we feel?" He sighed and leaned back in his seat.

Beatriz was fast asleep. He nudged her.

"And how do you feel?" she said, with remarkable timing.

"At home, I was very down, it was hard to see anything to look forward to" he went on, unaware of how pointless his slurred recollection was. "I wasn't in a happy place. Out here, I feel so different. It's been wonderful coming out and staying with Robert, relaxing, seeing something of Spain or at least Andalucia. And meeting you! That's something I could never have foreseen…and the way we met. You've helped me see things, like the Alhambra today. I could never forget that. Or you, I could never forget you."

Was she asleep again? He leaned forward and held her hand. Her eyes opened again.

"You've been so lovely to me."

Beatriz smiled as he let go and sat back in his chair.

"And yet. I'm still this other man that worries about his wife. And, of course, my family. It's very hard to cut off that connection after so many years. Her health issue obviously doesn't help, you know…I feel guilty for not being there. And there's the children. They're not children anymore! I don't want them to think badly of me. The truth is, I don't know what they really think, so I try to do the right thing by everyone."

He smiled a drunken, crooked smile. Beatriz held out her hands, turned her head to the side and gave him a look of sympathy and understanding. Then as they leaned forward and Jack took her hands…she hiccuped violently.

"Oooh…sorry, Jack" she said.

Looking down at the table she tried to hold her breath like before, raised her head then puffed out the breath.

"I wonder if we should take you home?" said Jack.

She simply smiled, an exaggeratedly wide-eyed grin to be more precise. Jack paid the bill and they headed out slowly and deliberately, arm in arm, into the cool night air. It was at this point that Jack observed that she was looking pale.

"You're looking quite white, Beatriz" he said.

"A-ha!" she replied laughing. "I have turned into the White Lady!"

"Are you sure you're alright? What about a taxi?"

"No, no. The air will be good for us."

They struggled on through a few more streets until they were only a minute or so away from her apartment. She asked if Jack had enjoyed himself. Of course, Jack had been in seventh heaven, despite his worries back in England.

"Oh, Beatriz" he started. "It's been magical, just the best day I could have had."

They turned to face each other. Then embraced. And embraced. And embraced a bit longer. Jack inhaled the heady scent of her perfume on her collar, luxuriated in the warmth of her neck. The embrace continued…maybe they were unsure what to do next? Maybe Beatriz had fallen asleep again, but it was she who broke first, looking up into Jack's eyes. Surely this was the moment…a moment that could change the course of his life. Their lips moved slowly but inevitably towards each other. They were just inches away…when she jerked, coughed, heaved and threw up down his right arm. He quickly pulled her to the side of the street, where she pebble-dashed a section of pavement and a beggar's left leg.

"Oh my God" said Jack, looking at the poor guy, as

if things weren't bad enough for him.

He gave him €20 and apologised. The beggar seemed to think that was fair compensation. He simply shook his head, rolled up his freshly encrusted trouser, unscrewed his prosthetic leg at the knee, then stuck it in a plastic carrier bag. He hauled himself up against the wall, standing on his right foot, then hauled himself down the street with the aid of a crutch.

Jack turned his attention to Beatriz, who by now was stood, legs apart and hands on thighs, leaning forward dribbling slightly and spluttering. Various people passed by - grimacing, chuckling or calling out remarks, none of which Jack could comprehend. They all understood what this situation was like as they themselves were also 'revellers', to use a term otherwise only ever seen in tabloid journalism. Standing next to her with his hands lightly supporting her shoulders, Jack didn't look as if he was exactly revelling in his rather sudden appointment to the role of carer. He asked her if she was alright. Lifting her head Beatriz stood upright and took a deep breath. After a few seconds she turned and pointed.

"This way" she announced abruptly.

Jack simply followed, still holding her. It was like they'd entered a three-legged race, the uneven sloping streets appearing to tilt, giving them a further handicap. Despite a bit of huffing and puffing they reached the main entrance to her apartment without further spillages. Eventually Beatriz located her keys in the deepest, most far flung corner of her handbag which, in keeping with all bags during the later stages of drunkenness, had expanded internally to assume the spatial dimensions of a small removal van. She lowered her head towards the lock with the key never more than 150 cm away from her eyes…she head-butted the door and reeled away. Taking the key from her, Jack wasn't a lot better but suddenly they were in. It was an old building, very tastefully and respectfully modernised. They made their way slowly up the two flights of stairs. Holding on to the stair rail with her right hand, and Jack's arm with her left, Beatriz had to grip hard to counter Jack's occasional swaying to the left. The front door brought another test of coordination and balance.

Once inside, first port of call for Beatriz was the bathroom. In the lounge, Jack looked around at the pictures on the walls and then closed the window blinds before perching on the edge of the brown leather sofa. Returning from the bathroom, Beatriz looked washed out and tired.

"Can I get you a hot drink or something?" asked Jack.

"No, no. Just water is fine for me. That's all I need. What about you?"

"No, I'm alright, thanks."

He followed Beatriz out to the kitchen.

"It's a lovely apartment, Beatriz."

"Thank you."

Taking a bottle from the fridge, she allowed Jack to take it from her as she seemed to need one hand for leaning on something for stability. He poured her a large glass. A couple of sips and she turned to look at Jack, a little sad, a little wistful. Then she noticed his sleeve.

"Oh, Jack, your lovely shirt! What a mess, oh no…"

"It's alright, don't worry. It'll wash out."

"Here" she said, passing him a damp cloth. "You can't walk back into that nice hotel like that."

As he sponged his arm he thought it probably was a good idea, at least he might smell a bit better on his way back to the hotel.

"I'm so sorry to end the evening like this" she said. "It's been such a beautiful day."

"Oh, look…" said Jack "we just overdid it a bit in the end. It's been fantastic and I had a wonderful time this evening. It's usually me that ends up in this position."

More water was followed by a long sigh then a groan and she slowly lowered her head.

"Are you going to be alright tonight?" asked Jack. "I could stay if you'd like…I could sleep on the sofa?"

"No, Jack, it's fine. I'll be OK. Just need to sleep now. Besides…look at me. I'm a mess! It's less embarrassing if you go back to the hotel. I'm sure Christina will find it very amusing."

"Maybe we will too in the morning. Shall I call you?"

"Yes, please. Not too early. Maybe you can come here…then I won't have to see Christina. I can't have her see me in this condition."

Jack laughed. He moved towards her to embrace and she simply held up her hand and looked away. Trying to smile, she held out her hand. Jack accepted the invitation and kissed it gracefully, eyes closed.

"Ave Maria, Señor!" she said, inexplicably.

As he left, she gently blew him a kiss to reciprocate.

Chapter Twelve

Friday 29 June 2018

Robert had woken in the middle of the night in a hot sweat. Looking around the room in almost complete darkness he remembered where he was and laid his head back down on the cushion. Several joints ached from lying at an angle on the sofa. Hauling himself up properly he felt around for his watch but couldn't read the time clearly. He got up and ambled over to where his phone was on charge. England had lost to Belgium, but they were through already, so no big deal there. No messages, just a row of tiny heads and another imbecilic invitation from LinkedIn to congratulate people he didn't know on some inconsequential anniversaries. It was just after four. 'Might as well use the bathroom now I'm awake' he thought. These days a steady dribble was all he'd come to expect in the night. Perhaps he should have himself checked out? After standing listening to his own breathing for what seemed like a minute he managed to go. He'd heard someone say it was like pissing in morse code, as it came out in dots and dashes.

Returning to the sofa he pulled the cover up over himself and tried to relax. Nothing doing. By now his head was swimming with possibilities, made-up scenarios in which it always ends badly. He'd remembered fragments of his dream, more of a nightmare actually. In the dream they'd been chased and shot at, hunted by dogs and finally they'd been buried under tonnes of bananas. At the point where the bananas blocked out any light he'd woken, panic stricken but ultimately disappointed not to find out if he'd been topped off with ice cream, walnuts and chocolate sauce, which he thought would have been an altogether more acceptable way to go. The headlines would be able to say 'British Ex-Pat Found Chunky Monkeyed In Ditch'. He'd wondered if his pursuers were on LinkedIn. 'Celebrate Pedro's first anniversary as Cartel Hitman (Southern Region). Rate Pedro for Negotiation Skills?' This lighter pattern settled him and he drifted off again for a while longer.

As they'd not heard anything about the men turning up at the restaurant, and with no news from anywhere, the plan was to have breakfast and make a plan. Orange juice, bread, coffee…that was all they'd got. The plan turned out to be simple. Robert felt he had to contact Xavi and explain the story to him, they'd had a good relationship before, he must make him understand.

"Did you tell them about the guy at the Mercamadrid who didn't show up?" asked Alfredo.

"No! No, I forgot about that. Good point, Alf. I mean, that's probably where this has gone wrong for them, isn't it? It looks suspicious, for sure. I'll tell Xavi about that, he's the man they need to find."

Robert tried Xavi's number several times but no response. He was wary of leaving a message so left it for now.

Meanwhile as staff at El Jardin are opening up to clean and prepare for the day ahead, visitors arrive. Both men wore black suits with white open-necked shirts. One looked wiry, sharp and lean; the other was big, beastly and mean. They entered the restaurant slowly and removed their shades. A young mop-haired man with glasses and a wispy goatee asked if he could help.

"Are you Pepe?" said the lean one.

"No," he said, "I'll just get him for you."

Pepe had an inkling what this was about as soon as he set eyes on the two men.

"I'm Pepe. How can I help you?"

"We're looking for a friend of ours…Robert - he's with another man too, I think. We believe they were in your restaurant last night."

"It was very busy last night" said Pepe. He shrugged his shoulders. "There were several tables during the evening with two men together…what does he look like?"

The lean one brought out a picture and held it up for Pepe.

"I'm not sure" said Pepe. "Do you carry pictures of all your friends?"

As the man's demeanour started to change, Pepe realised he needed to play more helpful and quickly thought of what to do.

"I tell you what, I will check the receipts for last night. If he paid by card he will be there, yes?"

Wiry man nodded showing a hint of a smile that said 'That's more like it'.

"OK. Just a minute and I will go through them."

As he walked towards the office, he suddenly turned and called back. "What's his surname?"

The men looked at each other and muttered a few things under their breath. Wiry man took out his mobile and started checking through messages. If it hadn't been evident to Pepe before it was crystal clear now, they were no friends of Robert.

"Harrington" he called eventually.

In the office, Pepe surreptitiously beckoned in the young man who had initially greeted the two strangers.

"I want you to do something for me."

He wrote on a small note: '2 men are here. You need to leave now. Keys to bike in outside store. Go to Playa de Monsul and stay low. Quickly. Will be in touch.'

"Here…take this to the men in our apartment, right away, as quick as you can. Don't say anything to anyone. Understand?"

The waiter quietly walked out clutching a brush and went out to the front as if to continue working, before scooting off up the road. Once out of sight he started to run. Pepe continued to look methodically through the pile of receipts knowing that he'd find nothing, given that they left without paying.

The young waiter, meanwhile, arrived at the apartment out of breath but clutching the note. He knocked on the door and waited. Inside, Robert and Alfredo stayed still and looked at each other. Another knock and this time the waiter spoke at the door in Spanish. Alfredo urgently told Robert what he'd said and that he had a note from Pepe. They unlocked and opened up, quickly shutting the door behind him. Taking the note from Pepe they read it and Alfredo put his hand on the young man's shoulder.

"You have the keys for the bike?"

"Si" he said, holding them up.

"Hey Alf" said Robert, "why don't we leave the keys to the van with Pepe? We might need him to get it to us. They'll know my car and there's a chance they may spot it here, but they don't know the van."

"Yes, good idea."

Alfredo explained to the waiter and handed over the keys to the hire vehicle. The waiter thought it was important to tell them that the road to Playa de Monsul was only open until 10:00 to restrict the number of people using the beach.

"Gracias amigo!"

The poor young guy went off, seemingly excited to be caught up in something he had no idea about but which was clearly dramatic and important. He looked around him before taking to the street. Robert and Alfredo unlocked the shed and wheeled out the bike. It was a scrambler.

"Jesus, Alf!" Robert looked a touch anxious. "Can you ride one of these things?"

"Sure. But with a passenger? First time for everything, hey?"

Robert put his hands together and looked to the heavens.

The dirt and dust encrusted red and white machine confounded expectations and started first time. The last thing Robert had said before they climbed on was to remind Alf that they weren't wearing helmets. He hung on to the underside of the pillion for dear life as the bike wobbled onto the road. Taking it easy for the first few streets Alf seemed to have his balance sorted and headed towards the edge of town. The last building behind them, Alfredo opened up the throttle, just as the quality of the road deteriorated. Clearly maintenance of what was essentially a track to a beach hadn't exactly been a high priority for the authorities. Alfredo wore a look of steely determination as he navigated the bumps and holes in the road, relishing the challenge. Robert's demeanour spoke more of terror as his teeth clattered and unknown elements of his skeletal frame announced themselves to each other.

A ball of dust trailed the bike as it sped along the

road. All around them was dry desert, punctuated sporadically by bits of bush, rough scrub and the odd eucalyptus tree. To the left, the azure blue of the Mediterranean. The sun's intensity built as it worked towards full power by midday. Just then Robert's assessment of the road surface was proved wrong as it became decidedly worse. They hit a bump that sent his backside leaping up from the seat, forcing him to grab Alf with his right hand until his left got back round the pillion. Within seconds, as Alf tried to avoid another bump, a sudden thud…they hit a pothole. Robert let out an immediate guttural response as his whole body seemed to shudder.

"Sorry!" shouted Alfredo over his shoulder. "You alright there?"

"Yes!" Robert shouted. Then quietly added "Fucking wonderful, amigo."

The road curved left towards the sea. Robert thought to himself that it couldn't be too far now. And then the bike started sliding around, Alfredo wrestling with the brakes as a tractor came out from behind what must have been the only large bushes for miles, where a track crossed over the road.

"Woooah! *Bastardo*!" screamed Alfredo.

They slowed enough for the bike to go around the back of the vehicle as the laid back farmer made the universal gesture for 'slow down'. Alfredo continued to mutter obscenities as he opened up the bike again. To the left was the idyllic, gently curving beach of Playa de los Genoveses, which meant another three kilometres to go. Speeding on, they lost sight of the coastline just around the same time Robert lost the feeling in his buttocks. At last the sea returned to view and straight ahead was Playa de Monsul.

Careering to a halt at the top of a path that leads directly to the beach, Alfredo lowered his feet to the ground as the two men exchanged thoughts on where to go. Robert pointed towards the car park, just a little farther on the right. It had a building in front of the parking area, there could be something there. As they entered the car park they looked around. It was quite busy already. They stopped by the building, enabling Robert to slide off the pillion. He bent forward and groaned, his hands on his thighs. Then, moving them to the small of his back, he stretched and extended, still groaning after his ordeal. But he knew time could be of the essence so he stumbled along to see if there was somewhere they could hide themselves. He wasn't optimistic.

"I don't think that's a good idea, in there, Alf" he said on returning outside. "Seems a bit obvious as it's the only place here. I'll have a quick scout round the car park."

Back at El Jardin, Pepe had been operating as coolly as he could under the circumstances. Having almost exhausted his visitors' patience, he'd finally emerged from his office only to advise them he hadn't been able to find any receipts in the name they'd given.

"Are you really sure about that?"

"Look" said Pepe. "I've been through the card payment receipts three times. There's no-one of that name. Then I thought…OK, maybe they paid by cash. That's not unusual. There would still be a receipt, so I go through them all…nothing."

"Nothing, eh?"

"Nothing. I'm sorry." Another shrug of the shoulders for effect.

"Maybe you run a crooked business here" said the wiry man.

"Crooked business? What are you saying?" said Pepe

with mock indignation.

"Maybe you don't have receipts or records so you don't pay the taxes. I think you understand."

"No. That's not the way I work. Now and again, we have a close friend or family, maybe we don't have the usual formalities, but things are run properly here. Maybe your friend was at another restaurant? Now, I have a lot to do today…"

At that moment, big beastly man passed his mobile to his boss to show him a message.

"They've been seen on a bike heading to Playa de Monsul" said the big guy in Spanish, smiling.

"I can read!" said the boss, looking daggers at him. Big guy stopped smiling. "Come on."

They turned and left with no word of thanks to Pepe, who breathed a sigh of relief and took out his mobile.

As Robert reached the far corner of the parking area he came across a blue trailer, naturally very sandy but otherwise covered by a tarpaulin sheet. He took a peep underneath, walked back round the front and waved to his partner, beckoning him over. Alfredo switched off the ignition, propped up the bike and, as the dust settled behind him, walked to Robert, who was examining his mobile.

"Just had a text from Pepe" he said. "There's been a couple of guys at the restaurant, quizzing him about us. They had a message to say we've been seen on a bike heading down here and we need to hide. He said one of them's a big bastard and not to worry, he'll get us out."

"I hope so" said Alfredo.

"Look at this" said Robert, holding up the heavy sheet. "There's nothing under here. Apart from sand. Do you think we could get the bike under here? Gets it out of sight then, doesn't it?"

"Yeah, let's see if we can lift it."

Alfredo wheeled the bike round, then put it back on its stand. Pushing it against the back of the trailer, they lifted from the seat and handle bars and heaved it on. Scrambling up themselves they dragged the bike along then hauled over the covers. Job done. Alf scrubbed out the tyre tracks leading to the trailer.

"Let's stay here and look out for them. Anyone suspicious and we'll dive under, but if we go in there too early we might just fry in this sun. In fact, one of us should stay in the shade anyway. You stay by the side of the trailer there, I'll look out for the first five minutes."

Time inevitably dragged as the two men took turns to look out. Every now and then one of them would come up with a new line in conversation. In the first fifteen minutes they discussed the beauty of the location, the boredom of sitting in the sun without a book or an iPod, how long it would take before Robert's skin turned to crackling, what Indiana Jones might do in this position and all interspersed by a common theme…what these thugs might do to them. Another swap round, Alfredo climbed up on the trailer for his second tour of duty.

"I'm just going to have to be Indie if it gets sticky" said Robert, clenching his fists as he jumped off.

"What?" Alfredo exclaimed. "That's not possible. How could I be your father? I have to be Indie."

"Well…not necessarily."

"Yes, necessarily. It's just the right way round."

"But I'm nowhere near old enough to play his Dad, am I?"

"And I am? I don't think so, that would be crazy."

"Ah, I suppose you've got a point. Alright, at least I get to be Sean Connery, that's not bad."

Just as Alfredo turned to crouch down, he saw a speed boat drawing in towards the beach.

"Hey Robert! Look."

"What's up?" he said, groaning as he lifted his considerable weight onto the trailer.

"That boat coming in - two men."

"Shit! This is them I reckon. Of course, the road'll be closed now, won't it? Crafty bastards."

As the speedboat slowed towards the sand, Robert texted Pepe to let him know what was happening. Pepe replied almost immediately. A vehicle was on its way. Two men. They'd look like maintenance. Clever, Pepe. Robert messaged back to say where they'd be hiding. Pepe didn't like that much. He thought they could get trapped. He said they needed to be able to mobilise themselves. Quickly. Mobilise? Robert thought this could be a first for him. They could now see the men walking across the beach. The leaner of the two was leading. Side to side his head turned, surveying assorted sun worshippers. He was struggling in the drier, deeper sand. Inappropriate footwear. The big guy was suffering in the heat…and he sunk deeper into the sand as he walked.

Robert had given Alfredo a running commentary on Pepe's messages. They decided they'd have to stand behind the trailer. Move round the vehicle as covertly as possible if necessary. The men were talking. The boss pointed down the beach. Away went the big lackey as they split off in opposite directions.

"Alright, Alf?"

"Yeah."

"Good. We've got to be ready for them. Let's get down off here, we'll still be able to see them standing up."

They stood at the rear of the trailer. Robert noticed that there was a van parked in the row in front of them. If they took the tarpaulin sheet from the trailer, would it stretch across the gap if they tied it to the van? Alfredo thought it might. They were bound to come into the car park soon and this would provide cover for them to sneak behind if they had to leave. At least it might give them a chance. They dragged it over the side, exposing Pepe's scrambler. It had ties on the corners. While Robert attached it to the van's wing mirror, Alfredo tied it round one of the trailer's sides. It meant it would be higher at the van's end but that was alright. It was cover. It could be vital.

By now Little and Large were back together and after a few exchanges they looked towards the car park. They followed the road track rather than the footpath. Great, thought Robert. That would mean they could stay to the left of the trailer and move along behind the tarpaulin. The now familiar figures entered the parking area. The big fellah took the outside. Checking the cars' doors. The boss was more circumspect. He moved towards the centre. Looking around at all the vehicles, he seemed a bit of a wily fox. Just then Alfredo's mobile bleeped. Robert glared at him. He stuck his finger sharply to his lips. He switched the phone to silent. Robert beckoned him then pointed ahead along the side of the sheet. He shuffled quietly along, head crouched down. Robert stopped at the front of the van. Alfredo remained at the other end where he could peer out over the trailer. From the back of the van was a short gap, maybe five or six metres, to a small building. The big man was now moving along the back of the car park, his boss even more central. Alfredo ducked down and swiftly walked under cover of the sheet. As he reached half way a strong gust blew across and lifted the sheet. 'Where the hell did that come from?' thought Robert. 'Why right now?' It was only a couple of seconds but enough for the boss man to see a pair of legs scurrying across and behind the van. He whistled to his hit man and pointed to the corner of the car park. Time to cut loose.

To the left of the building the two fugitives ran, Robert clearly feeling his age and weight handicap. Following the pedestrians' track to the beach seemed safest, where there were other people. They'd established a bit of a lead by the time the footpath crossed the road.

"Make for the big rock" called Robert, all out breathless as they trundled along an even more uneven path towards the beach.

To their left was a huge rock, as if a giant toad had crouched in the shallow waters of the Mediterranean and been turned to stone…where it had remained forever. The fine sand underfoot was no help to Robert and Alfredo. They now understood why their two pursuers, who by now had also crossed the road, looked so ungainly in their own attempts. The cliffs shielding the beach dazzled with their many hues and tints, the sun's brilliance illuminating the consequence of volcanic eruptions many years past. Apart from a few trees in bloom to provide some colour, only the odd palm tree and cactus punctuated the no-mans land from the cliffs to the beach. The sight of two pairs of men acting out a slow-motion chase across the dunes was surreal to bemused sun-bathers…the cumulative effects of age, heat and size, but mostly gross unfitness. It was like the Keystone Cops on cannabis.

Alfredo made it first behind the rock. Turning to urge Robert on he saw that their pursuers were themselves half way across the beach and heading straight after them. He grabbed Robert's arm as he came round the rock, pulling him round so he could see they appeared to be trapped.

"Are you saying this was a slightly flawed strategy, my friend?" he said in between gasps.

Alfredo simply looked at him wearing an expression crossed between exhaustion and abject panic.

"Well, you're bloody well right" said Robert. "Now think!"

There were a variety of bodies dotted around the beach, a few of whom were sitting or lying close by. All bar those listening to music with their eyes closed were following this intriguing spectacle. There were also lots of birds congregated on the beach, mainly seagulls. Just then a dark blue pick-up truck marked '*Mantinimiento*' on the doors slowly drove along the track until it stopped adjacent to them. Alfredo told him it meant 'maintenance' just as a text came in to Robert's phone. 'In the car park. Back of the truck, stay low.' He showed Alfredo.

"How are we going to do that?" said Alfredo.

"Hold on…"

With the two men only about twenty metres away, they were now walking slowly, tired and perspiring but with the confidence of hunters who knew they had their prey. Robert went over to a couple with their picnic box open, ready to tuck into lunch. Taking two ten euro notes from his pocket he looked pleadingly at the pair and stuck the notes in the man's hand as he swiped their box of bread rolls and various fillings.

"*Lo siento, lo siento*" he apologised as he rushed away. "Come on, Alf!"

He took out a roll, ripped it in pieces and threw it between the birds and the men. The big man tried to make a move towards Robert just as he threw the rest of the food at the pair. Within seconds an uprising of excited hungry seagulls had flocked around the less than dynamic duo. Peckish was an understatement as the birds hovered over them, landed on their shoulders, danced around their feet and, yes, occasionally crapped on them. It was carnage. Even the people who'd lost their picnic laughed. Probably the highlight of their day.

Robert and Alfredo had taken off up towards the road. As they looked back, it was like a puppet show, two pairs of arms flailing around amongst the seagulls, their heads facing down, their feet shuffling forwards and backwards in a strangely choreographed dance.

"*Super genio*, Robert! *Super genio*!" Alfredo was impressed.

"Spielberg meets Hitchcock, that's what it is. Let's just say I remembered my Charlemagne…Come on, mate."

The excitement of this unlikely victory had given them a shot of adrenaline that powered them on, loosely speaking, around the building and into the car park. There was the pick-up and two men in overalls waving them over. They lifted the covers on the back of the pick-up as Robert and Alfredo clambered up and under. They told them 'no noise', they'd be putting some other things in there with them. One of the men quickly went towards the building and returned with a couple of black bin liners full of rubbish and waste. Handing over to his colleague he threw them under the cover with Robert and Alfredo, who wretched at the smell.

"Shhhhh!" said the maintenance guy.

Underneath the cover there was a lot of suffering. The bags wreaked. More rubbish was heaped in. As one of the men got into the passenger's side, they could hear voices. From the conversation, at least the words they could make out, it was their hunters asking the maintenance guys if they'd seen two men. They said they had seen a couple of guys…a youngish man and an older fat man, sweating a lot. 'Bastards!' muttered Robert under his breath. He told them he'd seen them near the top of the car park going into the bushes and trees. They had evidently turned and gone to search. The driver's door banged shut, the ignition turned and the engine stuttered into life. Off they went…out with the garbage and ready for recycling.

—

"Buenos dias, Jack."

He stops mid-stairs and looks round.

"Ah, buenos dias, Christina" he replies gingerly, as she walks briskly along the corridor and meets him at the foot of the stairs.

"Did you have a nice evening with Beatriz?"

"Oh, wonderful, thank you, yes. I'm just going to try to wake up properly with a little breakfast and then go over to meet her."

"A late night?"

He could see Christina slipping effortlessly into interrogation mode.

"Not too late really…just a very tiring day with the Alhambra, the food, a few drinks…you know."

But Cristina was a hotel manager who'd seen it all before.

"Ah, of course, you have the hangover! Poor you." Then as she walked off, the advice… "Churros! That's what you need."

Jack walked into the breakfast area. Helping himself to a glass of freshly squeezed orange, he looked around the room. Stage two…bread with ham and cheese. Not bad, but better with a bit of olive oil. He didn't finish it. No sign of churros. Black coffee? It could only help. At least people were quiet, as if they'd entered a library. Not very Spanish, he thought. Probably all tourists. Checking his phone he found a message from Josh that had come in last night. He wanted to speak to him again about his Mum and suggested a time. Realising he needed to agree, despite hopefully being out and about with Beatriz, he said he'd call him at mid-day. Then, thinking of Beatriz, he decided he'd better call to see if she was awake.

"I didn't wake you did I?"

"Good. How do you feel?"

"Of course you've never felt better! That's the spirit."

"OK…if you're sure. I'll go out for some fresh air. Be with you in around twenty minutes. Bye."

He took a gulp of coffee, stood up, stretched while no-one was looking and headed for the door.

There was almost a spring in Jack's step by the time he arrived at the apartment. The paracetamol had started to act. He called up and she let him in. Still in her dressing gown she apologised that she'd need longer - everything was moving slowly for her, she said. Waiting for the tablets to act on her headache, the coffee was yet to kick in. She fell into a chair, pulling her gown across to preserve her modesty.

"Help yourself to coffee."

They recapped on various aspects of the evening, those that could be recalled clearly, and gradually saw the funny side of their drunkenness. Although she knew she'd been ill, she had no recollection of the beggar and was mortified when Jack told her. Eventually he noticed the copy of Tales of the Alhambra, the Washington Irving book, on the coffee table. Inspired by their day out, she'd been looking at her favourite story, The Legend of the Rose of the Alhambra.

"It's about a page who is following the Queen's

falcon and discovers a princess in a tower. She's forbidden to open the door by her aunt, but the handsome page is very persuasive."

Standing up she ran her right hand through her hair.

"I won't spoil the romance of it for you." Then as her bedroom door closed… "Won't be long."

Jack poured another coffee, sat down and picked up the book. 'The heart of the little damsel was touched by the distress of the page.' Mmm…Jack thought. Perhaps he could see if he could do a distressed page. How do you pull that off? 'He was gentle and modest, and stood so entreatingly with cap in hand and looked so charming.' OK…not such a stretch for me. So, she lets him in. 'Her Andalucian bodice and trim *basquiña* set off the round but delicate symmetry of her form which was as yet scarcely verging into womanhood.' Wow! Still quite young by the sounds of it, but Beatriz isn't, so he just needs the strategy, he thinks. 'A freshly plucked rose in her hair' plants an idea for later. '…her complexion was touched by the ardour of a southern sun, but it served to give richness to the mantling bloom of her cheek and to heighten the lustre of her melting eyes.' Oh yes, he liked the sound of melting eyes. Why does the princess look just like Beatriz in his imagination? So…what's this? The page picked up a reel of silk from the floor and '… seizing the hand extended to receive it, imprinted upon it a kiss more fervent and devout than he had ever imprinted on the fair hand of his sovereign.' She says 'Ave Maria, señor! … blushing still deeper with confusion and surprise.' That's what Beatriz had said last night, he recalled, when he kissed her hand. He felt a quiver of excitement.

Reading on, Jack discovered that the maiden was only fifteen and at the sound of her aunt arriving, the page only agreed to leg it if she'd give him the rose from her hair.

Which she does, naturally. It's a rose now, thinks Jack, but what will he be asking for next? The poor old aunt has had a life of celibacy and a particular description makes him wince '...Nature having set up a safeguard in her face, that forbade all trespass upon her premises.' Very subtle, he thought. Just then, Beatriz emerged dressed and looking much better. No such dastardly acts visited upon Beatriz, he thought, even with a hangover.

"Ah, it is my very own princess of the tower!" said Jack with a flamboyant waving of his arms.

"I'm afraid it's more like the princess of the make-up cabinet" she replied. "Where have you got to?"

"Well, she's been fed up of waiting for the page to visit again. But, having rubbed a trinket for this apparition of an earlier princess, she's now able to play the lute with supernatural melody. She's suddenly like Hendrix on LSD, entrancing people with her tunes. What did it say? Hold on...oh yes.

'She drew forth such ravishing tones as to thaw even the frigid bosom of the immaculate Fredegonda, that region of eternal winter, into a genial flow.' So what next?"

He answered his own question by adopting his best documentary voiceover delivery.

"Reports of her powers spread across the land and soon she was headlining festivals..."

"Oh, stop it! It's a lovely old story" protested Beatriz.

"What? He started it. His descriptions of the aunt with her ice cubes for breasts and so on are quite cruel but very funny too. I'm more than happy to finish it."

"It's time to go out."

"Alright, but you can't keep me in suspense. Tell me what happens whilst we're walking."

There's a lot more to Granada than the Alhambra.

It may be a small city and visitors may flock to its main attraction, but Beatriz wanted to ensure Jack realised what else it had to offer. Its baroque cathedral, for a start. On the way there, Beatriz tried to convey the finale of her favourite Washington Irving tale.

"Right…for the Princess' next challenge, she plays for the King, who is a hypochondriac and very miserable. He had become very ill, at least in his head, and stayed in solitude as if he was dead. The Princess played with all her heart and soul and amazingly he lifted his head and sat up. The demon of melancholy was driven out, sun shone through the windows of his chamber and it was as if a dead man had risen again. And then, at the end, the Princess fell to the floor, the lute dropping out of her hands."

"Oh, poor thing. Probably exhausted."

"When she awoke she was clutching the bosom of Ruiz…the page of the court!"

"Where had he been then? Sounds like a bit of a chancer to me, turning up to bathe in her glory and take advantage."

"No! Listen…that was his father's fault. But the Queen took care of that and so…they were married very soon."

"And they all lived happily ever after?"

"Of course!"

"Aaah" said Jack. "Thank you for sharing your favourite tale with me. It was very sweet of you."

Did he really mean that? Or was he just having a bit of fun with her? As they strolled on through the city, Beatriz was still a little fragile but improving slowly. Every now and then Jack would have a flashback to the night before, the moment they seemed about to kiss. Had it simply been delayed? Was it passion that led to the possibility or had it been the drink? Unlike the princess and the page, perhaps it was not their destiny to be together? And then his thoughts switched to monochrome as he remembered his wife, about to go into hospital.

And so they reached Catedral Iglesia del Sagrario-Capilla Real, otherwise known as the cathedral, a feast of marble and gold built between 1523 and 1561. Before they go in Jack tells Beatriz about having to call his son at 12 noon. He also messages Robert to ask how the journey home went. Continuing their visit they took in the cathedral's splendour, including its 17th century artwork and statues. Beatriz then reminded Jack that it was almost twelve o'clock. With a casual acknowledgement he left her to mooch around, walked outside and found a seat nearby. He had mixed feelings. He looked forward to hearing Josh's voice but, in the midst of a great couple of days away with Beatriz, he was also apprehensive about his wife's situation, which appeared to be edging closer to putting the kibosh on his holiday.

The six minute call, comprising the obligatory inquiries after everyone's health and the details of arrangements for his wife's operation, felt more like two. Josh had a lot on at work and needed to be somewhere else shortly after. He walked back into the cathedral. Beatriz was sitting down in contemplation facing the altar. He quietly sat down next to her and they looked at each other.

"A penny for your thoughts?" said Jack.

"What do you mean?"

"Oh, back home when we want to know what someone's thinking about, we offer them a penny, one pence, in exchange for them telling us. A quaint, very old expression, no doubt. Not a great deal, is it?"

Without waiting for an answer, Jack began to explain that his wife has a date to go into hospital. She goes in on Friday next week and the operation will be carried out the same day, not the following day as originally thought. He tried to convey how he felt. He really didn't want to go back. Yet he thought it important to be there and really, he knew he should. Something he didn't want to express was his fear of becoming too close again when he'd started to see that there could be another way, a freedom in living that he hadn't experienced for a long time. He needed to think carefully. Maybe speak to his children again, take a sounding from them. He'd also been slightly peeved to discover that the temperature in the UK is 30°, the same as in Granada. Beatriz took his arm and stood up.

"Come on. Let's walk."

Leaving the cathedral they strolled along, basking in the magnificence of Calle Gran Vía de Colón, Granada's central shopping artery. They walked around the Plaza del Campillo and pointed out things they liked in the artful window displays. Walking up Cuesta de San Gregorio saps their energy and Jack, spotting a small flower shop, calls a time out. He sits Beatriz on a nearby bench and tells her to wait a minute. Walking out of the quaint old florist's with one hand behind his back, he approaches Beatriz, smiles, leans over her and, with a swift flourish, deftly plants a crimson rose in her hair.

"Oh, what's that?" Feeling the petals, she takes the rose, breathing its scent. "Mmm…it's beautiful, thank you."

"A little something from your very own page of the court" he replied.

"Ah, that's so cute of you. You did read it."

She took his face in her hands and kissed him lightly on the cheek, dropped her hands to his shoulder blades, pulled him in tighter, tensing her shoulders as she hugged him passionately. Standing, she took his hand and they walked to the top of the hill. Entering a convoluted web of small streets, they finally emerge with Jack not having a clue to their whereabouts, on Placeta del Comino. Once again dominating is the Alhambra, high on its seat of dignity and authority. Just then, a text comes in from Robert. It simply says 'Return journey not quite gone to plan. Not home yet. Will call asap'. Jack is a little perplexed and shares it with Beatriz.

"Oh no" says Beatriz. "What do you think has happened? I hope they haven't had an accident."

"Hopefully not. I'll reply to him and ask if they can speak now."

She agreed. Jack fired off his message.

In the meantime, they proceeded to Restaurante El Agua, where Beatriz had planned to have lunch. They were shown to a table outside, with some shade. Jack said his hat would do the rest. And there it was again, the Alhambra, casting its spell over the city from another vantage point, itself watched over from a distance by nature's own Sierra Nevada. Two glasses of chilled white wine arrived in what seemed like seconds.

"I don't think I could ever tire of this view" said Jack. "If ever there was a spot for lingering in, this is it."

Just then, a message pinged into Jack's phone.

Still only mid-morning on the Cabo de Gata coast, the maintenance truck rumbles along the bumpy track at a steady pace. If it could go faster it would probably draw attention, but luckily 40kph is flat out. All the same bumps appear in reverse order. It may be slower than their arrival but Robert is certain he'll never forget the stench of their departure. It's so bad he's worried he may never be able to remove it from his nostrils. Who knows what waste is travelling alongside them, but in the murky light of their cover the faces they make to each other suggest it's pretty gruesome. By raising their heads a little they can see the outside world pass by in narrowscape, a small gap between the sides of the truck and the tarpaulin sheet. Robert has the sea view, Alfredo has the hinterland, which largely amounts to an intermittent display of shrubs and scrubs.

They begin to see buildings either side of the road and figure they're arriving back at San José. As the truck heads across the first junction, a right turn at Calle del Cerro Gordo, Robert spots a guy in dark clothing watching them go past. He's sitting on a car bonnet parked close to the junction with Camino de Monsul, which leads to the centre. At the same time Alfredo sees another man on the other side of the road, a little farther on. The two men in the back of the truck remain silent as the vehicle trundles on. After another minute or two it stops. The ignition is switched off. The doors open and shut. The sheet is lifted on Robert's side and the maintenance guy says something which Alfredo translates.

"OK. We can get out."

They struggle up, Robert in particular finding it hard to lift himself to his feet, let alone clamber over the side of the truck safely. With a bit of help he's down.

"Thank you so much, guys" says Robert, Alfredo doing the instant translation. "What's happening now?"

The other guy says they've had a text from Pepe while they've been driving. It's not safe to stay in San José, but Pepe would like to speak to Robert. He offers him his mobile to make the call.

When Robert gets through, Pepe explains that there is too much activity around with the two men at Monsul then at least two in the town. He wants to know what he's done to upset these people and how did he become involved with their sort. Robert explains simply and honestly what they've done and what he thinks may have gone wrong. Although he protests their innocence regarding the potential cargo that the clients had expected, he knows it's a little disingenuous. Nevertheless, he chooses naivety as the best policy under the circumstances. He concludes that it's been a real lesson for them and, although he needs the opportunity to clear up this mess, he doesn't want to tangle with these men, who are not the people he was working for. Pepe takes it on board and says it's too dangerous to return to the apartment or pick up the car or van. Robert says if there's somewhere they can lay low for a while longer he can contact a friend for help and continue trying to communicate with the man who employed them.

Pepe says he has a customer leaving shortly for Rodalquilar. There are plenty of empty buildings in the disused part of the village. They'll be hard to find there. As requested he passes the mobile back to the maintenance man. They sort out a location. It's back under the covers for another couple of minutes while they move outside San José to a small development off the AL-3108. After another couple of minutes stationary, a car pulls up alongside and there's a knock on the side of the truck and a few words of Spanish. Manoeuvring themselves out once more they shake hands with the customer from El Jardin, who hasn't realised that they'd literally been travelling under cover and tells them to jump in. Before they do, Robert thanks the two maintenance men and asks them to give the key to Pepe for his scrambler, which is in the back of the trailer at Playa de Monsul.

Robert jumps into the back leaving Alfredo to converse from the front seat. As he's explaining that Pepe had told him to drop them in the old village, he broke off his line of thought to comment on the terrible stench outside of the town, it must be the drainage.

"Yes, it's bad" says Alfredo, looking sheepishly over his shoulder at Robert. "I've heard it's like this all the way to Rodalquilar."

He looks back again. Robert has cocked his head to one side, eyebrows raised. He's quietly impressed with Alf's improvisation. If the driver asks questions about what they're doing in Rodalquilar, he shudders to think what else he'll come up with. At least the road to Nijar is a proper road with a decent surface.

Now heading along the AL-4200 in a north-east direction back towards the coast, they skirt past Los Escullos and La Isleta. Spectacular coastal views dominate their focus for the journey. El Jardin proves suitable common ground for discussion for much of the journey as they each go through their favourite dishes. When the talk inevitably comes round to why they're going to Rodalquilar, Alfredo tells him they're interested in researching the old gold mining history of the village. The driver shares a few tales of old and some of the local mythology he's heard about its mining and cinematic heritage. As they approach their destination Robert looks back behind them and can still see the twin peaks of Los Frailes, the two volcanic summits, and an empty landscape save the eucalyptus trees and odd indigenous hazel lining the highway. After a sharp right hand they find themselves in the modern part of the village. A tall metal statue of a miner stands at the side of the road giving a symbolic welcome and a reminder of the area's past role in the gold mining industry. As the driver says, there's been no gold mining here since 1966. Not dissimilar to England's World Cup record, Robert ponders. After that, many properties were abandoned and have remained empty. Unsurfaced streets lead to derelict homes, fenced off to protect people from their dilapidated condition. The driver tells them that, when they've finished their research, the modern village has a few nice bars they should try. And with that he bids them farewell and goes on his way.

Robert and Alfredo make their way back to the empty homes they saw as they entered the village. Although they've been left to rack and ruin over many years, it's still evident that all the streets are named after metals like bronze, zinc and nickel. It's lunch time, so there's no-one about, no-one to see them mooching around the empty places.

"Hey, Alf" says Robert, "I got a message from Jack while we were in the car. So I've replied saying we've had a problem and he's asked if we can talk as soon as possible."

"Shall we find somewhere for shelter first?"

"Yeah, we desperately need some shade, especially this time of the day. It's so hot."

They decide to stick with the first one that looks remotely safe or, more accurately, less dangerous than the others. Checking their mobiles, Robert is almost out of juice but there's still 25% battery left in Alfredo's. While they've got battery left they need to ring Alf's van hire friend to see if he can collect from San José. They need to try Xavi again and agreed reluctantly that it's time they let Jack and Beatriz in on what's happened, even if it does spoil the end of their break. So they decide it's Jack and Beatriz first - a potentially tricky call.

Jack and Beatriz were wondering whether to order lunch on the sunny terrace at Restaurante del Agua when Jack's phone buzzed in his pocket.

"Oh, it's Alfredo."

He listened intently as Robert appraised him of their situation. He tried not to let his expressions worry Beatriz and remained impassive, asking the occasional question of his friend. He finished the conversation by saying he needed to speak with Beatriz and he'd call him back.

"Let's just go in here where it's quiet" he said to Beatriz, indicating the inside of the building.

Jack then tried as best he could to relay the position as he'd understood it from Robert, as Beatriz' face increasingly betrayed her anxiety. Having summed up what he thought he understood and tried to answer her questions, he acknowledged that there must be a lot more to understand. But ultimately, they agreed they had to help. Luckily Jack had packed before leaving the hotel this morning and just needed to collect his case and check out. They decided to go to the apartment for Beatriz to collect her things for the weekend, then take her car round to the hotel. It would be at least a two hour drive, if not two hours twenty. As they walked to the apartment Jack called Robert back and told him what they had to do but that they'd be leaving in no more than twenty minutes. He urged him to save their battery and they could call when they got to Rodalquilar.

"Do you think they'll be alright?" asked Beatriz.

"I hope so. It would be funny if it didn't sound so serious. We've got to work out a way to resolve this, even if it means going to the police. Robert's assured me that there was no intention to be involved in anything illegal and that he's somehow been set up."

"I remember hearing something on the radio about drugs in a supermarket around Madrid but I thought no more of it."

"Oh, yes!" Jack said. "So do I now you mention it. I found an English language station in my room this morning. It was rather amusing when it came on but I didn't think for a minute that it could involve my friend and your brother. I wonder if it's connected?"

Back in the derelict hideaway, the boys are starving, so it's time to open the food box. Inside Pepe has put a note. 'Hey! Don't forget you haven't paid for your dinner last night. Then there's the accommodation - no charge, but a good review on TripAdvisor would be nice. Then there's your lunch. Make it last in case you're there all week! Good luck friends. Pepe'

The old derelict house was actually quite cool - that is, it wasn't too hot inside. It wasn't likely to be winning any design awards. It smelt pretty badly too, but no worse than they did. When it came to making their calls they realised they hadn't got much service. So they walked off until they found a signal and decamped to the nearest empty house. It was otherwise just like the first one.

"This would be a challenge to sell" reckoned Robert. "Mind you, it's only a matter of time before an estate agents' photographer wins the Turner Prize."

Alf went first and phoned his friend. He'd wondered what was happening about the van so had been pleased to hear from him. And it was no trouble at all to pick up from San José. He'd collect the keys from Pepe at El Jardin. Before signing off Alfredo invited him to have a drink there and tell Pepe to charge it to Robert's account. Sitting in the opposite corner on the floor, the senior partner shook his head and grinned.

Robert then tried Xavi's number but once again there was no reply.

Having picked up Beatriz' weekend bag, she and Jack arrived at the hotel to pick up his case, Beatriz said hello to Christina and explained simply that they had to rush back because of a family issue. With a kiss on each cheek from Jack and an invitation to come back and see them again from Christina, the Granada dream was abruptly curtailed. And they hadn't even had lunch!

The journey from Granada was a frustrating one in many respects, not least because they still had places to visit. And then there was their blossoming relationship. They seemed close and maybe on the cusp of something more meaningful. And now what? They kept replaying the telephone conversation with Robert and coming up with yet more questions. It was all so puzzling. But they were both of the same mind - they had to do whatever they could to help. They acknowledged that they'd never have met if it hadn't been for Robert and Alfredo, and in doing so revealed a little more about their feelings towards each other. But would either of them dare to take the next step?

After they'd stopped to pick up drinks and a quick snack, Jack asked "So what would you have had in store for me this afternoon?"

"Oh, it's difficult" Beatriz said, "there was so much more to show you but we would have only had a few hours at the most."

As they drove she reeled off the names of places that had been on her shortlist.

"So what would you pick?" said Beatriz.

Jack's mind had wandered elsewhere while Beatriz was talking, although it was her he'd been thinking of. Whatever feelings he'd felt towards her before their Granada trip had accelerated. He felt close to her. He'd again been luxuriating in her presence, as he recognised he'd been prone to on several occasions over the past two days. Quite apart from any physical attraction, he'd experienced both her character and vulnerability. At times he thought she might be attainable but at other times his confidence left him. And time was running out. And as a consequence...he'd hardly heard a word she'd said.

"Oh there's so much...I don't know" Jack mumbled. "Didn't you mention the Lorca museum, he was a poet, wasn't he?"

Beatriz sat up and leaned forward, more animated. He might just have got away with it.

"Yes, the Casa Museo de Federico Gorcia Lorca is dedicated to him. He was born near Granada and murdered by fascist thugs from here soon after the start of the Civil War. He was a great, great artist: a poet, musician and he wrote plays too. But he was outspoken and made enemies here and these things, along with his homosexuality, went against him. He was forced to dig his own grave by an olive tree outside the city. He was shot, his books burned and his work banned by Franco. Yet today, he is honoured as a legend and the city has to live with its shame."

"Wow. I'd like to know more about him."

Jack was impressed by her passion and her evident irritation at the injustice.

"Maybe one day, I will take you on the trail of locations associated with Lorca in and around the city."

"I hope so, it sounds fascinating."

In all probability it would have sounded fascinating to Jack if Beatriz had suggested that they take a party of school children round the caves of Nerja.

Jack and Beatriz made decent time and having passed Almeria were now motoring across Cabo de Gata. Beatriz had earlier managed to move the conversation round to Jack's immediate future. It was less than a week before he returned to the UK. How long would he stay? Had he thought about what type of work he might do in the future? Could he see himself returning to Spain to live, like Robert? These were not easy questions for him. Of course, he'd given them consideration, but as yet he had no answers, no clear path that he should be taking.

"How long I stay really depends on how long I feel that either Amanda or the kids need me to. And that's got to be balanced by my financial needs of course. Amanda's living in our house and I guess if I want to sort out my own accommodation more permanently the house would need to be sold. If I had to force the issue, I'd need to file divorce proceedings, that'd be expensive and time consuming, not to mention divisive amongst the family. Ultimately I have to decide on what I want to do - that'll have a strong bearing on where I live. Then again, if I have a stronger feeling for living in a particular place, especially Spain, that would influence the work I could do. Suppose I'd have to learn Spanish quite quickly."

"Naturally. Of course, regular Spanish lessons would

be essential but at least they would be very cheap."

"How so?" asked Jack.

"Well, I wouldn't have the heart to charge you…but I would be a very good teacher. Very strict too!"

"Would you give me homework?"

"Lots!" she said with a mischievous glance from behind the wheel.

"Truth is, I've thought of a range of different things I might like to do, but I don't really have any clarity about anything right now. Maybe when I'm faced with having to make a decision…"

As they drove on he confessed that when he'd imagined working back in the UK it hadn't made his heart sing. He'd also envisioned himself living and working in Spain and curiously that made him feel more optimistic. Just talking about the prospect energised him. It seemed more exciting. Real change in his life. Yet perversely he also felt a little afraid. Beatriz recognised he was troubled by it and that this was a big stumbling block for him.

"Perhaps you need to seriously put time aside to think about options. Maybe writing them down would help? When it's in writing, in front of you, choices sometimes become clearer."

Jack agreed. He thought this could help and the time was probably right to do this. Beatriz was interested in why the prospect of returning to live in England didn't make him feel happy. He attempted to explain that it was partially a consequence of his personal circumstances, his career and family struggles squeezing him from each side. That it was all happening to him at a time when the social, economic and political climate was so antagonistic perhaps made it feel even more oppressive. Beatriz noticed that when he spoke like that, he appeared tired by it, as if it drained him of his natural energy. After a short silence, she turned to him and smiled.

"But apart from that, you're happy?"

He laughed. He had ranted on a bit.

And so, as the afternoon sun bore down and the road continued its way through the rugged dry terrain of Cabo de Gata, Jack had a little time for reflection. He realised that when he was around Beatriz he was brighter, but was it realistic to think about any sort of relationship? Wasn't she out of his league? Yet isn't she the reason he's so enjoying it here? How would he have felt about living in Spain if they'd never met? But they had met…and he felt she was special. And he couldn't help thinking that she appeared to like him too. He hadn't asked her to take him to Granada. Surely it couldn't just be out of gratitude for saving her brother? Beatriz broke his train of thought…

"It's only a few kilometres now to Rodalquilar. Shall we telephone soon."

"Is it? OK, suppose we better had."

Robert and Alfredo were relieved to hear that the cavalry were approaching. Directions were straightforward and within a couple of minutes Beatriz' car pulled up outside. The front door of the house opened and Alfredo beckoned them in. As the fab four were reunited it was hugs and high fives all round. It wasn't long however before Beatriz was wanting some answers…

"How on earth have you got into this position? What's been going on? Who are these people?"

"Hold on, Beatriz" said Robert, "Let me explain briefly. We were contracted to do a job, to bid for a consignment of bananas and bring them back. That's exactly what we did, and that's all we did. It seems the people we were distributing them to were expecting more than just bananas. And they seem to think we're responsible. Fact is, we haven't got a clue what's happened."

"What about these drugs turning up in supermarkets round Madrid, it's been on the news?" asked Jack. "Do you think it's related?"

"Well, it's possible. We just don't know. I mean, you can't imagine anyone at Lidl knowingly buying cocaine, can you? So, yeah, doesn't it just smack of a real cock-up somewhere?"

"Oh, smack!" said Jack. "Very good, mate."

"Unintended" said Robert. "Listen, we'll tell you the whole saga soon, but right now we need to get out of here so can we just focus on sorting out a bit of a plan?"

Beatriz agreed. She was just relieved to see that her brother was fine, although he was not too keen on receiving a lot of attention, he just wanted to be seen as Robert's partner. Robert emphasised that he'd still been unable to make contact with Xavi. After some discussion, they agreed it would be safest for Jack to return to Mojacar to try to contact Xavi, in person, to appeal to him for help. Beatriz was happy to stay with the fugitives, partly to support her brother but also because the gang would not be looking for three people in a car.

Despite his misgivings about leaving Beatriz with two men on the run from a dangerous gang, Jack reluctantly agreed, but how would they secure Robert's car from San José? They would have to expect it to have been discovered by now and monitored. They couldn't just walk up to it, jump in and drive off. Even if they could, they'd at least be followed. And there was no way Robert and Alfredo could do it. So how could Jack and Beatriz pull it off?

"Look" said Beatriz "in my experience men can be easily distracted."

Robert and Jack each exchanged furtive looks and nodded sagely.

"So," Beatriz went on, "I'll take responsibility for providing some distraction. Jack, you will then need to steal the car so to speak. If I can get back to my car we can meet up at the edge of town and return here."

"That's a smart plan, that is" said Robert, clearly impressed. "Are you sure she's related to you, Alf?"

"Very amusing" said Alfredo. "Are you sure you'll be alright? These guys don't look too friendly."

"Of course I will. They're still only guys. I'll be careful, I promise." Then she looked at Jack and said "Besides, Jack will be there watching out for me."

"Too right I will" said Jack, looking right back into her eyes.

Whether it was love, devotion or a gullible audience, Beatriz had injected a sense of mission and camaraderie into the adventure.

"Let's go!" she said, marching to the door then purposefully walking down the path.

It was as if Stan Lee had invented a new character and Jack could only marvel at her.

—

The red Seat swiftly negotiated the road back to San José, a rare flash of colour against the arid desert landscape. Jack had the name of the street written down on a piece of paper and sought it out on his phone. They agreed to leave the car two streets away and to approach from different directions on foot. Beatriz told him to keep her in his sight until she'd engaged with whoever was monitoring the vehicle, assuming there was someone there. Then he could go round the block to access the car from another street. The nine mile route took them just about seventeen minutes. As she switched off the engine, Beatriz turned to Jack, took his hand and smiled.

"Have you got the keys?"

"Yes, in my pocket. We can do this, Bea!"

Her smile grew wider.

"You've never called me Bea before."

"Oh…sorry…I…"

"I like it" she interjected.

They walked together to the top of the road. They could see two youngish men on the opposite corner at the end of the street. They decided to circle round to observe them from a different vantage point and to see how close they were to Pepe's apartment, where the car was parked. When they get round to the end of the street where the apartment is, they can see it's about 150m from the two men, who are sitting loosely on top of a garden wall. Jack suggested he should stay there, then move across to the opposite corner, out of sight but where he could see her and the men through the foliage of a garden. He'd cross when she had their attention. That would also mean he'd be on the same side of the road as the apartment and it would be easier to access without their noticing. Beatriz nodded her assent and whispered that she'd go back to approach them from the top of the street near where they'd parked. He put up his thumb and wished her luck.

Before she turned into the street to approach them, Beatriz unbuttoned the top of her blouse then hoisted up the lower part and tied it, ensuring her midriff was revealed. Tying her hair up into a bun, she completed the new look by rolling up her blue jeans to just below the knee. Within a minute she'd transformed from classy to sassy. She began the walk. About twenty five metres away, one of the men turns round and clocks her. He quickly turns to his colleague and they both turn to her. As she gets closer she calls across the road to them.

"Hey guys! Are you local boys?"

"Why d'you want to know?" said the nearest from behind his sunglasses, a man in his early twenties with black hair and a slightly hooked nose.

He was sporting a black t-shirt and black jeans. Unknown to Beatriz, he was the man who'd been monitoring Robert for the past week.

"I need some advice. But if you guys aren't local then you're probably no help to me."

"Well, we don't exactly live here but we know a lot of stuff, so just ask us."

He stood up and turned to face her as he spoke. The other man followed suit and flanked him to his right. He was slightly taller, skinny with mousy hair and wanted to offer his assistance too.

"Yeah. We could help you in lots of ways."

He wasn't quite drooling but…

"You could?" said Beatriz. "I would be very surprised, but hey!"

She walked slowly and seductively across the road, looking around her and then back at the two men.

"So, what do you know about the restaurants here in San José?"

"All along the waterfront, just two minutes walk," said the first guy.

"Maybe we could take you for a drink later, maybe have dinner?" said the second.

"Oh, how lucky could a girl be? Well…I could probably use some company later. A lady like me is not used to being lonely."

As the two guys grinned and their levels of smugness went off the meter, Jack was creeping along the street towards Pepe's place. Keeping close to the wall, he opened the gates quietly. Tiptoeing round the back of the building, he quickly unlocked the car door and jumped in. Closing the door quietly seemed impossible but he figured it wouldn't matter too much initially - it felt secure. After a few mirror adjustments, he started the engine and moved off. As he drove out of the gates and onto the road, he could see the three players down the street still talking. Beatriz, having had her back to him before hearing the sound of an engine, figured it could be Jack and had moved along a few metres to the other side of the men. In doing so it caused them to turn their backs on the vehicle and allow her to see whether Jack could complete his stage of the exercise. By now she was telling them she was from Barcelona, down on holiday. Meanwhile Jack, looking behind him in his mirrors for any signs of reaction, slowly headed towards the end of the street. Keeping the revs low he pulled into the next street and slipped away up the hill.

"So listen, boys" said Beatriz after watching Jack disappear from view, "I've got to get along right now but hopefully I'll be back this evening. Which restaurant is the best one to go for, where do you go?"

They looked at each other. The one with the mousy hair shrugged his shoulders and deferred to his partner.

"You like Italian?"

"Sure. I love Italian food."

"OK, we'll be at Il Brigantino Puerto. Great pizzas, pastas, yeah. What time?"

"Tonight, let me think…let's say 8:30, yeah?"

"That's good, OK. We'll look forward to seeing you down there. Ciao!"

"Ciao, amigos - and thanks for your help."

With that, Beatriz pushed down her shades and walked across the road.

"Hey!" called the dark haired guy. "What's your name?"

"Maria" she replied with a smile.

"You got a friend you want to bring tonight?" called the mousy one optimistically.

"Maybe. We'll see."

Having wrested control of the situation and become comfortable with her act, Beatriz felt her heart beating faster as she walked up the road. How long would it be before they noticed the car had gone? She knew that the lecherous slime balls would be watching her initially so to ensure their attention a little longer she exaggerated the wiggle in her walk. As she passed the half way mark each of the two guys started to claim 'sotto voce' that she was theirs for the evening. Then they began to push each other like a couple of juveniles. The mousy one took out his mobile to photograph her but his arm was pushed as he tried to focus, cue further irritation. Once she'd gone round the corner the macho rivalry increased and their abuse of each other became louder. After amusing each other for a few minutes and speculating what sort of evening they'd have with the mysterious woman from Barcelona, they took a stroll along the street. The dark haired one went round the back of the apartments but quickly came running out to the street.

"The car! It's gone!"

"Oh Dios mio!"

They both ran round the back to where it had been parked. Still gone. More arguing, this time with intent. They both knew they were in the cart. A simple task like watching a car. How could they have failed to notice? How long has it been gone? When did they last check? At last one of the half-wits made the connection and realised it must have been taken while their attention was on Maria from Barcelona. As they stumbled around in the road berating each other and themselves, it dawned on them around the same time. Could she have been part of it? Was Maria distracting them intentionally? They set off to follow the direction she'd taken, running in the blistering heat of the afternoon. Nothing doing. She'd vanished. A couple of streets away, she was waving to Jack in Robert's car. He pulled up behind her and they sped off towards Rodalquilar.

As the two cars pulled up outside the hideaway in the old mining town, the two fugitives were already heading down the path. Jack leapt out of the car to run round to Beatriz as she got out.

"Bloody hell, Beatriz. Wow! How on earth did you manage to distract them?" Robert said sarcastically.

Alfredo just shook his head.

"You were amazing!" said Jack, smiling all over his face. "Well done! Nice look, you should dress like that more often."

"I was professional, I had a job to do. And if you don't stop teasing me I might just turn up for my dinner date with them tonight in San José"

"You arranged dinner? Amazing."

"Not at El Jardin" said her brother.

"No, some Italian place."

At that point Robert reminded them that it was only a matter of time before they were tracked down and told them the ideas they'd had about going somewhere public - essentially, they didn't have anywhere else secure to stay and, as the car may have been spotted around where they were, staying in Rodalquilar didn't seem like a good option. When he was asked if he had anywhere in mind he first looked at Alfredo as if for reassurance, paused a few seconds and then declared they thought the best place would be the airport.

"Why?" came the harmonious reply from Jack and Beatriz.

He explained that it was only about 45 minutes away and there'd be lots of people.

"Yes" said Beatriz, "and lots of security and police. I agree that should be good for your safety, but you could be attracting a lot of attention."

"I'm not convinced" said Jack. "If I can find Xavi then we might be able to get this sorted out. This whole thing sounds to me like you wouldn't really want the police involved apart from as a last resort. What about a bar or café somewhere in a well populated area?"

"Another alternative is that you could stay at my apartment in Granada which would give Jack more time."

"Look" said Alf, looking more than a little troubled, "maybe if we can't get hold of Xavi tonight, Granada would be a safe bet. At least we might sleep soundly. Otherwise, what about staying around Almeria, close to the city, to give Jack a chance to find Xavi and get things sorted out tonight?"

Against the odds they all agreed this sounded like the most sensible approach yet. Alfredo came up with a café he knew where they could sit inside and be able to watch the street, Cafeteria La Tana. Jack asked them to send him the details on his phone so he could find it if necessary. They could lie low in there and there'd be people around in the area. If they needed to leave quickly the autopista was close and they could take several directions from there. It was as good as they could come up with. Beatriz would drive her car, Jack would take Robert's back to Mojacar.

"What about your phones, guys?" said Jack.

"I've got a charger in my car" Beatriz replied.

"Great" said Robert, "we can keep in touch on any progress or developments."

Then Alfredo chipped in.

"Jack, I think it would be best for you to wait here a few minutes. They know Robert's car and if we're close together they may spot us too. It would give us time to get away and by the time you reach the autopista we'll be well towards Pechina. We'll take the same route to the autopista because we don't want to go back on the road that goes to San José - too risky."

"Yeah?" asked Jack, looking round. "OK, seems like a good idea, Alfredo. I'll give you five minutes. Let me just check with you that I've got the right contact details for Xavi."

At the edge of town, two young men sat low in the front seats of a car, parked adjacent to the road on a piece of rough track. They saw a red Seat Leon emerging from the old disused part of town, head to the junction and turn left to come towards them. The car accelerated at a reasonable pace as the men watched. The driver sat further up in his seat as they passed.

"It's her!" he said. "Maria!"

"Maria from Barcelona?" his partner said in disbelief.

"Yes, Maria from- no! Who knows who she is and where she's from, but it was the girl we're supposed to be having dinner with. Let's go."

He started the car and in his impatience gave the engine too many revs, causing them to slalom along the track until he joined the main road. The driver was the dark haired one and he told his colleague to let them know they'd found her and there were two guys in the car, possibly the men they were looking for. Whilst he made the call the driver kept a good distance behind, waiting for orders.

As Jack had five minutes to kill, he thought he might as well try Xavi's number. Robert had tried contacting him several times to no avail and hadn't felt it was a good idea to leave a message. A Spanish voice answered.

"Habla Inglés?' asked Jack, delivering his most frequently practiced Spanish phrase impeccably.

"Yes, I speak English" replied the man in a rich deep tone.

"My name is Jack, I'm a friend of Robert..."

Having established that he was talking to Xavi on behalf of his friend, he listened to Jack explain what had happened. He understood the consignment had been delivered as agreed but was unaware that there'd been any problems. As Jack described how Robert and Alfredo had been pursued and threatened and how they were having to hide for their own safety, Xavi betrayed no emotion. Finally he expressed concern at the situation, although in such an ambiguous way that Jack was uncertain whether it was for Robert or for himself. Why had he not been made aware that something was wrong? He said he wanted to meet them and would leave Garrucha immediately. He told Jack to wait just off the autopista at the junction with Nijar. Jack understood.

Before he left Rodalquilar, Jack rang Robert and told him of their conversation. He was surprised at how quickly Jack had got hold of him. He sought assurance that it would be safe to meet Xavi and to bring him to Robert. He agreed it would have to be, it was their best chance and he felt he could trust him. Jack then took off, following the same route as his friends but now he was only going as far as the Nijar junction so could take his time. Working out where Xavi would see him easiest on leaving the Autovia del Mediterraneo, he pulled up at the side of the road in a safe place. The heat was still intense and he had to leave his engine on to prevent frying. Just as he sat back his mobile rang.

"Nicole! What a lovely surprise, how are you?"

"Sorry, love…can't hear you very well. No, still can't. You're breaking up…the reception's awful."

Then the line went dead. About a minute later she rang again but it was no better. Jack messaged her, explaining he was in the middle of the desert and clearly the signal wasn't good. He'd call her later. Five minutes after, she replied saying she needed to speak to him and would try again shortly. Jack let out a sigh, muttered a few expletives, cursed the timing and flopped back into his seat.

Further west along the autopista, in a village north east of Almeria, the red Seat is parked down a side street close to the centre. The intrepid trio have found their way quietly to Cafeteria la Tana, a smart modern establishment. Its big windows are perfect to look out onto the street but equally perfect for people to see in, so they take a table set back under an arch where they can have a reasonable view without being too conspicuous. A pot of tea for Robert and coffees for the siblings, the lads actually find this a rare treat after the past twenty four hours.

"It must have a been a bit hectic for you two" Beatriz acknowledges. "I imagine it was quite scary at times?"

"Well" said Robert, "it hasn't been short of excitement, has it, Alf? Stopped by the police and examined by sniffer dogs, beautiful dinner at the seafront, a night in a holiday apartment, hung on to the back of Valentino Rossi here as he attempted a new world record for the San José to Playa de Monsul dirt track, chased across the beach by Joe Pesci and the Incredible Hulk, return journey to San José buried under bags of rubbish, then a picnic in an abandoned hovel. Eventful? It's been a rollercoaster of sweat and soiled clothes. But we've loved every minute, haven't we, Alf?"

"Oh yes, every minute. Just like I'm going to love every second of the hot shower that I've been dreaming of."

Beatriz nodded with a grimace.

"Yes, I understand a little more now. And if we have to take you to Granada to stay overnight, we can maybe buy you some new clothes."

"Yes, sorry," said Robert, "we must be a bit nasty by now."

"Hold on" said Beatriz, "look across the road. On the corner there…it's one of the guys from San José. You know, one of the men I had to distract for Jack to get the car."

He was on the phone too. Most likely ringing others to say he'd found them. How had he got there? They quickly figured they must have been followed.

Having barely touched their drinks, they asked if there was a back way out. There wasn't. Leaving a note to cover their bill they waited until their stalker was out of the picture and chanced it. Once onto the street they moved quickly along in front of the cafe's white walls and yellow sign, crouching down behind parked vehicles to the bemusement of shoppers then heading up the road towards the car. As they walked, Beatriz picked up a message from Jack to say he was waiting for Xavi who was meeting him near Nijar. At least that was good news. They each had a quick look around them before jumping into the car. Beatriz handed her phone to Robert and suggested he reply while she drove.

"Where shall we go?" she said urgently.

"Let's just get back onto the A-92 and head north for Granada. I'll think of somewhere."

They drove up to the junction and swiftly pulled out, hoping that they hadn't been seen. Yet even as they spoke, the second of the men from San José stood hiding in a doorway watching their departure.

They soon hit the motorway, Alfredo looking out of the rear window as they accelerated away, trying to see if there was anyone trailing them. Initially it looked good but after a kilometre or so, a black Renault emerged at some speed before settling to an even distance a couple of hundred metres back.

"There's two men in the front" said Alfredo. "They're just keeping pace with us now."

"That'll be them alright. Damn!" said Robert. "Keep going Beatriz and I'll tell you when to get off."

"OK - just give me a bit of warning which junction."

"Yeah, sure" said Robert. "I know it's asking a bit much but if you could be in the fast lane as we come up to the junction and work it so you can shoot across the inside lane to leave the autopista at the very last moment that would be wonderful."

Beatriz shot him a look, raised her eyebrows and blew her cheeks out a little. Passing a sign for destinations ahead, Robert had an idea.

"OK. Next destination we're off. Less than a thousand metres."

The reluctant getaway driver took a deep breath, put her foot down and moved out to the overtaking lane. Robert looked across and saw a focused determination etched on her face. With the junction looming in sight she slowed alongside a couple of vehicles. Thinking about making a suggestion, Robert thought better of it and kept his mouth shut. Abruptly Beatriz slammed her foot on the accelerator pedal and moved past the lorry and the car inside her. Leaving it as late as possible she lurched right, straight across the inside lane, no indication. Horns blared, lights flashed. The red Seat carried on down the slip road, braking urgently as they came towards the give way sign at the roundabout. Behind them, adding to the irritation of motorists left in their wake, the black Renault, stuck in the outside lane, caused havoc as it braked hard then cut up a queue of vehicles in the inside lane.

"Go left here and back under the autopista" Robert said suddenly, as if it were a spur of the moment decision.

There are roundabouts off each side of the autopista, forming a figure of eight below the road.

"Are we going back down the same way?" Alfredo asked, as Beatriz eased the car out onto the roundabout and into the inside lane.

"No. I just want to confuse them."

"They're just about to pull out, look" Alfredo says, straining over his shoulder to watch the other car.

"Great. Take your time, Beatriz - slowly round the next island and come back on yourself again and under the autopista. Then head off for Oasys at the first island."

"The Mini-Hollywood theme park?" Alfredo seems surprised.

"That's the one. There'll be people around and we can find somewhere to hide. Let's hope Xavi can have some positive influence when he gets to Jack. Hey, Beatriz, go back round the island…take your time."

They turn off the island to head back under the A-92 running overhead. Robert has another spur of the moment idea and tells Alf to duck down with him. As the two cars approach each other along this stretch it appears to the two pursuers that Beatriz is on her own in the Seat Leon. They both peer at her across the central reservation between the routes. She smiles and blows a kiss at them. They don't look at all impressed while she thinks to herself 'why did I do that?'

—

It was May 1965 when the great film director Sergio Leone started work on 'For A Few Dollars More', a sequel to the original spaghetti western, 'A Fistful of Dollars'. Building a huge set on 40,000 square metres of land near Tabernas, he created an authentic wild west town. Despite being used for many more films it fell into dilapidation in the 1970s. Then, in 1980, it was rebuilt and rebranded as Mini-Hollywood, recreating shoot-outs and saloon bar can-can dances for the entertainment of tourists. Now more of a theme park it's known as Parque Oasys. And that's the name on the sign at the exit that Beatriz aims for as she accelerates off the island. More unhappy drivers but hey…they're away.

"Well done, Beatriz" says Robert, "brilliant driving. Just a shame this car's bright red, isn't it? I'd love to know what they're thinking. Especially if they're wondering where we are, Alf."

Luckily the road is relatively clear on their side, but there's a lot of traffic coming the other way. They figure it's tourists leaving the park, all shot out and completely can-canned. Alfredo asks what time it shuts. Robert doesn't know. He assumed it would be open late but now he's worried.

—

Over near Nijar, just off the Autovia, Jack has had a hard time from his daughter. On a badly distorted line he's tried to hold a conversation with her, despite being cut off several times. Trying to explain why it's difficult to talk was not exactly straightforward either. It feels like they've had a series of miscommunications and her frustration was palpable. And now she's under the misapprehension that her father is on the run from hitmen in the middle of the desert following his friend's bungled banana delivery. Just as if! When his phone rings again he's relieved to hear it's Robert.

"Any news for us, mate?"

"Still waiting" said Jack, "but he should be here soon. Oh…hang on. This could be him on the slip road. Yeah, I think this might be Xavi. He's just pulled off."

"Lucky old Xavi! That sounds like him. Listen, we're under pressure here, they're on our tail. Get back to me as soon as you can."

"Right. Will do. Hang in there, mate."

Xavi gets out of the car and Jack does likewise. Strolling over in a blue open necked shirt and beige chinos, his sleeves rolled up, he extends a hand and a curt greeting. There's another man with him, a short rotund figure who appears to be grinning. This must be Luiz, he reasons, recalling Robert's description. He wants to know how much Jack knows about this business and asks him to start at the beginning. Jack obliges, setting out what he understood the purpose of the mission to be - to buy a consignment of bananas in Madrid and deliver them locally, to whom he has no idea. When he's finished, he goes back as instructed by Robert to emphasise what happened at the market - that the man who Xavi had told him to contact was not there and wasn't answering his phone. They told him at the market that he was off sick. So did something go wrong with him? Were the consignments changed? Robert bought and delivered exactly what he'd been asked to.

Xavi makes no comment initially. Why is Luiz still grinning? After thinking carefully he takes out his mobile and proceeds to make a call. There's no reply. He tries another number. This time he speaks to someone, in Spanish and quickly, so Jack's none the wiser.

"OK, amigo. The man who works at the Mercamadrid, he is not answering. But my friend says there has been some problems there. What has happened? He does not know. He understands that right now it is very difficult there to talk to people because they have a lot of pressure from the police after the situation involving the supermarket. Maybe you have seen this on the news?"

Jack nods. He has.

Xavi then asks him questions about what has been happening today. Could he describe the men? Of course not, Jack hasn't seen any of them - he mentions seeing two men when he picked up Robert's car, but from a distance and his descriptions don't ring any bells. He makes sure to remind him that they continue to be pursued and only a few minutes back Robert sounded like he was anxious about their position. Xavi wants to make some more calls.

—

"Are you sure this is a good idea?" asks Beatriz.

"Too late now" Robert answers.

Approaching the car park there's just a couple of vehicles. The gates are still open.

"Keep going! Leave the car round the side there,

between those industrial units or whatever they are" he says, pointing at one of the tracks running between several long structures.

All the time Alf is looking out through the back window. They've done well to put some distance between them and their pursuers but they know it's only a matter of time before they turn up like a bad penny. They leave the car and make a bolt round the back of the buildings. Scampering across some rough scrubland they head for the gates. Once through, they can see a few people clearing up. It looked very much like they were closing down for the day.

"Let's hide over there" says Robert.

"But what if we get locked in?" Beatriz reasons.

"As long as they're locked out, that's fine. I'm sure there'll be a way out. We've got to stay safe. Come on!"

They nip down the main path, past the First City Bank on their right and the Casino, before taking refuge behind some foliage. They huddle behind it where they can see the gates and anyone entering the park, but where they're reasonably well hidden. For the next few minutes they have to imagine what's going on. Voices, the sound of distant discussions, laughter and the occasional calling of names. Doors closing, gates banging. The odd person walks by on the path, unable to see them. Then apart from the occasional car going by there's an eery silence about the park.

"Right" says Robert, "we better move. "If they come through the gates, or over them now they're shut, we've got nowhere to go from here. Let's go see what's round the corner."

"Nicole! Can you hear me alright?"

She could. Why was it so difficult to speak to him, she wanted to know. She'd spent so long trying to get through. He'd been engaged, poor signal, inopportune moments. What was going on for goodness sake? Jack tried to explain that he was in the middle of something important for his friend and apologised. It sounded very much like she was annoyed and her frustration grew when her father told her he was still driving and didn't have a hands-free facility. No, he couldn't very well pull over as he was following someone. He would definitely call her later.

"Oh Dad! For goodness sake, I'm not impressed at all and we need to know if you're going to be back to see Mom. There's so…"

"I'm coming back so don't worry. And I'll call you later…I promise. Just bear with me please."

He hated people who drive with their mobile stuck to their ear so it was a relief to put it down and focus on the job of keeping up with Xavi.

Following the buildings round in Oasys, the threesome continued their quest to remain elusive and reached what appeared a central point in the street, with wooden stairs immediately in front of them running up the side of the building and leading to a first floor balcony. Alfredo went up to see if he could secure a better vantage point. It felt a bit strange to be up there, surveying a wild west town in silence, surely it should have been in black and white?

"What was that?" said Alfredo.

"What was what?" Beatriz replied.

They looked up to Alfredo, who moved along the balcony quietly to try to find a better view. There was some movement by the gates. Two men. He couldn't see who they were. There was another just appearing over the top of the gates. They were coming their way. Without making a sound Alfredo gesticulated frantically for them to move quickly. Robert looked out into the middle of the make-believe town. He beckoned them to move round the front of the place where they'd been lying low. Looking up they saw it was the Saloon, above it the wooden balcony ran round the whole establishment and at the top of the brick-faced facade in large capital letters was its name, The Yellow Rose. Just then they saw someone walk into view at the top of the street.

"Come on" said Robert. "They must be covering both sides, we'll have to stay here."

"Better upstairs?" said Beatriz.

They walked round swiftly and up the stairs as quietly as they could. The evening sun was still strong and they'd have nowhere to go after this. They lay low, literally lying on the floor of the balcony where they hoped they couldn't be spotted. They heard voices below them, out front of the saloon. Whilst they spoke as quietly as they could, their words were nevertheless audible in the silence of the empty town. They were splitting up…taking separate areas. Up on the balcony the heat and the tension combined to make it increasingly uncomfortable. All that was missing was the mournful tone of a church bell and a plaintive harmonica wail. Then footsteps could be heard, like someone ascending stairs. They weren't close though. Robert tilted his head round and knew that their game was almost up. He saw a man reaching the top of the stairs at a building across the street known as the Meat Market. He'd be able to see them. 'Damn!' he thought 'why hadn't we spotted that?' Within seconds of reaching the top he'd seen them and called out to his colleagues.

As four men advanced on The Yellow Rose, Alfredo, positioned on the side of the saloon, was up first and away down the stairs. Looking around him on the ground, he headed down the street that they'd initially taken, back towards the gates. Beatriz was looking certain to be caught by the two young men who'd expected to be meeting her for dinner later when Robert leapt out from the foot of the stairs brandishing a wooden pole he'd picked up on his way down. Challenging them both he allowed her to flee. Alf was keeping close to the walls of the buildings in the block. Beatriz got round the corner and saw a large barrel - there were many of them lying around in a western town. She pulled out the lid, looked around her quickly, then climbed inside closing the lid behind her. Robert meanwhile danced round his would-be captors wearing the look of a crazed fanatic and gripping the pole with both hands as he moved it about as threateningly as he could. In truth he resembled someone on a day out who'd managed to shake off his carer. After he'd grunted and awkwardly thrown wild shapes with his baton for a minute or so, the one with the hooked nose took out a knife. Breathless by now, Robert dropped the pole.

"Alright" he said, "I've seen that film too."

The older, smaller man from the beach arrived and admonished his young colleague.

"Hey, put that away" he ordered. Then, looking straight at Robert, "But be under no illusion, my friend, we will use force if you don't co-operate. Understand?"

Robert nodded.

"Take him over there" he said to the other two. "Keep him by the hangman's noose, to focus his mind. And make a better job of it than you did looking after his car! We'll soon find the other two."

The hangman's noose was just outside the Meat

Market and Robert walked slowly across. Round the back of The Yellow Rose, Beatriz was sweltering inside the barrel. The big fellow was mooching around and she heard the footsteps. She felt some momentary movement in the barrel, then noticed that one of the small holes punched into its side - bullet holes, perhaps - was no longer letting light through. She figured he must be leaning against the barrel. He thought the barrel seemed heavy not to have moved more when he leaned against it. Turning round he looked through the small hole in the lid but couldn't see anything. He crouched down to look through a hole in the side, firstly from about 30 cm back, then by putting his eye to the hole.

"Aaaaargh!" he squealed and staggered back as Beatriz poked him in the eye with her front door key.

She burst out of the barrel clutching the wooden lid, clambered out and, as 'big but dim' clutched his eye, she thwacked him over the head. Unsighted with head down and legs akimbo, she followed up by giving him an almighty kick between his legs. More agony as he crumpled to his knees with his testicles quite possibly lodged somewhere between his ribs. The groans must have been heard in Morocco. Unfortunately his mates were a little closer and were soon on the scene. She tried to flee but found herself trapped and face to face with her evening dinner dates. Beatriz stood defiantly in front of them.

"So. Now what?"

"Looks like you have some hidden talents" said hook nose.

The fair one looked back at the big lump who was still doubled up and squinting. He couldn't help sniggering but merely attracted a stern look from his partner.

"Walk! Let's put you with the other one. One more to go…"

Alfredo had been able to move past the Casino and had advanced to the far end of the First City Bank. There was a cactus in front of a fence which, if he could get behind it, would shield him from view from the main street and enable him to reach the other side of the town. It looked all clear so he made a dash for it. Keeping close to the buildings and fences he was soon peering out into the main street from behind a wall. Robert appeared to be handcuffed and was sat on the steps that lead to the hanging platform. There was no sign of Beatriz. The top man had his back to Alfredo so he stealthily set off across the street. That done, he carried on round the back of the next block until he found himself at the rear of the Meat Market and an access to the first floor balcony. Slowly and quietly he scaled the steps, pausing at the top to hide behind the wall, from where he could sneak a look at what was happening. He heard voices…they'd got Beatriz. She was made to sit higher up the stairs so she was behind Robert.

"Where's Mario?" asked the boss.

They explained that he'd been injured by the woman.

"What?"

He was incredulous. Not so super Mario. Alf clenched his fist and grinned like they'd scored a minor victory. The big man then came into picture, hobbling along with his legs at an uncomfortable angle, still squinting. The boss just stared at him, shaking his head slowly.

"Where's the other one?"

The young men shrugged, gesticulated a bit and mumbled something. Their leader was unimpressed.

"You" he said, pointing at the fair one, "go find him!"

"Now, señor…it's time we talked."

"Fine" said Robert, "what do you want to talk about?"

"Let's go straight to the big question. You were supposed to deliver something and you failed to do so. Who has the goods we paid for?"

"What? Are you serious? I was contracted to buy bananas from Mercamadrid. I was told to buy specific cases and that's exactly what I did. I don't know what else you were expecting but I have never had any knowledge of that. Oh, and so far, I've only been paid in part for the job."

"And you expect me to believe that?"

"Well, that's the truth. I came back with what I was asked to. Perhaps you could tell me exactly what it is that I didn't bring? Because I don't know what you're talking about, mate."

Boss man's expression changed instantly and he looked a little more serious, a little less the chilled master of ceremonies holding all the aces. He walked around in a circle, looking down at the ground, then turned to face Robert.

"I think you know what I'm referring to. Just tell me where it is, who has it…and all this will be finished…once I get it back."

He was smiling cynically again.

"I was given clear instructions. I followed them to the letter. You've received exactly what you asked me to buy and bring back. My instructions came from Xavi - have you asked him about what went wrong with his arrangements?"

Boss man laughed.

"Oh please, señor! This has gone well past Xavi. I will deal with this. And if I don't have co-operation from you soon I will have to deal with you too."

He was now starting to show some irritation. It had

become evident that when his mood deepened and he was struggling to contain his anger or frustration, his left eye began to twitch, almost as if he was winking. Another circle, this time anti-clockwise, saw him looking at Beatriz just as his tick kicked in. She smiled and winked back at him…which made him worse. After some deep breathing he returned his gaze to Robert.

"Now, my friend, I would like to conclude this situation. We've come a long way."

"Depends whether you're talking distance or evolution" said Robert. Then looking across at super Mario nursing his groaning gonads he added "'Cos if it's evolution, he ain't come far, has he?"

Feeling a little piqued by Robert's mockery, he returned fire.

"Very soon we shall also have your young friend, your assistant…another buffoon no doubt."

"He's not a buffoon" Beatriz piped up.

"If he's working for this clown then I'm afraid he must be! Ha! He, he he…"

He seemed very pleased with his logic and his humour.

Just then his other two junior henchmen came round the corner and he stopped them some metres away by raising his hand.

"Woah! Where is he?"

"We can't find him, El Perrito."

"El Perrito?" cried Beatriz, incredulous. "You are called 'The Doggy'? Seriously?"

"I don't like to ask why you're called El Perrito, but…no, perhaps we shouldn't go there, Beatriz. Bloody hell" said Robert, laughing. "The Doggy!"

"Shut up!" said El Perrito.

"No, it's just that, you know…here we are on the film set where they made A Few Dollars More and I'm thinking of you as The Man With No Name. But you're not. You're The Man Named After An Animal."

"It's my nickname!" he erupted and promptly broke into a series of rapid fire winks leading Beatriz to wink back again.

Now breathing heavily and struggling to contain his ire, he shouted at his two men with incandescent rage.

"Find them you fools!"

They looked at each other but embarrassment quickly turned to confusion with a loud rumbling noise that seemed to come from above. They all looked around in panic but by the time the two men saw the wooden barrel rolling down the stairs at them they just had time to jump as they were comprehensively skittled. Lying in the dusty street they slowly picked themselves up and, as they realised this could only be the work of the missing accomplice, their distress turned to mortification.

"There you go" said Robert. "Are you sure he's not in the barrel, then?"

"You'll check, won't you, Mario?" Beatriz chimed in. "You're good with barrels, aren't you?"

El Perrito began to twitch yet again.

"You see, El Perrito, my friend's got the stupid idea that you were laughing at him."

Then Robert directed himself at the two dust-covered failures by the barrel.

"You boys may just have been having a laugh, but he doesn't know that. He's riled 'cause he thought you were laughing at him."

The big bruised bruiser Mario starts to shuffle off round the side of the Meat Market building while his two partners in ineptitude dust themselves down and walk crestfallen around the other side. Robert shakes his head and smiles.

"He's great, isn't he, old Mario?" he says. "He's like a Greek statue…only with less flexibility."

Beatriz is amused even if El Perrito isn't, his face betraying the fact that he's trying desperately to keep his twitch under control and regain his authority. Alfredo may have struck a blow against their opponents in an entertaining fashion but he's rather given himself away somewhat in the process. As he speeds down the back steps he runs into the lumpen figure of Mario near the bottom. Exercising a body swerve worthy of Lionel Messi he feints to go left then weaves to his right, leaving him floundering, only to run straight into Dumb and Dumber. The game's up for Alf and they drag him unceremoniously back to El Perrito.

"At last" says the man with the canine moniker.

"You probably think you're in a good position now" said Robert. "But you're not. But at least we now know what your favourite position is, El Perrito, don't we?"

Alfredo tries to wriggle and is dumped on the floor for his troubles. Despite protests from their captives, there's no repentance.

El Perrito decides he wants them lined up together, so Robert is unfastened and one by one they're taken over to the sheriff's office and tethered to the hitching rail used for horses. After walking up and down a few times the boss starts his questioning again. Robert sticks to his guns and continues to challenge him about the arrangements. He urges him to check out the contact person, Señor Nunez, who had gone off sick on the day of the exercise. Surely that was no coincidence? He's still not impressed and threats are made. As it looks like things could become a little sticky they hear some noises coming from the area around the main gates. The young guys head off to see what it is. As they reach the side of The Yellow Rose saloon they see two men rushing towards them with a short dumpy one shuffling ten metres behind them.

"Where's your boss, El Perrito?" demanded Xavi.

"Who are you?" said hook nose.

"I'm Xavi and I need to see him now."

Jack is given confidence by Xavi's authority and general demeanour, although the presence of Luiz will merely add to the ranks of those unlikely to trouble Mensa. El Perrito beckons to his charges to let them through.

"So you're El Perrito? I'm Xavi, I'm the one who set up this deal. What's going on? Why do you have a problem with these people?"

"Why? Because they've only delivered half of what we wanted and paid them for and not even the most valuable half."

"Did you check the numbers on the boxes that the bananas came in?"

"Of course."

"And they were the ones we asked him to buy?"

"Yes, but they've double-crossed us. The product we wanted has, in my opinion, been disposed of and this man is pretending that he knows nothing about it. He claims the police opened the boxes but I'm not falling for that. We've never had a problem before and now we change to use this man, it all goes wrong. Then again" he says, "I think you are new too in this process. Maybe you're the one who has messed up, eh?"

Xavi shakes his head and walks closer to El Perrito.

"Have you been in contact with Nunez at Mercamadrid?"

"Nunez? No, I haven't spoken with him."

"Well if you'd tried to find out what had happened from Nunez himself you'd find that he's not been at work. On the day these boys turned up to buy, Nunez was not there, they thought he was sick. But let me tell you, El Perrito, he's still not there. He's not been home and he's not answering his telephone."

El Perrito looks confused. Xavi gestures for him to move away from everyone else to talk in confidence. He gives him the name of a shared contact in Madrid and suggests he ring him to check out the facts. He promises him it will be confirmed. He makes the call. It's brief. He now knows that Xavi was right about Nunez. And so was Robert. He looks very unhappy.

"I will leave them to you" said El Perrito. "This is all very frustrating. What about the parcels? Who has got them?"

"Don't know. We need to find out. Madrid better have some answers, hey?"

El Perrito walks over towards his team, his tail between his legs, so to speak.

"Let's go. It's finished."

"What about the drugs, boss?" said Mario, still walking with the gait of a man who's had an accident.

"I said let's go!" he bawled, and they followed.

Xavi and Luiz untied the captives, who expressed considerable appreciation for their release.

"I'm sorry this happened" said Xavi. "It shouldn't have done. You fulfilled your job and I will see that you are paid the outstanding amount."

"Fantastic" said Robert. "This has been one helluva long day."

"OK, now let's see if we can get out of this place"

Xavi said, leading them back towards the gates.

Ahead of them the four crooks were just approaching the gates. They stopped in their tracks as a few clunks were followed by the gates opening to reveal a semi-circle of armed police, stood in front of about eight vehicles. A few of them advanced as the men were searched and disarmed. It was surprise enough to see this happening, let alone to see how well armed their captors had been.

"Oh my God!" said Robert in disbelief. "I mean, I knew they had a knife, but…"

Not only could Jack, Beatriz, Robert and Alfredo not properly take this in, they had no comprehension as to what was happening and whether they themselves would be arrested next. Their mood was picked up by Xavi, who was reassuring and told them not to worry. For now, he said, he wanted them to go home and relax as soon as everyone was out of the way. This must have been a real ordeal for them and he would be in touch.

"But Xavi…all this time? Are you…" said Robert, as the situation started to become clearer to him.

"There's no time to explain now" said Xavi. "Later there will be time."

"Well, amigo" said Robert to Alf, "I think we should look for more jobs in fruit and vegetable distribution. It's quite exciting, isn't it?"

Coming out of the shower Alfredo picked up his phone to see a text from Robert. 'Got us a table at La Candela. See you in fifteen so get a jog on.' He read it out to Beatriz, who asked him what the last part meant. He said he thought it meant they'd better hurry. As he rushed to get dressed he was wishing he hadn't let her go first in the bathroom. Over the other side of town Robert had gone beyond relief and was feeling very chipper. As he and Jack walked out the door he sent another text to his mate. 'Just leaving Casa de Roberto.'

Robert's rough charm and pigeon Spanish appeared to serve him well locally and he'd managed to blag a table outside on the terrace. Perfect for a warm, balmy evening. There were hugs all round when Beatriz and Alfredo arrived with everyone declaring themselves to be starving. Drinks were ordered, food chosen and they sat back to wait. A toast was made to 'freedom', then 'the rescuers', to 'business partners', even 'bananas'…It was a giggly start to the evening. Then, just as the food started to arrive, Robert's phone rang.

"It's Xavi…excuse me a minute, guys."

He walked away from the table to find a quieter spot. Xavi told him that this whole episode had been part of a wider police operation and he apologised that essentially it'd been necessary to use Robert as part of a big police sting. He couldn't say anything about other exercises that were part of the strategy, but he did concede that they were behind the switching of the drugs to a supermarket in order to send a message to drug runners and the public alike. Best of all, he assured Robert that he would be paid the additional money to ensure that their bargain was fulfilled. Finally he cautioned him to be more careful in the future. When he was asked if he realised that the delivery would contain illegal substances when he agreed to undertake the job, Robert said he hadn't explicitly understood that, but it had crossed his mind as it had been a bit cloak and dagger. That was the correct answer according to Xavi. He told Robert that he may be required to come in to speak to detectives and answer questions to help with their investigations and otherwise wished him a quiet and relaxed weekend.

On return to the table he shared the revelations with his chums as they tucked into their food.

"Are you sure you didn't know what was in the bananas?" asked Beatriz, like a concerned yet dubious parent.

"No! Of course not" he replied, somewhat artfully. "Just my luck. I find myself an opportunity to make some money from a simple-looking exercise and it turns out to be part of an undercover police operation. Story of my life!"

The food was good, the atmosphere lively and the company convivial. From their colourful table on the terrace, with its brightly patterned cushions, they could look across the square, the lights of Mojacar twinkling against the town's white walls. As they ploughed through their food it was inevitable that conversation would keep returning to the boy's adventures. Robert insisted that his buttocks would never be the same again after riding pillion behind Alf, who protested about how difficult it had been to retain control of the steering with him on the back, not to mention his intermittent yelps of pain.

"It wasn't all pain" said Robert, "some of it was fear. I kept my eyes shut most of the time 'cause every time I opened them I screamed."

Of course, the chase on the beach was recalled with much glee, Robert exaggerating every possible detail. If only someone on the beach had filmed it there'd be every chance it would go viral, they were convinced. When Jack wanted to know how on earth he'd come up with such an idea under so much pressure, Robert admitted he was inspired by the scene in Indiana Jones and the Last Crusade where Indy's Dad brings down the Nazi fighter plane, which was actually filmed on that very beach.

"Who was the slowest" asked Jack, "Robert or big Mario?"

"There was not much in it" said Alf. "But Robert was just quicker I think because Mario didn't know where he was going and Robert was scared out of his wits."

"He didn't know what day it was most of the time" added Robert.

They wanted to know what had happened between Mario and Beatriz. Her blow-by-blow account met with laughter and cheering with a round of applause at the end on hearing exactly why he was walking so strangely when he reappeared. That was the cue for Jack to heap praise on her for her brilliant performance in distracting the two men monitoring the car in San José.

"I peeped round the corner when I heard the voices and there were these two young men being addressed by this flirtatious seductress! It was fully deserving of an Oscar nomination. They were so powerless against her that I almost felt sorry for these guys."

Beatriz insisted he was going over the top but she was rather pleased that she'd so impressed him. Another toast, this time to Beatriz. And Alf reminded Robert to show them his selfie whilst the police searched the van.

When Robert asked Jack how he'd got on with his daughter, shortly before the end of the evening, his response provided the only dampener on their night out. With some difficulty, he explained. The timing of her calls and lack of a decent signal had made communication tough and so conversation had been fraught. Explaining that he'd been caught up in a drugs heist and was being chased across the desert by bandits hadn't helped - she'd told him in no uncertain terms this was no time for messing about. At least he'd reassured her that he would be returning so that he could visit his ex-wife in hospital and maybe see what he could to to help. The glum expressions were tempered by an understanding that this was the right thing to do and certainly this appeared to have been expected by his offspring. He understood she'd be having the operation on Friday some time so he was planning to take a flight from Almeria early on Friday morning. Urged on by all three, he agreed that he'd have to return to Mojacar at some stage to see them. He said he'd miss them, as everyone does on such occasions, but he genuinely meant it. Nevertheless, would he really return?

Chapter Thirteen

Saturday 30 June 2018

Saturday morning started slowly and quietly. Beatriz and her brother were up first and shared plans over breakfast, including lunch back at home with their family on Sunday. Robert, however, stayed in bed. He was shattered. Jack brought tea up to his bedroom and sat on the end of the bed. He told him he was going to do a little bit of shopping in town before meeting Beatriz for a coffee and asked if there's anything Robert needed. He mumbled then asked if there was any chance of a blood transfusion. Jack decided he'd leave him to rest.

Taking Robert's car, Jack popped down to the modern shopping precinct at the end of the Avenida del Palacio, before driving along the coast road to the café. He'd miss the beach, he thought, and especially the beautiful bright blue sky, which lifted him every morning. It's better than coffee, he reasoned, but second to Beatriz. Confirmation of this comes the moment he claps eyes on her, sat at a table outside. A crisp white short-sleeved blouse, pink chinos, red flat shoes, shades, that ebony hair tied back. And her smile, even though she's not feeling entirely at her best this morning. Kiss on each cheek, embrace, breathe in scent…breathe out, let her go. They compare notes on their sleep and the state of Robert and Alfredo respectively. Coffees are ordered, along with some pie of course for Jack.

"So…" Beatriz opened. "You're going back on Friday?"

Jack simply nods in a resigned fashion.

"Well, I'll be back at work in Granada on Monday and you'll be gone when I come back for the weekend, so I wonder if you would like to come to have lunch tomorrow with my parents? Alfredo will be there and Robert can come too. Mama especially has asked frequently about you and Robert as he has been working with Alf, so I knew they'd like to meet you both. She is quite excited!"

"Yes! Yes, of course, that would be great. I'll ask Robert as soon as I get back."

"Oh good, Mama will be so pleased. I will warn you now, you will have plenty to eat and drink…you won't need to eat until you return to England!"

"Wow. Sounds terrific. It'll be great to see another part of the region too while I'm here" said Jack.

What was really more important to him was that this would be like bonus time with Beatriz. When she asked him whether he'd had any more thoughts about the future, he still hadn't a clue, attracted by the promise and potential of a new beginning and a different life, not to mention her, yet inclined to be a little afraid of making such a change. Beatriz told him she'd miss him once he'd returned to England.

"I feel like we've become really good friends since we met. Like we've known each other a long time, but it's what…two weeks? It's not like me. As I said in Granada, before I drank too much…" she giggled at recalling the evening, "I've kept my distance from people since my marriage didn't work and particularly with men."

"I suppose we should be grateful to your brother. It made you so angry at the time!"

"Yes, I was, he was so stupid! But now? I'm glad he was so stupid."

"And you didn't have to take me out to reward me, I was just doing what I thought was the right thing."

"It was quite courageous of me I think, looking back. You might have been a serial killer or something."

"No, I haven't got the eyebrows."

Jack smiled and leaned forward, his elbows on the edge of the table and his hands clasped. He looked up at her.

"Well, at least you know now I'm not! I should also say thank you properly for Granada. It was an abrupt end when we had to rush back. But such a magical time. The Alhambra and two lovely nights out with you, it was just... well." He shrugged his shoulders then added, "You're a great tour guide too!"

"You'll come back to see me one day, won't you?"

"Oh, absolutely. I will. But first I just need to..."

"I know."

Driving back to Mojacar Pueblo, Jack promised himself some quality beach time before he went back. He picked up the bags from the car's boot and went into the house. Dropping the bags in the kitchen, he saw that nothing had moved since he left and reckoned Robert must still be in bed. He thought he'd had long enough, it was going on for midday.

"Rise and shine Mr Sleepy!" he called as he pushed open the door.

There was a bit of commotion under the duvet as not one, but two heads surfaced.

"Oh my God. Err...sorry boys...what..? Do you

want to tell me something?"

Jack was stunned. Robert and Alfredo looked at each other. Equally stunned. Alf shrugged his shoulders and held out his hands, palms up, like he didn't fully comprehend how this had come about himself. Robert attempted to answer twice but words failed him. Then finally, he dragged his considerable frame from under the duvet and sat upright, adjusting his pillow behind him to buy a bit of time.

"We must have fallen asleep" Robert started. "Look mate, I guess me and Alf have become quite close over the past few days."

"Quite close? That's probably an understatement. How long have you been…"

"Well, we haven't…you know. It's just happened this morning. Alf came round to see me, see how I was after everything, and we started thinking over the things that have happened and how we got on so well and, well, it just happened. Spontaneous it was. Straight up, mate."

Jack's eyebrows arched. Robert grimaced slightly.

"You know how I meant it."

"I'll let you sort yourselves out and we can have a drink when you come down."

"Aye, alright. Good idea."

Jack smiled at them and shook his head.

"Well, well, I wasn't expecting that!"

Around the table it was quiet to start with - not frosty, just a touch subdued. Jack took the bottle opener to three San Miguels from the fridge.

"So this isn't going to affect your working partnership I trust?"

"Look, come on, Jack. This has just happened, it wasn't planned or anything." Robert glanced across at Alfredo and continued. "We feel quite close and, I mean, it's not like either of us has been in great demand, has it? You know…you didn't see a queue outside the door this morning, did you?"

"No" said Alfredo, shaking his head.

"So I guess we'll just see what happens, see where it takes us."

Alfredo nodded his assent.

"He's still the boss."

"Here's to you pair then" said Jack, raising his bottle.

They all drank to that.

Jack then told them about Beatriz inviting them to lunch with her parents at Velez Rubio.

"What - me and all?" said Robert, startled. "Did you know about this?" he asked Alfredo.

"No, it's news to me. Did she invite you this morning, Jack?"

"Yes, just now while we were at the café."

She must have phoned her mother while he was out, he reckoned. Jack said he thought it'd be great fun for the four of them to be there and meet Mama and Papa.

"You're taking the piss, aren't you?" said Robert.

Jack laughed alright but insisted they should go. Besides, it would be rude not to. Robert started to come round to it but said on no account should they know about him and Alf, who was quick to add that his sister shouldn't know just yet either.

"OK" agreed Jack. "But after a few drinks, ooh, tricky… well, I'll do my best."

"You say a bloody word, mate…"

Chapter Fourteen

Sunday 1 July 2018

"That's that then" mutters Jack at the kitchen table as he closes down his iPad. "My ticket's booked, I'll have to go home now."

"Break it to me gently then. What unearthly time have I got to be up to get you to the airport?"

"Ah, it's not that bad actually. I'll buy you breakfast there. Anyway, we'd better make ourselves look presentable, we haven't got long."

Just before 12:30 they strolled down the road to wait for their taxi. Jack clutched a colourful bunch of flowers and Robert's bag contained a couple of bottles. Right on time, there was the red Seat Leon. Robert watched Jack's face.

"Hey. Are you sure you're not…you know?"

"What?"

"I just noticed your face, that's all, when you saw her. It was like someone had put new batteries in."

"Before I woke you two up yesterday I took a few photos…"

"Alright. Point taken."

They opened the doors and jumped into the back

seats. Pleasantries exchanged, Robert glanced over his shoulder.

"Now, Beatriz, are you sure there's nobody following us?"

The roads were predictably quiet and it was to be a relaxing journey, punctuated by the occasional knowing looks and glances between Jack and Robert whenever the subject of the banana boys' future partnership came up. So far so good as they approached the outskirts of Velez Rubio. They drove past what was referred to as the Grand Entrance to the town, with its letters separately standing large before an arch. Beatriz made a point of taking them past the Iglesia de la Encarnacion, a national Historic Monument built in the 18th century.

The childhood home of Beatriz and Alfredo turns out to be an old stone-built house at the end of a road on the edge of town. Alfredo whizzed inside to alert Mama and Papa, who rapidly emerged from the front door, the lady clearly excited and proud to be welcoming her guests and appearing to drag along the lord of the manor, typically playing it all down. The Spanish greetings went well for the boys although Jack for one hoped they'd speak English for the rest of the afternoon. It was all smiles and, as they entered the house, sat in the corner of the living room like Father Jack on valium was the old man.

"This is mi abuelito" said Beatriz, introducing her grandfather.

He held up his hand and, whether he really knew who the two men were, he was smiling. Or it could have been wind. They shook hands and were all ushered outside by Mama onto the terrace. But first, Jack insisted on presenting the flowers to her, which she'd artfully pretended not to notice but was delighted to receive, revelling in the attention.

Robert waited until they were outside to reveal his boozy offering, firstly placing the wine on the table, then quietly presenting a special bottle of beer to Papa. He looked mightily impressed and also appreciated the subtlety of the presentation, not usually one of Robert's strengths. The house was in a great position, occupying a vantage point that looked out across the valley. As they admired and discussed the view it was difficult not to be distracted by the aroma of barbecuing meat. Jack asked what was cooking and Beatriz showed him and Robert that it was a goat. Papa came over and explained that he'd rubbed its skin with harissa. As this North African paste is hot and spicy, he'd mixed it in with olive oil and some garlic. Whatever he'd done to it, they agreed it smelt divine.

Once everyone had a drink and a seat at the table, a variety of small plates were passed round with cheeses, hams, nuts and some thinly sliced aubergines baked in honey. With the exception of the nuts, the source of each food was announced - all people known to Beatriz and Alfredo and nothing seemed to have travelled beyond Velez to reach the table. Naturally, Mama and Papa wanted to know how they'd got on with their respective trips. Equally naturally, there was a lot of fudging and disguising of what actually happened, particularly on the part of Robert and Alfredo. Every chance they had to divert attention to the short break in Granada was duly taken.

"Did you go to see Flamenco?" demanded Papa.

"No" said Jack "but I'd love to see a good show sometime."

That turned out to be the right response.

"I do love to hear a good Flamenco guitarist" he added.

Beatriz rocked her head back and let out a groan.

"Ah! One minute..." said Papa, launching himself out of the chair.

It was Paco time.

The sun illuminated the mountains on either side of the valley while the guests sat back and sipped their chilled manzanillas and beers. As the calmly sorrowful strains of a Paco de Lucia rondena drifted over the terrace, his guitar eliciting a spectrum of singing tonalities, as the master virtuoso interacted with his instrument to draw space and silence into the equation, a chicken walked into Mama coming out of the kitchen and seven smashing soup bowls delivered an unexpected crescendo to the movement. It was all Jack and Robert could do to keep a straight face as a torrent of rapid fire Spanish invective blasted the poor hen, whose odds on appearing as the centrepiece for next Sunday's lunch increased dramatically. The men all gathered round to clear up. Eventually Mama laughed, which allowed others to join in. More bowls were found and caldo de huevos was announced, a local soup recipe made with eggs and garlic. Mopped up with piquito bread, it was delicious.

Papa then took centre stage, removing the goat from the spit, laying it on a very large metal tray before proceeding to expertly carve the meat, setting it out on a white oval dish. Mama began surrounding the meat with roasted tomatoes and roughly chopped onions. The dish was placed at the centre of the table. Around it were various salads and a couple of bean dishes.

"Carne de cabra!" announced Papa.

"To the chefs!" proposed Jack and Robert.

The meat was succulent and so, so tender. Robert asked if he could come again next week. The guests' Rioja was very good and Papa was smiling. After second helpings of goat had been carved, Mama brought up the beach incident and thanked Jack for his courage. Of course, he played it down, but Alfredo's parents were having none of it and regaled them with a few stories of drownings as if to emphasise how lucky they had been to have Jack there. Hearing it again simply reminded Alfredo how stupid he'd been and was something he could have done without.

"He has been spared" said Papa, before a long pause as he looked down at the table - was he exhibiting early signs of intoxication or had he forgotten that he'd not finished his sentence? Perhaps he had finished. No, finally he went on…

"He has been spared so that he can fulfil his destiny, to find a good woman to be his wife and to give him children."

'Oh hell' thought Jack.

"And a man with a family" he went on "cannot take the same risks with his life. He has the responsibility…the responsibility to take care of them…to provide a home and food on the table. Then he will take his place in the world…"

"And you will take these plates to the kitchen! Never mind babbling on about the boy."

He made a half-hearted attempt to protest at being cut off in what was hopefully some way off his prime, recognising not only that Mama had taken charge of the situation but that she hadn't drunk as much as he had. The rest of the family stood up and carted off the remaining debris from the table.

"What strength was that beer, Robert?"

"7.5% I think"

"Bloody hell, mate. Nice one."

"He didn't half enjoy it though."

"Sure he did. Just a pity he'll have no recollection of who gave it to him."

"Vino rosso!" cried abuelito from the shaded corner

of the table.

Jack and Robert looked at him. He was holding his glass up.

"D'you think we should pour him one?"

"Has he had one already?"

"His glass looks clean, so I don't think so. He's had a sherry."

"Vino rosso" he said again, this time banging his glass on the table three times.

Robert looked at Jack, shrugged his shoulders then picked up the red wine. It was the last of the second bottle. The old man said 'gracias' and slurped a mouthful, smacking his lips afterwards.

"Did that hit the spot then?" asked Robert.

He burped. He smiled. He went back to sleep.

After a few minutes Mama and Beatriz emerged from the kitchen with more food. Time for dessert.

"Pastel de almendras" said the matriarch, placing a stand on the table displaying a beautiful almond cake.

"And this is licores y donas de naranja" added her daughter, "liquor and orange donuts."

With taste buds already primed to the max, along came Papa with a plate of cheese, which he either felt needed no explanation or he'd worked out that while his mouth was shut he wasn't slurring his words or getting into trouble. That didn't work for long.

"Tell us what the cheeses are, Papa" said Beatriz.

"Oh…right" said Papa, slowly locating his powers of recall. "This one is Venta del Chaleco - the one you brought us, Beatriz, from Las Alpujarras in the Sierra Nevada. Next to it is Queso de Leyva, it's a hard cheese from Guadix. And here, this is Queso de Murcia. The rind is very deep red, almost purple, because it is soaked in wine for a time when it is maturing. Some call it wine cheese. It's softer and very creamy and I think you will like."

Fruit, nuts and fresh bread accompanied the cheeses and, of course, the desserts. Alf poured the boys a glass of 2014 Late Harvest Navarra. The low murmuring and facial expressions suggested they liked it. Followed of course by a few flamboyantly exaggerated descriptions. It was evident that lunch would last for a good while yet. They dug in, intent on doing justice to the efforts of Señora and simply reaching the end of the afternoon without bursting.

Late afternoon and coffee arrived. Strong coffee. It was probably what they needed. Predictably only Mama and Beatriz could be described as fully compos mentis. The gentlemen looked a little tired and the worse for wear, their wit and repartee was by now less than sparkling and Papa was yawning with a frequency that suggested a snooze was not far away. Abuelito, who was arguably not compos mentis to begin with, was not far away in body only. He'd been away with the fairies for nearly an hour, head back in the chair, mouth open, his every in-breath sounding like the sucking tube used by the dentist to keep your mouth dry. In the kitchen, dishes were loaded, glasses washed and some order returned.

Papa then emerged, beckoning the boys into the house. With a click of the remote, the screen displayed the World Cup hosts and rank outsiders Russia, lining up for the national anthems with their opponents, the highly rated Spain.

"La Furia Roja!" announced Papa proudly, a fist clenched in the air.

"Ah, yeah, 'the red fury'" Robert told Jack, "that's their nickname over here, mate.'

They all sat down to watch, everyone hoping for a

Spanish victory to send them into the last eight and ignite the hopes of the nation.

At half time, Beatriz asked Jack to 'let me show you the garden'. Despite Jack being fairly certain that he could see most of it from the chair where he was slumped, he took her hand and was hauled away. References to the foliage and the soil were soon dispensed with. She seemed very conscious of him returning and this being their last time together. Whilst there was some anxiety on her part about not seeing him again, he wasn't in the best shape to talk sensibly let alone seriously. Once again, he promised to keep in touch.

"But not just like a pen friend, you will come back again some time?"

"Yes" he replied. "I can't imagine not coming back here again. Never seeing you again. And I've got to come back to see Robert again, I've got that excuse, you know, I can't just…"

"You don't need an excuse! Life is short and time goes so quickly."

"I know, I know."

They put their arms around each other and clung tight. Jack was slightly wobbly.

"As soon as I'm back and I've caught up with my children, I'm going to make a plan."

She stepped back and held him at arms length. She looked intensely into his eyes.

"I'd like to be in your plan, Jack."

They embraced tightly again.

"Beatriz! Beatriz!" It was Mama calling.

"OK, Mama!" she called back. "It's not a great place to say goodbye."

"No. Not really. It's like we keep being cut off. First Granada, and even now, we can't be alone. I'll go back to the football, it'll at least keep your Papa happy!"

If it did make him happy, it didn't last. Finishing 1-1, the score remained the same through to the end of extra-time, before the unthinkable happened. It all hinged on the final penalty. Iago Aspas ran up for Spain to strike the ball left footed to the centre of the goal, the Russian keeper Igor Akinfeev dived to his right but swung his trailing left foot high to deflect the ball wide of the net and they were out! 'La Furia Roja' instantly became 'La Verguenza Roja'. The red embarrassment was no doubt felt more deeply by Papa and Alfredo for happening in the presence of two Englishmen. Jack tried to console them by proclaiming that 'we know what's it like to lose on penalties' but it didn't really help. He and Robert tried to remember the last time England had actually won a penalty shoot-out, then recalled that it was in the quarter final of the 1996 Euros…against Spain. They decided not to share this.

Some of them thought it was all over. It was now, as Beatriz appeared swinging her car keys and announcing that it was time to go. The handshakes, hugs and compliments commenced, promises were made. A good time had been had by all. The men were herded into the Seat and there was lots of waving as Beatriz drove off, expecting a reasonably quiet journey given the heavily sedated state of her passengers. Within twenty minutes or so both Robert and Alfredo had drifted off in the back seats. Jack was working hard to stay with it. This would be his last hour with Beatriz before returning home and he was talking to stay awake as much as anything. Ten minutes later his eyes had shut.

A roundabout approaching Mojacar caused Jack to stir, momentarily followed by the sleeping beauties in the rear. Into the centre of town and the car pulled over. Robert and Alfredo exchanged thoughts on meeting early in the week to talk about possible work opportunities. In the front, there were meaningful looks and brief hand-holding. It was difficult and a little awkward.

"Can I ring you in the week?" asked Jack.

"Of course. Please ring. I'd like that."

A kiss on the cheek. As he waved towards the accelerating car Jack knew this had been a frustrating way to say goodbye. It was an anti-climax to what had been a wonderful afternoon out.

"How special to be invited to Sunday lunch with a Spanish family and have them make such a fuss over us?" said Robert, plonking himself down on the sofa.

"Wasn't it? All that food and wine, such a warm welcome too."

"So, what's going to happen between you and Beatriz?"

"I don't know. I've got to sort out my future I guess."

"You don't want to think too long about it, mate. I saw the way she was looking at you this afternoon, she really feels something for you I reckon. You've got to come back - your plan needs to be focused on her."

"Do you think so?"

"I'm not joking, pal. I can see you together, I really can."

"Well, she did say she wanted to be in my plan."

"There you are! I told you so."

Jack sat back and shrank into the chair, his hands behind his head. Right there he looked like a man with the weight of the world on his shoulders.

Chapter Fifteen

Monday 2 July 2018

It's a mixed up Monday for Jack as over breakfast he thinks about what he needs to do before his flight on Friday. Not having seen his brood for the best part of a month, he's looking forward to that, yet he remains apprehensive about seeing Amanda, and in hospital of all places. There's a few mates he'd like to catch up with too. Despite all of that, it's Beatriz that dominates his thoughts. No matter what he trains his sights on, his mind meanders off to reflecting on the times they've spent over the past couple of weeks and fantasising over what could have been or maybe still could be. He wonders what she's doing. Is she thinking about him? He supposes she'll be distracted by work. Should he text her? No, not yet.

Robert, on the other hand, is relatively buzzing for a man who drank as much as he did the previous afternoon. He's looking to his future and, undaunted by dipping his toe in the waters of fruit distribution and almost having lost his foot, he's scouring the internet for information and especially opportunities for business. Every now and then he chunners something which interferes with Jack's process of internalising all his worries and concerns, something he's pretty good at. He has a bit of a whinge at Robert.

"Look, mate" says Robert. "You're doing my head in. You keep rabbiting on about this plan you're going to make. Why don't you get on with it? Why wait 'til you get back to the UK? You could start by writing down all this crap you're worrying about. I thought you were going to do that, help clear your mind a bit."

"Yeah, yeah, I know. Maybe I should."

"The danger is, if you wait until you're back in England, there'll be all sorts of other factors to influence you. This is your plan, it's about what you want."

"You're right. Sorry for being a grump."

"It's alright, usual fees apply for my therapy sessions."

"What's that, lunch?"

"Yeah, lunch'll do nicely."

Jack insists on going to Lola's for lunch. He wants to enjoy the beachside location one more time, breathe in the sea air, he says. But Robert's not falling for that and insists it's because he wants to rekindle memories of when he first clapped eyes on Beatriz. Despite the strong denials, he won't budge from his view.

"The smitten tourist doth protest too much, methinks."

At least Jack's able to tell him that since their earlier exchange he's listed everything that needs to be done before he goes and he's finally written down what's worrying him. He's already claiming to feel better and he'll send Beatriz a message once he's been out later to buy presents to take back to the family. Inevitably he can't stop himself reminiscing about seeing her on the beach with Alfredo, his thoughts and reflections. Once he's stopped, it's a minute at least before

Robert playfully punches his arm to ensure his attention.

"I told you, didn't I? I knew that's why you wanted to come here."

"Oh piss off!"

Over lunch, Robert wanted to know if, Beatriz aside, Jack had enjoyed the beach. Of course he had, and he always loves strolling through the shallow water to pass the time away, observing the variety of characters at play. They went through some of the "usual suspects", the ones you always expect to see. They agreed that selfie-stars were a relatively recent category, their social media posts no doubt ending up photoshopped to the extent that no-one they knew would actually recognise them anyway.

"I've seen a few Siamese couples" said Jack. "You know, the ones so newly in love that they just can't bear to be separated. Oh, and I saw a really incompetent teenage body boarder demonstrating the variety of ways you could fall off. So entertaining."

"And at the hottest time of the year in southern Spain," said Robert, "you must have seen some joggers".

"Oh yes! Lean, angular frames sheathed in taut, tanned leathery skin, each turn of their head shooting out bullets of sweat."

"There must have been a guy with a man-thong," said Robert. "He's usually maturing physically if not mentally, he's pleasantly plump and takes 'cheeky chappy' just too literally."

Jack recounted how one day he'd taken a knock to the back of his head. A frisbee. He liked watching exponents of the art playing on the beach, but novices are dangerous and need plenty of space. As he was reminded when he attempted to return the orange disc and struck a dog, who promptly picked it up and scampered down the beach pursued by three young screaming boys.

"Ah! Dogs on the beach… don't get me started" said Robert. "Another thing, last time I was on the beach there were these four Spanish mums, three of them yapping heatedly whilst the other was on her mobile. Their sweet little rascals could have been skewered by a swordfish or lobotomised by a jet-ski and they'd be completely oblivious. I swear they see the lifeguards as a free nanny service and let their kids run amok. Bless them".

Reminiscing about family holidays in years gone by, Jack recalled those they used to call plonkers.

"Amanda would usually choose a spot well away from people. Then, despite there being acres of open sand around us, a family would come along and plonk themselves down right next to us. Always that little bit too close."

Talking about happier times with his wife, when the children were younger, brought a more wistful mood. One more beer after lunch and the two amigos left Lola's to catch a bus home.

Chapter Sixteen

Tuesday 3 July 2018

Over the course of a quiet evening in, there are sporadic bursts of texting between Jack and Beatriz, the frequently mundane subject matter betraying the fact that they're each skirting round what they'd really like to be saying. They know it but neither of them takes the plunge and so they settle for any contact rather than risk none. Jack doesn't sleep too well. After waking he drifts towards sleep only to find his thoughts becoming more lucid and invariably negative. The pattern recurs throughout the night and trying to fight it just makes matters worse. The more tired he feels, the harder it is to think positively. It's a long, dark night. Opening his eyes and surveying the bedroom, it's as if his eyelids are glued shut. He's thankful that he doesn't have anywhere to go. Over breakfast he makes a decision. This morning he'll catch up on his sleep by lying on the beach. Almost immediately he's transformed; with his brightness increased and his picture quality adjusted, his mood lifts. A few hours at the beach prove very restful but only to a point. Eating away at him constantly is what feels like unfinished business with Beatriz. He never expected to feel like this again about a woman.

And certainly not so soon. Imagined discussions where he lays bare his feelings for her are energising, yet always followed by fear of rejection and misunderstanding which make him feel morose and dejected. It's at another of their haunts, Heladeria Blu, tucking into tortilla for lunch, that he has an idea. It's only a couple of hours to Granada, he could borrow Robert's car and drive there and back. They'd be alone. He could say what he needs to say. After driving there he'd have to have the courage to tell her, he couldn't live with himself if he drove all that way there and back without doing so.

Excited by the prospect of what could lie ahead, he wants to contact Beatriz, he wants to tell her that he's prepared to drive to see her, he needs to know that she approves, that she's as excited as he is. Would it be sensible to ring her now? No. Not until he knows he can have the car. He rings Robert. Good job he did too, as he's going to be late home. Why not tomorrow night, he suggests? Or he could drop him off at the station in Almeria later this afternoon and he could take the train? No, Jack didn't fancy that, he wanted the flexibility of the car.

"Will it stop you worrying then?" Robert asked.

"Oh, who knows? Probably not. I promise I'll try not to."

"Yeah, right. And by the way, if you get lucky and stay over I need the car Thursday afternoon."

"Very funny, knock it off, mate."

Next...when would be a good time to ring? He texted her to find out.

It's funny how the nearer it got to making the call, the dafter it sounded and the less confident he was that she'd want him to come over. With Robert not home until late, he had privacy. The clock said 7:30 and she'd be home by now.

He tried to compose himself on the sofa, he was tense and feeling sick in the pit of his stomach. 'Come on, come on' he uttered to himself and took a few deep breaths. After staring at her name and number on his phone, he pressed 'mobile'.

"Hi, it's me."

"Oh, Jack, hi."

Her voice was warm and mellifluous. Feeling his heart rate increasing and his brain melting, he attempted to make conversation and they spent a while going through their week so far and saying what a lovely time they'd had at her parents. He was pleased and relieved that they'd appeared to have enjoyed the afternoon themselves. A slight pause arrived and suddenly it felt like now or never…

"I hope this doesn't sound silly but I've actually had a sort of unsettling day today, you know…erm…I just, well…I just can't stop thinking about you, Beatriz."

He let out a nervous laugh but Beatriz stepped in quickly.

"Me too. About you. It's been hard to concentrate at work."

"Really? I couldn't sleep properly at all last night. What it made me think is, I wondered about driving over to see you tomorrow evening? Robert says I can borrow his car. It didn't feel right, saying goodbye at your parents' home, or outside Robert's place, and I'd just like to see you and talk to you. But only if you want to, you know, you must say if you don't."

"I do, Jack! I do. It would be so nice to see you, just the two of us. But it's a lot of driving, are you sure you don't mind?"

"Oh look, Beatriz, I've not much to do this week until I go home and I can't honestly think of anything I'd like to do more."

"I'll try to finish a little earlier so…what time?"

"If I aim to be with you for seven? Will that be OK?"

"Perfect."

That was that. Done! Then just before they signed off Beatriz added:

"Oh Jack - thank you. Thank you so much for ringing and…well, I'm looking forward to seeing you tomorrow. Drive safely."

Jack rolled over on the sofa, brought himself into a foetal position, began kicking his feet alternately and muttering 'Oh my God' on repeat. Jack was a happy bunny.

Robert was almost as happy as Jack was. He told him he could stop fretting now over what he should do and enjoy the rest of his time here, starting with going out to find a bar showing the England v Columbia game. When they find one, it's packed.

"Half the people in here are ex-pats" said Robert.

"That reminds me of something I've been meaning to ask" Jack replied. "Why is it that we refer to Brits living abroad as ex-pats, but everyone else living abroad as immigrants?"

"Beats me, mate. Fair point though."

"I wonder if it's that thing about seeing ourselves differently, or is there an element of racism about it?"

"It's part of our make-up that's probably rooted in the Empire. You know, it's alright when we go to live in another country 'cause, being British, we're doing them a favour, aren't we?"

A decent football team, Columbia unfortunately put on a display of crude tackling and cynical gamesmanship that brought out the patriotism in Jack and Robert. Still 1-1 after thirty minutes extra-time and it was penalties. Showing coolness and determination under pressure, England banished memories of all those dramatic tournament exits of the past to go through. The locals could only look on enviously as the night air filled with the songs and laughter of the English, immigrants and tourists alike.

Chapter Seventeen

Wednesday 4 July 2018

Stirred by the illustrious peaks and ridges of the Sierra Nevada in all their glory, Jack took it easy on the route to Granada. He made it on time. Beatriz let him into the building and he made his way up to her floor, where she was in the doorway, waiting. For once he didn't particularly notice what she was wearing, other than a broad smile, that sparkle in her eyes just made him feel so alive. They threw their arms around each other in a tight, warm embrace. He could just about hang on to the bunch of flowers and the box of chocolates. Moving through to her living area, she edged her nose to the roses, inhaled their scent and rolled her eyes in a way that was effortlessly sensual.

"Oh wow!" she exclaimed, unwrapping the box. "Bombon de higo! I love them so much…thank you, Jack. Shall we have one now?"

"Yeah, why not. Let's live dangerously."

It was the first time Jack had experienced the utter fabulousness of a fig dipped in dark chocolate. He was rather pleased with himself. They put the rest away until later and sat together with some sparkling water. Beatriz suggested they stay in for a quiet evening, she'd bought in a few things for them to eat and he was more than happy.

"I'm sorry for being a little mixed up in knowing what I want to do with my future" Jack started. "I have to admit, I'm none the wiser right now, although I have started planning this week."

"Oh my goodness!" she reacted in mock astonishment.

"Yes, I really have. Before I go back, there are some things I just wanted to be able to say and for you to know, if that makes sense?"

She nodded and briefly put her hand on his.

"OK. First, none of this needed to have happened - going out for dinner, Almeria, Granada, your home yesterday, just meeting for coffee...I know I did something special in saving Alfredo but, nevertheless, your gratitude and kindness has gone above and beyond. Thank you so much - if nothing else, my holiday here would have been so dull without you. And each time I see you, each time I'm with you and share a little bit of your life, I feel closer and closer to you. Now I find that, maybe because I'm going back to England in a few days, the thought of not seeing you is eating away at me. I mean, I know I'll see you again but... how long? Will your feelings be the same? You may meet someone else...you may not feel the same as me anyway! And all this is against the knowledge that I have to go home and I have to make sure everything is straight there, you know? The place where I'm living has a few months more on the lease, I don't have a job or a clear idea of what I'd like to do, so...I need to sort out things but it felt important for me to share my feelings with you. I don't know if that makes sense to you, but..."

"Oh, Jack. It's very brave to tell me how you feel and

I understand. It's only been a few weeks that we've known each other. My time also has been better for having you here. I've loved showing you round places and going out with you. I feel like I've had more zest for life, an energy that I haven't felt for a long time. I've been worrying about you going back and maybe you won't return here. You have your family there and your friends, it's very emotional."

Beatriz stood and extended her arms out to Jack. He took her hands, stood and she hugged him. Moving away slightly she looked up at him, holding his hands.

"You know, Jack, you treat me so well, so graciously, it feels good when I'm with you. You've made me feel special and…it's like we're equals. That's not something I've felt with men before."

"Maybe you've just been unlucky?"

"Maybe. But don't play yourself down, Jack. You're a good man."

"I'm certainly a lucky man, which is not how I felt when I came out to Spain."

"Perhaps it was meant to be like that, it was our destiny to meet!"

"Ha ha! Now it's sounding like one of your Tales of the Alhambra."

They laughed. Then Beatriz said they should have a drink and she'd bring some food out. Jack was ravenous but said he'd better stick to sparkling water as he had a long drive ahead of him later.

"Look, you don't have to go back to Mojacar tonight. I have a spare room and, as long as you don't mind me being out early in the morning for work, you're welcome to stay."

He suddenly felt a nervousness again. The possibilities, the implications, the pressure!

"Oh, I don't want to impose on you, Beatriz."

"Jack! Relax. Let's enjoy being together this evening, it's fine for you to stay. Then it's one more day we'll see each other before you go back. OK?"

It was very definitely OK.

As she sets out the various small plates on the table, Beatriz tells Jack that she called in at the Mercado San Agustin, opposite the cathedral. It's great for fresh food and if there'd been more time last week she'd have taken him there, perhaps to one of the little tapas joints that are so popular. Why doesn't he go there in the morning to take something back for Robert? He thought that was a great idea - if Beatriz would be leaving early he'd have plenty of time to go round the market before driving back for Robert to have the car in the afternoon.

It was a laid back, unhurried sort of evening as they grazed over the food. They talked and talked about all sorts of things, filling in gaps in their knowledge of each other. It felt entirely natural. Eventually he confessed to bringing a small overnight bag with him in the car but blamed Robert - he said you might decide to stay over in a hotel for the night rather than drive back tired.

And then their evening was almost over. An air of melancholy pervaded their mood and their hearts became a little heavier. Yet there was also an air of contentment about them, now they both understood each other's feelings better. All they'd wanted to say had been said. Jack couldn't commit himself yet but the ideas they'd discussed left him optimistic that his future really could lie in Spain. The prospect of having Beatriz in his life was surely worth the risk? Leaving the kitchen after loading the dishwasher and tidying up, they moved back to the living area.

"Beatriz" he said, nervously, "I'm so glad that we've

been able to see each other and be alone for an evening. It's been great."

"Thank you for having the courage to make it happen. I'm so thrilled you should want to drive over two hours to see me."

"Well…"

Jack took hold of her and held her tight, their heads close together. His eyes closed. He breathed in her scent as if his life depended on it. Divine. Turning his head, he looked at her face, immersing himself in those dark brown eyes, like deep burnished pools of desire. As he did, he murmured her name. She reached up and slowly encouraged him towards her, quietly telling him to 'shush'. Her lips brushed ever so tenderly against his cheek and shivers ran down the back of his neck. He gently caressed her forehead, dragging his lips away in a languid arc across her skin. Opening her eyes, Beatriz used her left hand to coax him towards her face again. Her mouth was open and as Jack closed his eyes he felt her lips against his. She trembled, letting out a soft, low moan that caused Jack to squeeze her more tightly, the intensity between them increasing. When at last their lips parted, she lay her head on his chest. They stood listening to their salacious breathing, feeling their hearts pulsating, driving a rhythm against each other's chest.

"You'd better fetch that bag from the car if you're staying" she said.

Chapter Eighteen

Thursday 5 July 2018

The waiter sets down the two beers with a smile.

"Ah, lovely" says Robert. "I've been fantasising over a cold beer for hours. Funny how your fantasy subjects change as you get older, eh?"

Jack just laughed as he dabbed away the line of foam from his top lip.

"Hey, thanks for that goody bag from Granada, mate" he went on. "Some nice stuff in there. I had a couple of those little pastries when I got in before. Beautiful! Too many of those and a boy could spoil his figure."

"Talking of which, what about this running on the beach last week? Seriously, you need to take care of yourself and you should think about building on that."

"Oh, honestly, Jack, that nearly effin' killed me. The sun blasting down as well…aargh no."

"But you managed it because you had the motivation."

"What? Being chased by Attila the Honey Monster?"

"Exactly! You thought your life was threatened. Your health is the same. No disrespect, but you must have seen all the stuff across the media about diabetes? I mean, you're a prime candidate, Robert. Not to mention your heart. You could do some jogging? Even walking's great for you, just make it a decent walk and do it regularly, that's what they say."

"I heard some medical guy talking about it on the BBC World Service not long ago. When I heard him say that the NHS strategy and budget were being driven by Holby City I was appalled. You know, a TV drama having that sort of influence. Then it dawned on me. He'd actually said 'obesity'."

Deep down, however, he knew his friend was right and he knew he was heading for trouble unless he got himself in better shape.

Shaking his head, Jack said he wanted to see him acquire a regular exercise habit by the time he returned. So was this an indication that he'd made his mind up about his future? He wasn't giving anything further away, other than saying that he was looking forward to having his life sorted out. Instead, he turned the subject to Robert's plans. From having been quite gung-ho about his vision for wholesale fruit domination, he was now feeling somewhat more circumspect about his chances of achieving anything.

"Remember what Homer said? If at first you don't succeed, give up."

"Homer the Greek philosopher?"

"No! Homer Simpson, of course."

"Oh, come on, Robert. What went wrong on that job was nothing to do with you."

"Maybe not. But it paid well. Why? Because there was always something a bit iffy about what we were collecting. OK, I didn't know in what way or to what extent, but… Fruit distribution perhaps isn't that lucrative when it's for ordinary fruit, so is it worth it?"

"Does it have to pay a fortune for it to be fruitful? Fresh natural products are becoming more popular and here you are right at the heart of one of the world's biggest producers. If you could become more efficient at it, you might find it brings you more money. Then there's the job satisfaction. How much did you enjoy going up to Madrid, buying at the market, seeing a bit more of the world? Getting to know your new business partner, dare I say it?"

"You might have a good point there, mate. I suppose reflecting on things, I worry that this is just the latest in a long line of projects that's not worked out. I never quite manage to do the right thing, let alone do things right."

"You might be a bit frustrated by what happened but…what an adventure it was!"

"Yeah, but when all your projects go pear-shaped it can become a bit tiresome."

"Hey, I tell you what. Why don't you write a book about it? A spoof business book. How about 'The Seven Habits of Highly Ineffective People', or 'The Four Obsessions of an Extraordinarily Shit Executive'. 'Average to Crap'? Sorry, it could be something sensible like 'Learning From Failure', it's quite in vogue at the moment to be seen to be able to admit to weaknesses."

"Is it? Well, I could fill several sequels with my bloody weaknesses, mate. Two problems: I can't write and I don't exactly seem to have learned from any of my failures."

Oh dear. Robert was feeling a little jaundiced now the dust had settled on the previous week's events. His friend tried to encourage and cajole him into looking on the bright side. Just as he appeared to have accepted it would be a dull evening, Robert pulled his phone from his pocket. A smile grew incrementally as he read the message. Looking up, he told Jack it was Xavi - he'd confirmed his outstanding money would be sent tomorrow. He'd not expected that for a while. He texted Alfredo straight away to tell him and quickly received a response from a clearly very happy partner. It was enough to change his mood and soon he was back on the front foot. It was a good time perhaps to ask about his relationship with Alfredo.

"So do you think you and Alfredo might develop this relationship, or was it just a one-morning stand?"

"Oh, we'll have to see. He's a lovely lad and we get on really well but I think it sort of took us by surprise as well. I've chatted to him a couple of times this week and we met up the other afternoon but…I guess we don't really know how to behave around this. And I am a lot older than him. So I suppose we're just taking it steady and, while we don't want to hide it especially, we're not necessarily equipped to have it out there, if you see what I mean?"

Jack nodded.

"It's cool though, Jack. We'll see how it goes and, well, you heard his Dad going on about their hopes for him and so on. We just got to be very careful initially. But I'm comfortable with it myself. I've not had much love in my life."

"That's important, Rob."

"Thanks, by the way."

"What for?"

"Oh, just for handling it like you have. Not everyone would have reacted like you did, but it's helped us feel like it's natural and that's been helpful. Cheers, mate. Anyway, considering you weren't looking forward to going back you're very chipper this evening. Something happen last night that you've forgotten to tell me?"

"No. I've not forgotten to tell you anything."

The huge smile was now accompanied by an exaggerated roll of the eyes.

"Come on, Jack. You can tell your old mate Robert, can't you?"

"There's nothing to tell. We had a lovely evening and we talked a lot."

"But you stayed over. Do you mean to tell me you slept on your own? I've seen that glint in her eyes…come on."

"Look, yes, we are quite close and who knows what the future may hold but…we discussed a lot of things, she offered me her spare room to avoid a long drive at night… that's it."

"That's it? Give over, Jack. You know what I've been up to so…"

"That's not because you told me! I just had the misfortune to walk in on you."

"Did you give her a goodnight kiss?"

"Oh, God…yes. Yes I did."

"How long did it last?"

"That's all! Give it a rest."

"Aaaah. I still remember my first kiss, you know. I never had any luck with girls at school whatsoever so when I got to Uni I was quite keen to have myself some sort of experience. It was at a party and that mature student was there, Greta. Did you ever know her?"

"No, doesn't ring any bells."

"'Cos she was about thirty and from Scandinavia somewhere she seemed quite exotic to me. Had a throaty, deep voice."

"Not a deep throaty voice?"

"I didn't get that far, mate. We used to say 'looks like Greta, talks like Peter'. This one night she appeared to be sufficiently inebriated for me to approach with a little more confidence. The music was really loud in this house and we were in this dark corner of the room. Suddenly she fixed me with her stare, which was intense. Then after a few seconds she moved her face towards me. The first thing that struck me was her perfume, which I then realised was actually Harvey's Bristol Cream. She'd still got the bottle in her right hand. Before I could change my mind I found myself pinned to the bloody wall and her tongue was in my mouth. I could have been very pissed…but it seemed to me that Greta's tongue had preternatural powers, it had this immense vitality about it. It felt like having a writhing eel inside my mouth, indeed, inside my throat, such was its reach. It shimmied and squirmed. One second it was pounding against the roof of my mouth, the next it was throbbing against my tonsils. It went round and round at one point, faster and faster, like a motor cyclist riding the wall of death it was. I swear at one point it turned upside down and looped the fucking loop! Just when I thought I was about to pass out she withdrew. Still staring at me, she inhaled deeply, uncrossed her eyes and took another slug of sherry. While her eyes were closed I wriggled out and pissed off."

"Did you get her number?"

"I did not! Tried to put her to the back of my mind. It worked too, until I went to see Alien at the cinema and when that creature burst out the guy's stomach I started having flashbacks. Thought I was going to have to leave the film."

They ordered another drink.

"My recollections of you at Uni were of a bloke that used to lie in a lot, pretty well every morning," said Jack. "Certainly in the early days, when we had that shared house. For months I thought you were half-man, half-mattress."

Jack decided to push Robert a bit further.

"Was there anyone after Greta?"

"Oh, a few. Generally short-lived and occasionally traumatic, like Donna."

"Donna? Was she a student?"

"Yeah. We had a fling one night. The day after, she was going round the students' union bar telling people I'd got a three inch penis, the cowbag."

"Oh, no! What did you do?"

"Ah, whenever anyone mentioned it, I told them even a jumbo jet looks small if it's landing in the Grand Canyon."

"Fair point."

A few drinks and umpteen tapas later, the boys were ready to wrap up the evening. The world might be going to hell in a handcart but they vowed to keep the faith. They concluded that though the planet may be endangered, the world wouldn't end. It would simply be rebranded. The spirit of their old friendship had been rekindled these past few weeks and they sensed each other as a renewed presence in their lives. Each had possibilities ahead and, for now, the potential pleasure of exploration outweighed any problems or pitfalls. After an evening of reflective introspection, the quiet stroll home proved soporific. Jack's bags were ready and in the morning he'd face the next passage of play.

Chapter Nineteen

Friday 6 July 2018

Although they made the airport on time they weren't able to have that breakfast Jack had promised and settled for a quick coffee before he checked in and went through the gates.

"Hey, Jack" Robert shouted to him as he walked away. "Just remember, the first piece of luggage on the carousel never belongs to anyone."

As his smile wore off, it almost seemed to him that he'd just woken from a dream, it no longer appeared as his world. Reality was where he was heading to this morning. Once in the waiting lounge, he checked his phone and read a warm, heartfelt message from Beatriz. But it was the one from her brother that he'd not expected and which took him aback. Alfredo's words expressing his gratitude and his encouragement to return soon touched him deeply and helped make it clear that he was also, very definitely, part of that world too. Later came a text from eldest son Josh saying that as he'd be taking his Mum to hospital early this morning his brother Seb would be at the airport to meet him.

Stepping out of the plane, Jack descended the steps onto the tarmac at Manchester. The pilot had promised it was dry and sunny there. It was dry but not sunny as he'd become accustomed to it. The dullness of the light brought him down a little, just how he'd always felt on returning from a good Mediterranean holiday, no doubt how everyone feels. Yet this time it felt more so. Was it because this time he was re-entering his country divided over an uncertain future? Or was it about his lack of purpose, the first time he'd arrived back without having to think about refocusing on his job? He didn't know, he just knew it felt different. No 500 emails waiting for him though, that was nice. Coming out of the terminal, Seb was there, hand aloft at the back of the crowd. They embraced warmly and shared the bags. The journey back to Jack's place was useful, giving them time to catch up with what was happening. Jack's account of his few weeks in Spain was minimal and discussion centred on family.

Discovering that Amanda's operation was scheduled for late that morning, Jack sent her a message wishing her well. He thought it was probably a little late for her to pick up but she'd see that he'd at least thought of her and tried. Seb was of the opinion that she didn't know he was returning home. It was evident that the three offspring had not only wanted him back but thought that it would have been disrespectful not to have been around to offer help or support. He saw that Nicole ringing him last week was their attempt to ensure he returned, using the father-daughter relationship as their ace in the pack. Fair enough, he thought. And they were probably right about his being around.

Seb helped him again with bags when they reached Jack's furnished apartment. He couldn't even offer him a cup of tea as they had no fresh milk. Still, they sat for a while discussing what was going on. He admitted to his son that he'd be spending the next couple of weeks making plans about his future. He needed to check his lease although he thought there were two or three months left on it yet. He still had many of his personal items, such as they were, in storage. The sooner that stopped the better, he thought, money down the drain. Seb was interested in his Dad's ideas for the future but didn't get much out of him. Jack sensed he'd be subjected to further interrogation over the coming days. According to his son, it seemed that Amanda had been keeping herself busy and active, despite her health problems coming to a head. Whenever he rang home she seemed to have been out at some group or club, meeting friends or had somebody round, but she didn't talk much about stuff that she was doing. Josh and Nicole were not really any the wiser.

Later on, Jack was pleased to learn that Amanda's hysterectomy had been completed successfully. She was 'comfortable but a little groggy'. By this time he'd been shopping to stock up the place. He'd have a quiet night in, with the kids visiting their mother in the evening. They'd agreed he would visit next day, on Saturday afternoon.

Chapter Twenty

Saturday 7 July 2018

Visiting hours were 2:00 to 4:00 at the General Hospital, so he'd stop for a bite to eat before going in. By the time he set off he felt he was just about sorted at home. As he remembered the gift he'd brought her from Andalucia, he realised he hadn't bought flowers. Resisting the temptation to stop at one of several petrol stations, he called into a florist. They were very pretty, but he couldn't help thinking that it would've cost him less had he been caught stealing them from a garden and been fined. It meant he was a bit later than planned but he parked, then found his way through the labyrinth of corridors to the right ward.

A certain nervousness had gradually built in him since he entered the building. It wasn't helped by colliding with a bed being wheeled round the corner by a nurse, who grimaced at him as the horizontal patient, a pale man with piercings and a union jack tattoo wrinkled over his flabby right arm, told him to "watch where you're fucking going, numpty". Jack said nothing although he knew how he'd like to respond and spent the next few seconds imagining Mr Angry being turned over in the operating theatre to have a bunch of flowers surgically removed from his rectum. The ward was just ahead on his left. There was nobody on the desk so he thought he'd best just look for her. He was almost at the end of the ward, having passed all the usual suspects visiting their friends and relatives. Some wore the blank expressions of people who'd already exhausted the possibilities of conversation; children kicking the bed, or asking for stuff, or pulling the bed covers, or hitting the patient; women who hadn't stopped talking since they got there, talking to patients whose ailments rendered them too slow to interrupt or who appeared to have gone to sleep or even died; one or two were tucking into chocolates they'd brought, discovering the people they were visiting were actually unwell. The overall impression was of a quiet madness.

She must be at the very end he thought and he looked to his left as he passed the last curtain divider. There was Amanda, sitting, propped up in bed by some plump pillows, not looking too poorly. She'd probably put some make-up on. She was smiling, she looked happy and there was even the trace of a sparkle in her eye. The person she was looking at was sat at her bedside. It was a man, a man Jack hadn't seen before. He was holding her hand. And stroking her arm with his other hand. Someone she was quite close to, he thought.

"Jack!" she let out, pulling her hand away from the man. "What are you doing here?"

"Hello, Amanda" he replied. "I just got back yesterday."

"Oh my goodness. No-one told me you were coming."

"They must have thought it would be a surprise for you…and indeed it is!"

He laughed. The man, who'd initially looked round, had since averted his gaze, possibly through embarrassment.

"Oh, sorry…" said Amanda. "Ronnie, this is Jack. Jack, this is Ronnie, a friend of mine."

The two men mumbled their greetings and shook hands.

"Look" said Jack, "I don't want to interrupt, I really just wanted to see how you were and to leave these for you. I'll pop by another time."

Amanda looked troubled and slightly upset, maybe even close to tears. Was it simply embarrassment or was it the surprise of Jack's unexpected appearance, being suddenly forced to confront her circumstances? Or was it seeing the man she'd been married to for over thirty years momentarily bereft, a little boy lost. They'd both had a shock. There was nevertheless genuine affection in her face when she told him how beautiful the flowers were and how good it was to seeing him looking well. He felt he must ask about the operation, of course, and having got that out of the way, said his goodbyes quietly and politely.

Walking out of the ward, Jack felt the gaze of every visitor on him, imagined or otherwise. He retraced his steps through the whitewashed maze of corridors, wondering whether his kids knew anything about this relationship. How long had it been going on, could it have been going on when they were still together? Bloody hell! Then he reached the exit. He stopped, looked up at the sky, the unremarkable steely dull blue sky, and took a deep breath. As he exhaled he looked around and there just a few metres away was tattooed Mr Angry who he'd run into on his way in. He was staring at Jack and puffing on a cigarette.

"And you can fuck off staring!" Jack shouted at him.

And with that cri de coeur, he turned and strode off

across the car park. Into his car, seat belt fastened. Pulling down his sun visor, he looked into the mirror and addressed himself firmly.

"I. Am. Making. Plans. For. Jack."

He started the engine and turned up the radio. 6Music was playing Arcade Fire. And with the opening bars of 'Ready To Start' pumping through the speakers a new phase of his life was just beginning.

Glossary of Terms

Abuelo/abuelito	Grandfather/Grandad
Adios	Goodbye
Amigo	Friend
Andalucia	Southern region stretching from Cadiz and Huelva provinces in the east to Almeria in the west
Autopista	Motorway/Freeway
Autovia	Like autopista but no tolls
Basquiña	Short-sleeved overdress for outdoors, usually black
Bastardo	Oh, go on…have a guess
Beso	Kiss
Boquerónes	Anchovies
Borracho	Drunk
Buenos dias	Good morning
Cabra	Goat
Calamar a la marinada	Squid in a marinade
Calle	Street, lane
Carne	Meat
Casa	House, home
Cava	Sparlking Spanish wine
Chorizo	Spicy sausage

Churros	Like a long doughnut, usually dipped in thick hot chocolate
Come te va?	How are you, how's it going?
(Non) comprendo	I (don't) understand
Confiteria	Shop full of cakes
'Cuando Calienta El Sol'	'When Hot from the Sun'
Cuesta	Slope, steep hill
Desayunos	Breakfast
Dos besos	Customary greeting, a peck on each cheek
Drogas	Drugs or narcotics
El Pais	'The Country', national newspaper
El Perrito	'The Doggy'
Ensalada	Salad
Eras tan valiente	You were so brave
Estación	Station
Estoy muy agradecido	I'm very grateful
Estrella	Estrella Damm, beer from Barcelona since 1876
Flamenco	Dance rooted in musical folk-lore of Andalucia
Frutas	Fruit
Gambas rojas	Red prawns
Genio	Genius, ingenuity
Gracias	Thanks
Gracias de nuevo	Thanks again

Guiso marinaro	Marinaded stew
Habla Inglés?	Do you speak English?
Heladeria	Ice-cream parlour
Hola	Hello
Hora de las noticias	Time for the news
Hortalizas	Vegetables
Inglés	English
Jamon	Ham
Jerez	Sherry…from Jerez in Andalucia, of course
La Furia Roja	The Red Fury, aka Spain's national football team
Lo siento	I'm sorry
Magdalenas	Small traditional cakes
Mantinimiento	Maintenance
Manzanilla	Pale dry sherry from Andalucia - or chamomile tea, so beware!
Mercado	Market
Museo	Museum
Numeros	Numbers
O Dios Mio!	Oh my God!
Paella	Originally a workers' dish from Valencia, cooked in the fields with rice, chicken, rabbit… maybe a few snails?
Palacio	Palace
Paseo	A walk, stroll

Plátanos	Bananas
Piquito	Rustic bread
Playa	Beach
Plaza	Square, public space
Por favor	Please
Pueblo	Town, village, city
Puerta	Port
Qué puedo decir?	What can I decide?
Queso curado	Cured cheese
Raciones	Ration, next up from tapas
Ravioli de rabo	Oxtail ravioli
Rio	River
Rondeña	Musical form of Flamenco, from Ronda, Málaga
Señor, Señora, Señorita	Mr, Mrs, Miss
Si	Yes; if
Siesta	Afternoon nap
Supermercado	Supermarket
Tapas	Snack with drink
Torrejas	French toast Spanish style
Tortilla	'Small cake' of sliced cooked potato and onion
Tostada	Toast
Un momento	One moment
Vermut	Vermouth
Yo no hablo Español	I don't speak Spanish

Acknowledgements

It was when we were on holiday near Mojacar that John and Vicky Owen accidentally gave me the germ of an idea. With nothing to read on the flight home, the notes I made eventually became Outside Lola's. Thank you both!

The support and encouragement from my writing group friends Janet Banks, Libby Riddell and Mark Moore has been invaluable. Similarly, appreciation and gratitude goes to members past and present of #WriteHereWriteNow at Storyhouse for enabling me to road test key passages, and in particular James Eldridge, who actually read the whole thing.

Thanks to Roy McCarthy at kulastudio.com who designed the cover. And to Amber Burns at outloudpr.co.uk for connecting me with Roy and for the cake.

A special mention to Dylan the cocker spaniel and Penni the chihuahua, who's lodging with us, for putting a smile on my face and ensuring exercise and fresh air every day.

Finally, special thanks to Kate for your love, confidence and patience, especially for putting up with my moans and groans about problems and obstructions both real and imagined.

The author

Outside Lola's is Paul Diggory's debut novel. It follows a long and rewarding career in housing which saw him become President of the Chartered Institute of Housing in 2007-08 and presented with the 2015 Outstanding Contribution to Housing in Wales Award. You can find out more at pauldiggory.com where you'll also find some of his travel writing and short stories.

You can follow Paul on Twitter at @paulwdiggory.

Lightning Source UK Ltd.
Milton Keynes UK
UKHW011413250920
370518UK00003B/877